PEEPS

ERIN GORDON

ALSO BY ERIN GORDON

Cheer: A Novel

Heads or Tails

Beshert

For my ancestors,

especially Mom and Dad.

"This is the beginning.

Almost anything can happen."

— *Aristotle*, by Billy Collins

CHAPTER ONE

I had so many questions.

Why had she never tried to understand me?

Why had she been so cold to us?

If the situation were reversed and the funeral was for me, *would my mother have attended?*

Just as these thoughts arose, the service ended. The twenty or so guests began to mingle and nibble on bagels and fruit in the restaurant's small private room, my mother's ashes in a modest urn at the head of the table. I excused myself for the restroom, my brain swirling with everything I wish I'd asked before cancer claimed her lucidity.

Through the bathroom's partially cracked window, the squawks of seagulls and the pot my brother was smoking wafted inside. It hit me then.

I was no longer someone's daughter.

At fifty-one, I was an orphan, my father having died suddenly when I was a toddler. I sat on the closed toilet lid, my bones aching as if I'd been hit by a semi. Yet also emerging were the first sparks of what I always imagined I'd feel when my mother was gone: relief.

I washed my hands in the sink just to keep me alone with my thoughts a few moments longer.

I wished I'd asked my mother the seven questions I posed to all my podcast guests. Since she was now dead, what object, I wondered, would she have taken with her to the afterlife? I honestly had no guesses. I'd never been able to grasp what was important to my mother. I just knew it wasn't us.

Alex, my son, would probably take his collection of Stevie Wonder albums on vinyl. My ex-husband Jeff recently volunteered his answer: "I'd bring my wedding ring from my marriage to you," he said, "and the receipt from my first date with Milt — the two loves of my life."

Then another truth struck me as sharply as the almond-scented soap.

I was no longer someone's partner.

I needed to get back to the gathering as the mourners would soon disperse. My brother was still outside smoking so it was up to me to thank everyone who'd paid their respects.

I joined the tiny cluster of my friends who'd come not to say goodbye to my mother but to support me. One handed me a mug of coffee. Another draped her arm around my shoulder. I'd known most of these women for upwards of fifteen years, since our kids were in preschool. We'd seen each other through potty training and tantrums. We'd collaborated about when to allow our kids cell phones and social media access. We'd shared photos of our teens with their learner's permits. Now those kids were college freshmen scattered throughout the country.

Reality smacked me again.

I was no longer an active parent.

"Meg?"

I turned to see Jeff, my ex-husband, arms outstretched. "Milt's gone out to get our car," he said, enveloping me in a hug. He felt, he smelled as he always did, as familiar to me as my own body. "I'll call tomorrow, okay?"

I nodded. "Thank you both."

Soon after, the rest of the guests drifted out with condolences and embraces. Then it was just me and my younger brother Leith. I was settling up with the restaurant when Leith approached me carrying the urn.

"I assume you don't want this?" he said, holding it up like a trophy.

"Uh, that's a hard no," I said. Even if my mother had been warm and loving, the kind of mother I worked so very hard to be, I would have declined.

"I figured. I'll take it." He pulled keys from his pocket and jangled them. "Got a long drive back up north. I'm gonna hit the road. Thanks, Meggie, for, you know, handling everything. Especially these last few weeks."

Our mother died swiftly after a pancreatic cancer diagnosis. I'd arranged her care.

"It's what I do," I said with a shrug.

"Well," Leith said, half hugging me with the arm that wasn't holding our mother's ashes, "now you're free."

It was thrilling and terrifying.

Without parents, a spouse, my son nearby...

Who was I?

Brad and I met up in the shade of a huge Monterey cypress tree outside his house on Adelaide Drive about a mile and a half from my own in Santa Monica. He greeted me with a hug and a sympathetic smile with an extended lower lip that I'd seen from others that morning at the funeral. We walked three blocks to the beachfront path and then sauntered north. It was late afternoon. The sun was bright but turning a warmer shade of orange and the breeze was picking up.

Brad and I had been set up a few weeks before by mutual friends. Attentive and interesting, he was also surprisingly fit and attractive for a fifty-eight-year-old divorcee with three kids. I hadn't dated in twenty-five years but so far he'd made it far less awkward than it could have been. On our first date, we met at a wine bar and talked about books, raising kids and mid-life divorce. The next week we went to a movie that neither of us could concentrate on because the famous actor who was headlining that very film was sitting two rows in front of us. A week ago — two days before my mother died — we grabbed vegan hot dogs at Yum Dog and ate them while watching the sun set over the Pacific before going to an artist talk at a nearby gallery that his friend owned. We finally kissed that night, a very, very good kiss, the kind you turn over and over in your head, memorizing its breadth and depth so you can conjure it again at will.

"How was the memorial?" Brad asked as we dodged rollerbladers and cyclists. He'd offered to accompany me to the service but I'd declined, explaining that it would be a small gathering — Jeff and Milt, a few of my mother's former co-workers, a handful of my friends. My own son, I explained, wouldn't even be flying home from college to attend. After just three dates, it was far too early for Brad to meet my friends, my ex-husband. It was too early, too, for him to witness first-hand how conflicted, maybe even ambivalent, I was about her death.

"It was nice," I said. "My younger brother spoke. I read some words from my mother's brother Oscar, her only living sibling, who's too old to travel across country. The whole thing lasted less than an hour. I'm just glad it's over." I regretted that last part, fearing I'd over shared or, worse, revealed a callousness he wouldn't like. "Anyway, I'd love to talk about something else. Is that okay?"

"Of course," he said, putting his arm around me the way he did the night we roamed through the art gallery. Jeff had loved me — still loved me — deeply, but he'd never been affectionate like Brad. "Here's something:

tell me about Peeps. Since we first met, I've listened to two episodes. And now I have questions."

"Fire away," I said, grateful for the topic shift.

"How'd it start?"

"Short or long answer?"

He looked down and sideways at me and smiled. "Long."

"Okay, so, when I was in college at UCLA, about a hundred years ago, I wrote this column, kind of a man-on-the-street feature, for the Daily Bruin. I was a journalism major and wanted to hone my writing skills. But it turned out I learned way more about the human condition than I did about journalism."

"Go on."

"There's a proverb that goes something like, 'God must have really liked stories because he made so many people.' In stopping random students and faculty on the quad, in asking pointed questions, I discovered that everyone had a story. I could literally never miss, no matter who I interviewed."

"Did you write for newspapers after college?"

I shook my head. "Baby reporters usually have to cut their teeth at small-town papers in Arkansas or North Dakota or other places far, far from LA. I mean, I've only ever lived here."

"Really? Only LA?"

"Yeah. So I knew that, constitutionally, I'm just not cut out for that kind of uncertainty or isolation."

"You sell yourself short."

"Also, Jeff and I were seriously dating then and he was staying in LA after graduation. So I took a PR job downtown. For a think tank devoted to water resources. I churned out press releases about transfer water rights and wetlands permitting. You know, fascinating stuff. I worked there for a few years until I had Alex. Then I stayed home."

"My ex also stayed home with our kids. She referred to herself as the family's COO."

"I like that."

We reached a beachfront shack on the path. Wordlessly, as if we were in sync, we got in line. The scent of coconut tanning lotion on the teenaged girls behind us commingled with the fishy seaside wind. We ordered two decaf iced mochas, and returned to the path, heading south, back the direction we came. Nearby herons clucked their familiar *go-go-go* landing call.

"Then what?" Brad said, shaking his cup, the ice sounding like dice.

"Then what what?"

"How'd you go from staying home with your son to starting a podcast?"

"Ah, right," I said, mock smacking my head. "When Alex started high school four years ago and needed me less, my friend Dana hired me to write for her legal newsletter. It was nice to have a paycheck again. But the work was — still is — boring. I thought back to how much I'd loved writing that column in college, how I loved making art out of *life*."

"Did you apply for newspaper jobs? You know, like pitching that same kind of column?"

Sipping my mocha, I shook my head. "Who'd hire a forty-something part-time legal newsletter writer? A woman who'd done a bit of PR ten, fifteen years ago? A writer whose best clips were from The Daily Bruin back in the eighties? It may be the New Millennium but I know how the patriarchy works."

Brad lampooned pulling an imaginary arrow from his heart.

"Present company excluded," I clarified.

"So you took matters into your own hands and started a blog."

"Right. And I did it assuming that no one would read my man-on-the-street interviews except the sources themselves. But surprisingly, within about six months, I had lots of daily hits, a steady stream of loyal readers who commented on my posts, and a teeny bit of advertising that covered gas and a new laptop."

"Then came the podcast…."

"Yes. A couple of months ago, before Alex went away to college in Austin, he convinced me to convert Peeps the blog into Peeps the podcast. I don't know why it hadn't occurred to me because I'd long lamented that too many podcasts were about only extraordinary people. You know, scoundrels, killers, inventors, geniuses. I'd been searching for a podcast about everyday people but never found one. One of my college professors used to say, 'You can see the world in a grain of sand.'"

"Ah, the show's tag line!"

"You really *have* listened."

"You doubted me?" he simulated another arrow through the heart. "I heard the one about the grandson of sharecroppers who spent years as a postal carrier. And the one about the movie-loving priest who ties every sermon to a film."

"So, yeah, that's the premise of Peeps: that everyone's life — even the smallest, most insular life — is a story worth hearing."

We were about to turn off the beach path and onto the city streets. We tossed our empty mocha cups into a blue recycling bin. He placed a hand on my lower back as we crossed Palisades Avenue, which made me feel dainty.

"Was it hard?" he said. "Starting a podcast?"

"If I didn't have Alex, yes. But he taught me how to use Garageband to record, how to find a hosting service, how to submit shows to distributors. He helped me pick out a mic. Later, I added a mic stand, a pop filter, and found a do-it-yourself graphic design app to change my logo from simply 'Peeps' to 'Peeps Podcast.'"

"You must be happy you did it."

We'd reached the Monterey cypress in front of his house.

"I am."

"Do I detect a hint of hesitation?" Brad said.

Man, he was perceptive. "No," I said. "Well, maybe. I love doing the podcast. I just have this low-grade, nagging concern about keeping it sustainable."

"What do you mean? I thought the whole idea is that everyone's life is interesting. So unless you plan on making literally billions of episodes, you'll never run out of content."

"It's not that. Or not that exactly," I said. "With the blog posts, I interviewed people — people from all over the place — by phone. But a podcast requires sound and I've vowed to do all interviews in person. I don't want any over-the-phone hum. Even the most high-tech recording equipment can't mask that. And I want to be *with* the sources."

"Why does that matter?"

"I want listeners to hear for themselves the…nuances. The sadness behind an offhand laugh, the southerner's twang, the exhaustion of a new parent. I love the intimacy of the audio format, but I can't just keep interviewing people from Southern California. Listeners will get bored. I might too." A couple on a tandem bike jingled their bell as they rode past us. "So, anyway, that's a wrinkle I haven't sorted out yet."

Brad smiled at me but didn't comment on my conundrum. It didn't matter. I really just hoped that he'd invite me inside, the next milestone in our burgeoning relationship. Yes, my mother's memorial was that morning but I didn't want to think about it. I was ready for my second kiss.

But instead he said, "Well, I'm sure you're worn out from the day."

Had my mother's funeral really been just hours ago? He assumed, as most people would, that I was in mourning, exhausted from grief. But the truth was, I felt an enormous release, not just from the obligation of taking care of her in her final weeks. It was a release from my mother herself, one that I'd longed for as long as I could remember.

"Yeah," I said, hoping my disappointment in not being asked inside was interpreted as the grief I was expected to have.

"Let's talk soon." Brad hugged me, planting a kiss on the top of my head, and went inside.

I stood there on Adelaide Drive not wanting to go home but not knowing where to go instead. My friends would assume, like Brad had, that I was too sad to socialize. And I didn't want to intrude on Jeff and Milt.

Just then, a petite woman with blond hair that shimmered in the fading afternoon sunlight who may or may not have been Reese Witherspoon passed by me with an oversized orange purse slung glamorously over her shoulder. I remained still and watched her walk, her thick shiny hair swaying with each step.

I wanted to be someone with the need for such a bag. But I usually wore a fanny pack and I was not going for an ironic or retro look. I carried with me merely the essentials — hand sanitizer, my wallet, my phone — with no need for a big orange bag. Someone who carried a big orange purse like that had a Big Life. I don't mean big like chartering a private jet to Cabo on a moment's notice. No, to me, a Big Life meant living with a distinct joie de vivre, a conspicuous engagement with life, a desire to celebrate little things, which turned them into big things. A person with a bag like that had symphony tickets and dinner parties, a stack of hardcovers to read and knowledge of skin care.

If people won't have much to say about you at your funeral (as I observed that very morning), if YouTube thinks all you're interested in is "Secrets You Never Knew about the Cast of Friends," then you're not leading the kind of Big Life I'm talking about. People with Big Lives I know: the woman who threw a reveal party when she received her pet mutt's DNA results, complete with huge balloons spelling the dog's name, a guessing game and cake. And my neighbor who hosted free pop-up classes in her kitchen teaching how to make authentic pot stickers exactly like her grandmother taught her. And the man whose "Fridays with Mom" Instagram account cataloged the adventures he planned — "Tasting Afghan food for the first time," "Mom at a Beyoncé concert" — for his eighty-three-year-old mother.

I wanted to ask Big-Orange-Purse Reese what she was carrying in that bag. Then I wanted to ask about her life's pivot moment, one of my favorite Peeps questions. But she was already out of sight.

I remained still on the sidewalk, the setting sun beating onto my scalp, caught between longing for a Big Life and the momentum of how mine had simply unfolded. Mine certainly wasn't a bad life, but it wasn't a big one. And my longing was confusing — after all, with Peeps, I *celebrated* little lives.

Could I even have a Big Life? I shook the thought out of my head like a swimmer knocking water from her ear. Big Lives, for all of their allure, were scary, carrying risks like defeat or disappointment. Still, *foreclosing* the chance at a Big Life was as frightening to me as pursuing one.

Finally, with no other options, I crossed the street, got into my car and drove home.

Hi. Welcome to episode seventeen of Peeps, the podcast where you can find the world in a grain of sand.

The Oceanside Hill branch of the Ventura library is a sleek, recently remodeled mid-century building. It features glass-enclosed reading rooms, oak stairs and even a small cafe. There I met Marcus, a friend of Renee who was interviewed back in episode four, on a sunny afternoon where we sat in the courtyard with its view of horse property just beyond the library. The scent there was a mixture of hay and sea salt. A stout guy with a shaved head and an expansive smile that fills the entire bottom half of his face, Marcus looks like a high school football coach. But that's not what he does.

Marcus, seven billion people live on this earth. What's it like to be you right now?

I'm a librarian here in Ventura. After college, I spent eighteen crappy months selling industrial carpets. Thought I was going to lose it. Just lose it. Boring and pointless, that work. No offense to anyone who does it. Just wasn't for me. One day of particularly uninspired work, I asked myself what I really enjoyed doing. Where was I, you know, happy? When I really thought about it, library images popped into my mind. I still remember getting my first library card at a small library up north in San Mateo where I grew up. I was only about five but I remember it for sure. I love the smell of libraries. The near, but not total, silence. I was a jock in high school, didn't ever spend much time in the school library, but I loved it there too. Even someone with my large build could, you know, kind of hide among the tall stacks. Sometimes I'd tell my buddies I had to do research for a paper when actually I just wanted to be in the library.

Go on...

So, yeah. I got a wrestling scholarship to UC Berkeley. It has the most spectacular libraries. Most people studied in Doe. It was like right out of movie. Majestic like a church, picturesque like a centuries-old Ivy League college. It's got old-fashioned lamps in the reading room and long tables where everyone flirted instead of studying. But as pretty as Doe was, I actually preferred "sleeper" libraries, as I thought of them. The one-room library in the paleontology building, the earth sciences library with its displays of rocks and old, dusty notebooks. Anyway, the point is, I loved libraries. Being in them. But also — and this is key — the philosophy behind them. The intellectual freedom and democracy of it all. So I ditched that awful carpet-selling job and went back to school. Got a master's in library and information science. I started off in an Oxnard middle school library. Then came here about, let's see, nine years ago now. It's a wonderful job. Mostly. In recent years, I've come to fear that I'm, um, going to be shot.

You— I'm sorry, what?

I'm chief librarian. Here almost every hour we're open. And I'm in charge. So I've gotta be the one to deescalate conflicts. Ask people to leave when necessary. A homeless person using the bathroom to bathe or sleep or shoot up. I mean, this magnificent institution is also a de facto shelter. My degree is in library science but I'm as much a social worker. A homeless woman actually died in the bathroom upstairs. Or it could be two teenagers who get into it about...whatever. Or it could be the person who starts yelling because he knows he returned all the books he checked out and refuses to pay the seventy-five cent late fine. I've dealt with this kinda stuff and more. These days, librarians — of all people — are on the front lines of the opioid epidemic, of homelessness. I'm mostly okay with it. But as you saw when you came in, my desk is right by the front door. So the city requires me to attend active shooter training every year. It's utterly unnerving. I try to concentrate on what I love about being a librarian. Helping to preserve history, being a center of education. Recently, a teenager thanked me because for her, this is a place to go when she feels unsafe at home.

That does sound challenging. Marcus, tell me about your background.

Let's see…. Well, here's something: I was one of four kids growing up and I'm smack in the middle. Like really the middle because my two younger brothers are twins.

That sounds like a fun upbringing. And if you could take one physical object with you after you die, what would it be?

So my dad passed away a few years ago. I had the oh-so-fun job of cleaning out his house. I found a box of his mother's — my grandmother's — belongings. More like mementos, right? I didn't know my grandmother. She died before I was born. It was mostly junk, as you might expect. But I did find an old journal. It was old, probably from the sixties. Spiral-bound. Pages crisp and yellowed. Inside was a list of books. Things like In Cold Blood and Flowers for Algernon and The Wizard of Oz. Better than that, it included the names of her friends who'd borrowed each book, the date she'd given it to them and whether it had been returned. Took me a minute to realize that she was her own personal librarian! Remarkable to me. No wonder I ended up in this job. So I'd take that.

What's one thing you do every day?

I've got an eleven-year-old daughter, Izzy, who lives most of the week with her mom. We're divorced. They live about two miles from my apartment. Every morning, I go on a run. Izzy's house is the half-way point, the spot I turn around. At precisely five minutes after seven, I knock on her window. I'm her alarm clock. It's a way for me to see her every day.

What was your pivot moment? In other words, what was the moment when something shifted for you?

Oh, easy. After my divorce — this was, let me see, about four years ago — I was at a New Year's Eve party. Afterwards, the host posted photos from the party online. I saw a picture of myself. I was like, I don't know, stunned. I mean, I'd seen the number on the scale. But I hadn't quite registered how heavy I'd gotten. I looked bloated. Like someone made one of those blow-up Halloween costumes of me. I looked downright awful. A switch was, like, you know, flipped. I stopped overeating. Immediately. Quit smoking cold turkey. I was down, really down, about my divorce. Being separated from Izzy. But I knew I wanted to live. It's probably why I'm so afraid of getting killed at work.

Who is someone you never saw again?

What do you mean?

I mean, is there someone in your life, someone important or someone fleeting, who you once knew or briefly crossed paths with, who you think about but no longer know or see?

Oh, yeah. Definitely. First person who comes to mind is a kid who moved into my neighborhood when I was in fourth grade. Same home room as me. He was different than me, though. I was big and not much into school back then. He was skinny and studious. But we, I don't know, clicked. His name was David. I don't remember anything about him other than he had blond, kind of frizzy hair, a lisp, and he told me that his mom had leukemia. Super nice kid. His backyard had this cool tree house. It was the bomb. We hung out there after school many afternoons that year. At school, we were in different friend groups. Matter of fact, some of the dopey guys I hung out with made fun of David's lisp behind his back. Hope he never knew that. Summer after fourth grade, his family moved away. I don't know where, when or why. Don't remember his last name. He was only in my school a year. Your question makes me realize I actually wonder about that kid all the time. Did his mom die from leukemia? Does he still lisp? What kind of life did he end up having? I wonder if he remembers our time in the tree house.

What's your life motto?

Oh, I don't have some grand philosophy or anything.

Do you have any, I don't know, mantras? Codes you live by?

Now that you mention it, something I say to Izzy every time I say goodbye is, "Remember who you are and whose you are." I want her to think about her identity. I don't want her to end up selling carpet by default because she hasn't considered what interests her, what's important to her. And I want Izzy to know that she's her father's daughter. Not like I own her or she's my possession or anything like that. Just that she's part of a family that loves her.

I'd like to thank Marcus for answering my questions. Have a suggestion for a future Peeps guest? Send me an email and let me know.

CHAPTER TWO

The day after my mother's funeral, I sat on a faux leather chair with threads coming loose at the seams. To my right, a Hollywood bro tried on black leather low-top Chucks and to my left sat a teenage girl in a tank top and booty shorts who made me feel every one of my fifty-one years. I, in contrast, wore elastic-waisted leggings and hoodie with the logo of my son's new college.

I probably didn't even need to try the shoes on since I was planning to buy the same Asics I'd been wearing for the last eight years. That was me: buy the same thing, do the same thing, eat the same thing, wear the same thing. I worked relentlessly to minimize surprises by sticking to formula in my clothes, my food, my schedule, anything I could routinize.

While waiting to be helped by a clerk, a low-pitch buzz emanated from my pocket.

I pulled out my phone and the screen revealed it was my best friend Scottie. Her real name is Michelle but her parents took one look at her outside the womb and started calling her a version of her middle name, Scott, which was her mother's maiden name.

"Hi," I answered, curious why she was calling since she'd already checked in twice since my mother's funeral.

"Kegel," Scottie said, and hung up.

I guffawed so loudly that the Hollywood bro narrowed his eyebrows at me.

Scottie and I regularly shared tips to forestall the increasingly rapid onslaught of aging. We were going to do everything in our power to keep our brains active (we had a 700-game Words with Friends streak), our bodies producing collagen, and our pelvic floors tight. That last one was easier for me since I'd only birthed one baby and she three, but more necessary for her because she was still having sex with her husband and I no longer had a husband. Sex with Brad was not imminent as far as I could tell.

My index finger punching the phone keyboard, I texted Scottie a check mark emoji. (Try hearing the word "kegel" and not doing it.)

"How can I help you?" The shoe store clerk had gray hair and a round face to match the shape of his belly, which hung over his black-belted navy slacks. He wore thick glasses, which he slid back up his nose with a middle finger, and too much cologne. He struck me as old, but then I realized he was probably my age, maybe even younger. Becoming parentless catapulted me closer to senior status.

"Hi," I said, lifting my right foot and circling my ankle. "Can I try on the latest version of these? Size seven and a half?"

He gave a thumbs up and turned on his heel toward the back room.

While waiting, I decided to do 5-4-3-2-1, a grounding mechanism my therapist Melinda taught me when she'd discovered that I was too often in my head, plotting out a safe, predictable path for my day and rehashing recent obstacles or hassles so I could craft ways to prevent them from happening again. Constantly noodling, I'd often pull into my driveway on Spruce Street and wonder how I got there, remembering nothing I'd passed along the way. I was always just…elsewhere. Worrying I'd been inadvertently dismissive while chatting with a girlfriend about an argument she'd had with her husband, wondering if I'd forgotten to put cooking oil on the grocery list, outlining in my mind an article I was writing for the legal newsletter I worked for.

Melinda recommended that at least once a day, I label five things I see, five things I hear, five things I feel, then four things I see, four things I hear, four things I feel, and so on. The exercise forced me to be present even just for a few moments. Sometimes I'd forget whether I was on threes or twos and that was proof that even while doing a grounding exercise I got swept away by the whoosh of my thoughts.

I enjoyed 5-4-3-2-1. It injected something new into an existence that had become…monochromatic.

Waiting for the Asics, I said to myself:

I see a teenage girl thumbing at warp speed on her phone.

I see the long line at the cashier.

I see the scratched up metal foot-measuring thingy.

I wanted to go through life with ease. But that wasn't how I operated. To me, the world was unpredictable, chance-laden, scary. So I remained on high alert, sussing out dangers. It was a helpful skill when it came to big things. For example, years ago, my instincts suggested something wasn't quite right with my son's guitar teacher, who, a few months later, was arrested for distributing child pornography. But it wasn't so helpful when my nervous system kicked into high gear when, for example, I approached grocery store checkout lines like everything depended on getting in the shortest line. I knew it was ridiculous, but my heart pounded and my quads clenched nonetheless.

Thoughts, Melinda explained, can be medicinal. But fear had its grubby tentacles on nearly every aspect of my life. She assured me that with diligent work I could change my neurochemistry, even deep in middle age, as I was. So I committed to a good solid try with Melinda's cognitive exercises.

The clerk dropped a box at my feet. "Let me know if you need another size."

White tissue paper crinkled as I removed the shoes. They fit perfectly, which was unsurprising since I'd worn the same model for nearly a decade.

"Keep the box. I'll wear them out," I told the man. My worn out pair thunked as they landed in the cylindrical donation bin next to the register.

In front of me in line to pay, a thirty-something couple stood with their arms around each other, palms slipped into the other's back pocket. Their soft giggles were like whispers and made the hair on my arms stand up. I had the not uncommon urge to ask them a couple of my standard questions for Peeps, my podcast.

What's it like to be you?

What's your motto for life?

It was an occupational hazard.

Instead, I turned away from their display of youth, catching sight of a nearby table showcasing shoes on clearance, including a pair of rugged outdoor ankle boots. A chalkboard sign next to them read: "Great for hiking & snow!" A mahogany color with copper-like clips for the laces, the boots were meant for rugged paths. I was no twenty-something Cheryl Strayed, hiking hundreds of miles up the Pacific Crest Trail. I would simply never have the occasion to wear such boots.

Then, right there in that shoe store, I just finally got sick of myself, of the way I'd been living and thinking.

"Uh, go ahead," I said to the person behind me as I stepped out of the checkout line and squatted next to the stacks of shoe boxes under the clearance table, my knees popping with the move.

The boxes were out of order but after a quick scan I spotted at the bottom of the pile the last pair of boots in my size. I took it as some sort of sign. My attempt to deftly slide the box out of the pile failed and the tower of boxes toppled. After putting everything back together, there was no way I wasn't getting those boots. Even at the clearance price, they weren't in my budget. I was still waiting for the legal publisher I worked for to sell the company, hopefully to a big media conglomerate, making my low-salary-large-ownership-shares arrangement worth it in the end.

But those boots represented something to me then — a faint, hopeful notion that perhaps at age fifty-one my life was not quite yet set in stone.

I signed "Megan Gale Newlin" on the credit card slip for my Asics and the impulse purchase. I preferred Meg or Meggie from people who'd known me forever, like Scottie. But for some reason I always signed my complete married legal name. Jeff and I were no longer married but I had warmer feelings towards him than towards my mother, my family of origin.

The warm Santa Monica air, always salty and dense whether it was April or October, assaulted me as I left the store, a generations-old mom-and-pop place tucked between fancier shops. To the left was a store bearing the name of a celebrity "lifestyle influencer" who'd begun her multimillion-dollar career as a dating show contestant. To my right was a crepe bar that threw off a yeasty aroma. I glanced right and left — up and down Wilshire Boulevard — trying to remember where I'd parked.

"Ma'am," I heard, as I pulled sunglasses from my fanny pack. "Ma'am!"

I felt a tap on my shoulder.

Oh, I thought, *I guess I'm the ma'am*. Despite the need to kegel and add calcium supplements to my daily routine, in many ways I still felt twenty-five.

I turned around to see the shoe store clerk holding out a brown box like an offering.

"You forgot your new boots."

I expected Laura to be ragged and hollow. So I was stunned at how content she seemed. Just forty, Laura was raising her eight-year-old son by herself after her husband died six months ago from a swift battle with ALS, according to a previous podcast source who'd recommended her. That's how I landed most of my podcast sources: suggestions from previous guests. It's like a chain I can trace back and back and back to my earliest interviews when Peeps was just a blog. Like we're all linked by, say, twenty degrees of separation.

Laura was beautiful, almost glamorous, with auburn hair swept into a casual ponytail, full lips, and a warm smile. Wearing trendy yoga pants that accented her shapely figure, she guided me through the front door of her Marina del Rey home and into her living room, a magazine-worthy sanctuary featuring warm white oversized couches, a black coffee table and sunshine yellow accents like pillows and sleek vases. Her design sense was tasteful and distinctly feminine. Nowhere did I spot a man's touch. My own place, in contrast, was awash in browns and other neutrals and was "decorated" with furniture that Jeff and I bought together decades ago or had been handed down to him from relatives.

"Are you a knitter?" I said, fingering a black and white mohair throw resting on a tufted sofa.

Laura opened her mouth to respond but was interrupted by the "garrraaahhhh" of a boy blowing through the living room wearing a dark Jedi cloak and wielding a light saber. He charged right up to my face and yelled "gaarrrraaahhhh" again, thrusting the light saber towards the ceiling.

"Oooh," I said approvingly to the boy, remembering my own son's Star Wars phase. Now Alex was a freshman at UT Austin and the wisest person I know, which is remarkable because as a toddler and in elementary school, Alex was a certifiable pain in the ass — defiant and annoyingly fussy. He'd refused to wear shoes or eat anything other than mango and yogurt or stop yelling "What the F?" whenever his teacher announced that recess was over. But around seventh grade — ironically, the age that most kids *become* difficult — he just mellowed out, seemingly overnight and through no special efforts on our part. He handled our divorce — and his father's new existence — like a champ, even without a sibling to commiserate with. It probably helped that Jeff and I remained on good terms, all things considered.

"Brandon," Laura said mildly. "That's not polite."

The boy narrowed his eyes at me and ran from the room as quickly as he'd come in.

"Sorry," Laura said.

"No worries," I replied. "I once had an eight-year-old boy myself."

"He's…still working through everything," she said, the perfect segue into our interview. I quickly set up my computer, external microphone and settled back against an oversized, fringed pillow that I wanted to take home with me, and began asking Laura my standard seven questions.

"Laura, there are seven billion people on earth — what's it like to be you right now?"

This was always the first Peeps question. In high school, I had a five-foot tall social studies teacher who frequently remarked, "Seven billion people, seven billion paths," a notion I loved because it somehow sanctioned my rigid, my predictable habits. So I turned that idea into my first question for Peeps. Sources usually dove right into whatever makes them *them*, launching into an answer about their job or ambitions, who they're in love with or trying to become.

"I'm starting to look into—"

"I'm going to Aidan's," Laura's son hollered as he dashed back down the stairs and out the front door, Star Wars cloak fluttering in his wake. He slammed the door before Laura could even respond.

Involuntarily, I widened my eyes in surprise. Marina del Rey was less urban than where I raised Alex, but I didn't know any eight-year-olds who walked anywhere in Los Angeles County alone.

"He's fine," Laura said, flapping a hand in front of her torso. She used her hands frequently when she spoke, something I planned to highlight in my intro, the primary way listeners could visualize my sources before they heard their voices.

"We spent nearly two years being sad," she continued by way of explanation. "And, for us, the worst has already happened. We were so busy with Brandon, with sports, school, work and bills, that I never realized how happy we were. And now it's all gone."

I nodded, wondering if I could keep this unexpected exchange in the audio or if I should edit it out. It was a balancing act, knowing when to stick precisely to the seven questions, when to ask a follow-up question, when to verbalize empathy, when to remain silent, neutral.

What exactly did that feel like, knowing the worst had happened? I moved through life believing the worst was always *about* to happen.

I turned my focus back to Laura, who, in answering my next few questions, revealed that she was considering going back to school for a master's in social work, to help families who'd been through what hers had. Beach air, with its hints of seaweed, traveled gently through the French doors at the far end of Laura's living room. Sunlight landed in shards on my laptop resting on the coffee table between us.

"Onto question six. Laura, who is someone you never saw again?"

Her face blanched. "You mean like my husband?"

"Oh, no. I mean, maybe. Could be. But it could be anyone."

"I'm not sure I understand." This question often stumped people and sometimes required explanation, which oftentimes I edited out of the episode.

"No worries. It's a tricky one. So here's what I mean: I think so often of people in my life — maybe someone I had a fleeting but memorable interaction with like a flight attendant or maybe a person I'd known pretty well like a college dorm mate — and wonder what happened to them. Or wish I could tell them something like, 'Thanks for being nice to me that day' or 'I'm sorry I wasn't a better friend to you.'"

"I see. I think. Can you give me an example?"

"Sure," I said. "You're not the only one who's asked. Here's one example from my own life. Once, when my son was an infant, I was pushing him in the stroller down Bundy Drive. It was noon, the sun was bright and I'd deliberately not dropped the stroller's shade because he'd been fussy all morning and I was hoping the bright sun would force him to close his eyes and finally, finally nap."

Laura nodded in mothers' understanding.

"So in the crosswalk — I remember exactly where it was, on the corner of Bundy and South Barrington — this woman marched past me and said sharply, 'That baby *needs a hat.*' I was stunned. When I reached the other corner and turned back around, the woman was gone. I wanted to say so many things to her: 'Um, he's got sunscreen on and I'm just trying to get him to close his eyes,' or 'How is this *any* of your business?' The point is, I still wonder about that woman all the time even though that baby of mine is now in college. I wonder, Who was she? What became of her? Does she have any recollection of that encounter, a one-sided interaction that has stayed with me nearly twenty years? And what is remarkable to me is that no matter how hard I tried, I'd never be able to find her. Ever."

Laura answered, telling me about a hospital nurse assigned to her husband but who spent more time caring compassionately for Laura and Brandon. I found myself then strangely jealous of Laura. Like my own mother, she'd suffered a massive tragedy in losing her young husband. But Laura was still young herself and had nothing but freedom to design her life going forward. And like her living room furnishings, it would be solely her design.

There I was, finally free of the day-to-day grind of parenting, the binds of a partnership, *of my mother*, but compared to Laura, I felt my life dwindling.

We said goodbye at her front door and I wrapped my arms around Laura. It was something I did after every interview because anyone who answered my seven questions became a friend.

I drove away and felt a surge, a jolt, a feeling of something shaking loose. I'd spent decades on high alert, afraid of what might happen: illness, loss. But my interview with Laura brought a new kind of terror, a corollary to my Big Life obsession: a fear of what *wouldn't* happen.

At a stoplight on the outskirts of Marina del Rey on my way back to Santa Monica, I spotted a flashing sign outside a small storefront. It read, "Future Teller."

Oh, jeez, I thought. *Could this timing be any cornier?*

Still, how could I ignore it?

Remembering Laura's life motto — "Everything is temporary" — I clicked my blinkers and pulled over. A single parking spot right across the street opened up at that precise moment.

Of course.

I was skeptical, yet eager, feeling equally foolish and emboldened.

When I reached the storefront, the door was locked. I stepped back and took another look at the sign, which buzzed noisily with each pulse of light. I wanted in. I tried the door again with no success and then peered inside, my palm shading my forehead against the glass. It was dark but a sliver of light shined through the bottom of a closed interior door. I fisted my hand, prepared to knock when that interior door opened right then.

Jeez.

A middle-aged man approached and unlocked the front door.

"Welcome," he said with a British accent. "What can I do for you?"

"Hi, is the—" I backed up to re-read the sign. "Is the 'future teller' available for a, um, reading?"

The man widened the door and beckoned me inside. "I am indeed."

He motioned me towards the interior door. I smelled incense. Frankincense, perhaps? I remained frozen, fearful I might be entering a den of captured sex slaves as in Pulp Fiction or Silence of the Lambs. This Brit, this man was not what I expected. I imagined an overweight woman wearing ankle bracelets and a mumu, a grandmotherly figure who'd assure me my future was bright and give me tips for how to move forward. Motherless, spouseless and, in a way, childless.

I took a step backwards. "I, um…."

What to say? *I'm afraid you're a serial killer? I'd come in if you were a woman?*

Instead, I said, "How much is a reading?"

"Ah," he said, and picked a slick brochure from a stack on a nearby coffee table and handed it to me.

Nigel Rand, it read. Future reader certified by the UK Divination Academy, the Psychic College of Massachusetts. Bonded by the California Agency of Industrial & Client Relations.

I brought my gaze from the brochure back to Nigel Rand. His expression was calm, self-assured and amiable. He wasn't grandmotherly but seemed trustworthy.

"Oh, I'm sorry, this is a little more than I wanted to spend," I said even though I hadn't even looked at the pricing. "Sorry to bother you."

He nodded a knowing smile and walked with me to the door.

"I'm here any time you'd like to learn about your future," he said.

I held up the brochure, a response of sorts. "Thank you."

Screeching my car out of Marina del Rey, I called Scottie.

"Dude," she said, "you should have done it."

I know, I thought. *I know*.

"You wouldn't have been scared?" I asked.

"Of what?"

Your future, I would have said were I being honest with Scottie — or myself. "Serial killer, rapist. Disguised as a fortune teller."

"Neither of which is likely to have a *storefront*," she said dryly.

"Need I remind you about Zed?" Pulp Fiction was one of our favorite movies.

Scottie hesitated. "Okay, maybe. But unlikely. Damn, I'm dying to know my future!"

When I arrived back in Santa Monica, I told Melinda about my impromptu stop during our therapy session that afternoon. I expected her to explore my being afraid to follow through. But she surprised me with the focus of her questions.

"What, exactly, were you hoping to learn from the fortune teller?"

"*Future* teller," I corrected.

She shrugged as if the distinction didn't matter.

"Well, my future."

"And why's that?"

"I just want to know — I feel like I *need* to know — what's next. I mean, where do I go from here?"

"From where?"

"Just…this stage of my life. I've raised my kid. I've buried my last living parent. I'm no longer a wife. My job is…sort of…inconsequential," I shrugged.

Melinda nodded again, staying silent. I was aware of the technique. Whenever I wanted a Peeps source to dig deeper, to continue on, I bit my tongue, forcing myself to wait at least seven one-Mississippi seconds before diving into the next question. Interviewees usually met those awkward seven seconds with blurted statements, often resulting in the golden bit that illuminated their whole story or served as a breadcrumb for a follow-up question.

I took a breath. "I just need some direction, some certainty about what's next."

She clicked her pen closed. Our hour was over.

"Believe it or not," Melinda said, "it's far more interesting to live in the real world."

CHAPTER THREE

I walked to 18th Street to pick up tamales. The weather was decidedly October-ish, with winds yanking hair from my ponytail. My hip joints were cranky as I made my way to Pancho's, a place I got takeout from at least twice a week. I was picking up dinner for my nephew Nathan, who was in town for just one night with his new girlfriend on the way from Chicago to Japan, where they were beginning an eight-month travel extravaganza before starting grad school. Nathan's warmth, his success made me less concerned about the effects of epigenetics — my recent obsession — on my family. Epigenetics is basically the idea that *acquired* characteristics can be transmitted to future generations.

On the way back from Pancho's, I cradled like a baby the sturdy weight of the warm bag of tamales. Walking around the Mid-City neighborhood, I glanced around, scouting, as always, for potential people to interview for Peeps. For variety, I turned down Euclid instead of continuing on 18th, my normal route. Two blocks later, I spotted a man loading large plastic containers into the side doors of a sparkling blue van. He was late twenties and heavily bearded, wearing sunglasses and a ball cap featuring a cartoon dog's face.

"Hello, there," he said, smiling as he slid a shallow but long container into the van.

"Hi," I said, glancing briefly inside. It was streamlined, all clean lines of steel and pine, punctuated with round USB ports and electrical plug-ins.

"Here, come closer," he said with the air of a proud father.

Again, serial killer and rapist images from Silence of the Lambs, of Pulp Fiction flashed in my mind, as did the Marina del Rey future teller, whose services I regretted declining.

My instinct was to bolt. But I fought that, instead stepping six inches closer, peering further inside and to the left, where I spotted a sink and what looked like a queen-size mattress. What I called "the cozy feeling" descended on me then.

I've always loved compact living spaces and the sense of hunkering down. My first cozy feeling occurred when Scottie invited me to spend the night on her grandfather's sailboat in Newport Beach when we were kids. We didn't even sail anywhere. We just spent the night docked in the marina. But I loved the efficiency of the boat's living space, with tables transforming into beds. I loved the pared-down feel, loved that you brought only the essentials and they remained right there within arm's reach. Rather than making me claustrophobic, the tight quarters made me feel protected, like all I had to do to remain safe was to stay within those two hundred square feet.

After college and before I married Jeff, I had my own apartment in Westwood, a modern condo I rented from the parents of a friend of a friend. It had a burglar alarm and I loved the occasional afternoon when I knew I wouldn't be going out again until the next morning. I'd change into my pajamas in the daylight and turn on the alarm. That hunkering down soothed me. The "cozy feeling" was one I frequently longed for. It was why I dragged Alex and Jeff on camping trips when Alex was younger. Holing up in a tiny tent with my two favorite people, zipping us inside for card games and snuggles was heavenly.

"This is the coolest thing I've seen in awhile," I said to the man.

The van had a masculine feel, in the same way that Laura's house felt distinctly feminine chic. Both places reflected the owners in a way that my own house, with its hodgepodge of hand-me-down and utilitarian Ikea furniture, did not.

The bearded man patted the side of the vehicle, making a thunking sound, which revealed its sturdiness. "Totally custom," he said, proudly but not boastfully. "Solar panels, plug-in hybrid engine, electric awning and outside shower hose."

I shifted the tamales from my left arm to my right. The afternoon Santa Ana winds picked up and more hair swirled out of my ponytail and circled my face like tumbleweeds in a tornado. I needed to get home, to prepare for hosting my nephew for dinner.

"Where're you going?" I asked, staying put.

"From here? Down the coast to Mexico. Want to finally learn Spanish. I started a month ago in Seattle and just spent a few weeks exploring the Bay Area."

"Are you on some kind of sabbatical?"

I clicked into interview mode, an autonomic response.

"Could say that," he said. "I spent the last six years working for a large online retailer up in Seattle. Just when I was starting to get bored with my work, my routine, I stumbled on an article about hashtag vanlife. Got no debt, no romance. Decided it was now or never to try it for myself."

"I admire your decisiveness." The tamales were already cooling in the bag. I pulled out my phone to check the time. "How'd you get this van so... personalized?" I continued with my questions.

"Woman in Spokane builds them. Does all the work herself. Took about three months." The metal twanged as he gently slapped the side of the van again.

I wanted to ask the price tag. Instead, I said, "Forgive me for asking, but, um, where do you go to the bathroom?"

"Ah," he said, with the drama of a magician about to reveal your card. "Check this out."

He pulled open a tall, wide drawer near the door. "Behold the compost toilet. I don't use it a lot. I try to use gas stations and gyms whenever possible. But this works in a pinch."

There it was, that cozy feeling. From a toilet, of all things.

"I host a podcast. It's called Peeps. It's an interview show about everyday people. I ask every source the same seven questions. I'd love to have you on, if you're willing."

Shifting the food bag again, I unzipped my fanny pack and pulled out a square business card with my email, cell number and an avatar of my face. The man in the van took it from me.

"Cool beans," he said. "I love podcasts. You listen to Serial?"

Of course I'd listened to Serial, as had half the human race. His question was an unpleasant reminder that I'd probably bitten off more than I could chew with Peeps. I mean, my teeny little episodes were surely getting lost amidst the crowded field of professionally produced podcasts. Those with big money backers, real reporters, original theme music. I had no financial backing, no production company promoting Peeps. I'd joined a podcasters trade organization, Pod Path, and had recently spent hours on an application for one of their coveted grants. But I was still learning about advertising, finding more listeners.

"Yeah," I said, unable to mask a defeated sigh. "Serial's great, the gold standard."

"I'd love to be on your show. Can we do it tonight? I'm heading out for Orange County at sunrise."

I lifted the tamales up by way of explanation. "Wish I could, but I've got company coming over. Will you be returning to Los Angeles after Mexico?"

"That's my plan. From there, it's anyone's guess."

"Great. When you're a few days away from LA again, message me and we'll meet up."

He slipped my card into the pocket of his shorts. "Looking forward to it."

At home, I heated the tamales and quickly pulled together my signature guacamole, my one culinary specialty, so I could squeeze in some research on van life. I loved that feeling, the quickened heart rate and warm flush after hearing about something totally new, whether it was a useful new app or a must-see TV show. I quickly discovered dozens of articles and videos about the van life community, custom vans and various routes, and marveled at the courage of people who upended their lives for the unknown. It was similar to how I felt observing my ex-husband begin his own new life.

Fifteen minutes earlier than expected, the doorbell rang, bringing my research to an abrupt halt. Happy as I was to see Nathan, I felt a little like an energetic puppy called back indoors just moments after being let out into the yard. Still, I threw my arms around my nephew's neck before he even crossed through the front door. And on first glance, I liked his new girlfriend, a tiny brunette with a pixie cut and a gymnast's figure who greeted me with a half-dozen cookies still warm in the box.

"'Auntie Meggie loves chocolate,' I told her!" Nathan announced.

We skipped the formality of pre-dinner cocktails and appetizers and sat right down at the dining room table and dove into the tamales, my guacamole and my favorite, extra salty lime-tinted chips.

"How's your dad?" I asked. Rather than bond over our own father's early, unexpected death from cardiac arrest or the common foe of our difficult mother, Leith and I retreated into worlds of our own. Mine with Scottie and solitary interests like poetry and writing. His with skater dudes, pot and even petty thefts. Now almost fifty and living in Sacramento, my brother was still very much into skating and pot. Meanwhile, his son Nathan had put himself through college and earned a grad school scholarship. "He was only down here for a day and a half for the funeral so I didn't get to spend much time with him."

Nathan lifted his eyebrows and pursed his lips. "You know, the same."

I took my cue to change the subject. I turned to his girlfriend. "Here's one of my favorite Nathan stories."

"Oh boy," my nephew said.

"Not to worry — it's cute, not embarrassing. When Nathan was in kindergarten, he called me one afternoon to tell me that 'kids were teasing' him on the goat farm field trip he'd taken that day. Of course, protective auntie that I am, I was ready to drive up to Sacramento and beat those kids up! But then Nathan's dad got on the phone and explained that because of Nathan's toothlessness combined with his six-year-old lisp, I'd misunderstood that the 'kids' were actually baby goats and they were '*teething*' not teasing him."

We cut the salt of our dinner by digging into the cookies they'd brought and I brewed some decaf. They gave me a play-by-play of their upcoming trip to Asia.

"I want to hear about your podcast," Nathan's girlfriend said.

"I just heard the latest one — about the librarian guy," Nathan added. "I think your show is really gonna take off."

"Not sure about that," I said. "But it keeps me out of trouble." I explained to his girlfriend the premise of Peeps, the seven questions.

"Which question is your favorite?" she asked.

"Definitely the 'who'd you never see again' question. Not everyone gets it at first. I often have to explain what I mean. But I'm fascinated by people who are in our lives, whether momentarily or longer, and then just…disappear. People who are literally impossible to find again but who manage to stay with us."

"I've never thought about that," she said.

"Most people don't. I'm weird that way."

"No, it's cool. It has a bit of a…cosmic element to it."

I flashed back to the future teller. "I suppose so."

"So who is someone *you* never saw again?" she asked Nathan, rubbing the back of his neck. "A long-ago girlfriend you still pine for?"

He rolled his eyes at her playfully. "Definitely not. I actually *have* thought about this since listening to your show, Auntie Meggie. It really makes you, I don't know…scour your memories."

Something fluttered in my belly. That's precisely how I wanted listeners to respond.

"So," Nathan continued, "there was this kid I went to high school with. He went by RJ. I don't even know what that stood for. A nerdy guy, not a lot of friends. Nice kid, though. I didn't know him well. But one day senior year he called me at home. We weren't even close enough for him to have my cell number. He probably looked my home number up on the class list. Anyway, he said that his father had passed away. Asked if I'd come to the service the next day."

"What'd you say?" I said.

"I was pretty speechless. Not only because his father died but because I hardly knew him and yet he was asking me to be with him at his father's funeral. But I agreed. Hardly anyone was there. It was so small that it was in the family's living room. It was clear from the remarks that his father had died after swallowing a handful of opioids."

"How awful," Nathan's girlfriend said.

"Right? I felt so bad for the guy. I mean, if the same thing had happened to me, it would not have even *occurred* to me to invite *him*. That's how few friends this kid had. Anyway, that was during the last weeks of senior year. Don't even know where he went to college. Or if he did. I wonder about that guy a lot, actually. Did he recover from that tragedy? Tried finding him online a few times. But 'RJ Golden' is just too broad a search."

And with that, it was confirmed: Nathan was still as awesome as he'd always been. He showed no traits of Leith or, thankfully, my mother, his grandmother. Chalk one against epigenetics.

The conversation evolved and I smiled, elbow on the table, my chin in my hand, as Nathan recounted how he and his girlfriend met while working as servers in the same off-campus diner. But like a jazz standard in the background of restaurant din, the man with the van flitted through my mind.

The earlier flickers of twisted jealousy of Laura the young widow transformed by nighttime into an embryonic heartbeat, the thrill of a new notion. It was an unlikely idea until I remembered that my pathological need for predictability, for safety strangely co-existed with lifelong fantasies of escape. It's why The Fugitive was my all-time favorite movie. And it was probably why I loved that cozy sailboat, on which one could depart on a moment's notice with just the barest of necessities. It was why when I lived in that Westwood apartment after college, I periodically surveyed my belongings, maniacally purging whenever I sensed that I'd acquired too much for a quick escape, were it necessary, one of my strange and soothing rituals. It was why I harbored shameful fantasies about leaving Jeff long before he upended our marriage.

Nathan and his girlfriend helped bring the dishes from the dining room to the sink. As they stood in my kitchen, arms wrapped around each other, a thought rose to my pre-frontal cortex, hitting my psyche with clarity as their energy seemed to increase at precisely the same rate that my own eyes began to droop with exhaustion.

They're so young.

At the front door on their way out, I gifted Nathan and his girlfriend small, leather travel journals.

"It's old-school, I know," I said. "But one way or another, write down your experiences. Take it from an old lady like me, you'll be glad you captured this time so you can re-live the details someday."

"If you're an old lady," Nathan's girlfriend said, "then I can't wait to grow old."

"I knew I liked you!"

They set out, promising — just like the man in the van — to visit again on the return from their adventure. I left all the dishes and other dinner detritus in the sink and went to my bedroom, where I sat nude at the bay window with its sliver of Pacific Ocean view. Moonlight threw sepia streaks through the upper glass, which augmented the fluorescent light of the magnifying mirror I used every night to scan my chin for coarse hairs that had emerged throughout the day. They were always there.

Mexico, Japan. What would Nathan and the man in the van discover?

Meanwhile, my life was either half over — or I had half left to live. Would the second half be driven, as the first, by drift — or by design?

I knew I was no explorer. I was a certifiable scaredy cat.

The night I went into labor with Alex, a hospital triage nurse checked my cervix.

"Yup," she confirmed. "You're dilating."

I burst into tears, heaving, covering my face with my hands.

"What's the matter, hon?" she asked, snapping off her latex glove.

"I'm scared," I sobbed.

"Of what?" she said softly, placing a hand on my bent knee and looking sideways at Jeff, whose concerned expression matched hers. One consequence of my mother constantly telling me to "calm down," to "stop

39

overreacting" was that I wasn't much of a crier. So my outburst alarmed Jeff.

"Of *everything*."

That was true in that moment. It was true after giving birth. It was true as long as I could remember. Moving through the world with generalized fear not only limited my life, but it led to self-loathing. I wasn't a man who'd lost a son to gang violence, a mom with MS who was the sole caretaker for her severely autistic daughter, both people I'd interviewed for Peeps. Who was *I* to be afraid all the time? My surprise divorce was sad. But Alex was nearly grown so I lost little time with him. And Jeff and I remained as close as two formerly married people could be.

I started seeing Melinda because I wanted to root out that fear. She informed me that if I did not gather the strength to wrestle fear down to the ground, it would destroy me. I started studying epigenetics, cellular memory, DNA, because I wanted to get at its source. I was a quarter of the way through *Transgenerational Transmission of Environmental Information*, the 600-page hardcover on my nightstand.

Bzzzz. Bzzzz. Bzzzz.

The phone interrupting thoughts startled me so badly that I dropped my tweezers, which poked a tiny hole in my bare thigh. Caller ID revealed that it was Brad.

"Hello?" I answered.

"Hi," he said, his voice pleasant and deep. Sexy. "What'cha doing?"

I put the magnifying mirror down and gazed out the window. The sky was stripes of grey and black, punctuated by specks of stars.

"I just had dinner with my nephew and his girlfriend. They're heading to Asia tomorrow."

"Any interest in meeting up for a drink? Or coffee?"

On any other night, I would have tingled like a schoolgirl at his late-night call. But my body was already heavy with sleep, my mind occupied with the people I'd crossed paths with. "I'm sure I sound like a senior citizen but—"

"I understand. It's late. How about we watch something together? We can do it over the phone. From bed. Like Harry and Sally."

Any man who references When Harry Met Sally was a man whose interest was worth keeping.

"We could even watch that very movie," he added.

But I really was tired. And I needed to process my day, the strange urge that overwhelmed me, perhaps my own personal on-ramp to a Big Life. I was constitutionally opposite from the man in the van, from Nathan. There was a difference between curiosity, which I had, and boldness, which I didn't. And yet I sensed the urge I had was fleeting: if I didn't act soon, it would pass.

"Another night? I love the idea. I'm just not up for it tonight."

My heart quickened as I ended the call. Declining an invitation from Brad was something I wouldn't have done even yesterday. But I wanted to sit alone awhile longer with that nascent spark of an idea, to turn it around and inspect it from every angle, the way a child would examine a colorful marble. I knew that with a host of other middle-aged divorcees probably interested in him, Brad might not call again.

Looking back, in declining that phone call I'd made the decision to leave.

It's episode twenty-three, Peeps listeners. Thank you for joining me to find the world in a grain of sand. In this installment, you'll meet Alejandra in Long Beach. Alejandra frequently ends sentences with a soothing "ya?", a verbal tic that made me lean towards her, eager for her next words. Her studio apartment in a senior home is like Alejandra herself: warm and inviting. She has no fewer than three orchids — purple, white and yellow — blooming in her tiny home. A Rummikub set has pride of place atop her coffee table. One of her neighbors came over to play the moment we completed our interview, an illustration of Alejandra's bustling social calendar.

Seven billion people in this world, seven billion stories. Tell me what it's like to be you right now.

Well, this week I'm preparing for the annual "Walker Waltz" here. An old-fashioned dance-off like the ones we had in the fifties, ya? Downstairs in the big rec room. They move all the tables and all the chairs to the edges of the room. We dance. No partners. Just everybody dancing. You should see us! They play songs from our time. The forties, fifties, sixties. Then the judges — they're just the cooks and other workers here but they're judges just the same — they come around and tap us out if they're not impressed with our moves. You get tapped? You gotta sit down. The idea is that the best dancer is the one left standing, untapped. They have prizes for first, second and third place. The best prize is that you get to pick the kitchen menu for an entire day. Including dessert! I haven't won yet. But last year I came in fourth. So this could be my year, ya? My friend Jan, she lives down the hall. We've been practicing, testing out steps as fancy as we can make them. Building our stamina. Last year's Walker Waltz lasted ninety minutes! My grandnephew showed me some moves. But I can't do any of that crazy stuff. Looking like a robot or a sprinkler hose! He makes me laugh, though.

I'd love to know more about you and your background.

I met my husband in college in 'fifty eight. I was just there in school, minding my own business. And he was minding his, ya? We were walking along the main promenade. Separately. A guy with a camera approached me. Not one of those little cameras they have now. Not a camera phone or anything like that. It was a Kodak. Big as a brick. That guy asked if I could spare a minute. Said he had to take pictures of students "in action" for a campus brochure. I was on my way to U.S. History. I remember that because I had a little crush on the professor. But class wasn't starting for about fifteen more minutes so I agreed.

What happened next?

"Stay here!" he said, then dashed like a bullet back down the promenade. He grabbed another student, a big handsome boy I'd never seen. I couldn't hear what the photographer said to the boy but I saw him point over to me. The big guy nodded and the two approached me. The photographer instructed me and that boy to walk towards him but look at each other and pretend like we were talking. But, let me tell ya, we didn't need to pretend! Ernest, that was the tall boy's name, was cracking jokes. Really making me laugh. I didn't have to make believe a thing! I was wearing a short-sleeved turtleneck and a skirt. He was wearing a tie. You did that in those days, ya? Two minutes later, the photographer thanked us, then moved on to other students for more pictures. But from then on Ernest and I never stopped talking. We married the following year right after he graduated. I finished up my degree the next year. Our connection must have been clear because one of those photos of us was used for the front page of that campus brochure! It's right there in that frame behind you on the table.

So sweet. What a fun way to meet a life partner. Alejandra, if you could take any object into the afterlife, what would it be?

Ernest died about fifteen years ago. But my love for him didn't stop simply because his soul departed his body, ya? Neither did my desire to talk to him, to tell him everything. When they discontinued Product 19 cereal, I wanted to tell him. When the Giants finally won the World Series. When I was struck with the memory of the time we saw a perfectly good futon that had been discarded next to a dumpster near our first apartment and we lugged it four blocks to our place and I wet my pants because we were laughing so hard. I didn't want to stop having a conversation with my husband just because he was gone, ya? So I started writing it all down. Got myself a folder. Labeled it "Things I Wanted to Tell You." I need to get a new one soon because this one is almost full.

What's one thing you do every single day?

My younger sister Manuela lives in Seattle. Her birth date is one-twenty-three-forty-five! We're both getting up there, can't really travel much. She thinks she's plenty fine for a two-hour flight here. But her kids say she's too frail and won't let her. I'm not sure I'm up for it either. But we're still very close. We grew up playing music. She plays violin. I play flute. We hated all the lessons and recitals when we were kids. But we both kept it up even when we were no longer forced to. So every day we play one piece together on the phone. For a long time, our phone bills were through the roof. But rates have gone down. My niece, her daughter, showed me how to use FaceTime on my phone. She showed Manuela too. So now we can see each other when we play. We pick one piece, play it for a couple of weeks. When we get bored, we pick another. Right now, we're playing a Vivaldi flute concerto.

What was a pivot moment in your life?

My husband having the name Ernest was funny to most people because he was truly such an earnest man. Hard-working, loving, ya? The last words he said to me before he died were: "You made my life." In that sad moment I remembered back to the time of our ten-year anniversary. We'd managed to save a little bit of money by then. We were deciding whether to use it to recarpet our living room or blow it all on an anniversary trip. After a lot of hand-wringing, we decided to spend it on a four-day trip to Hawaii. Had the most wonderful time. Saw whales. Ate sushi for the first time. Took hula lessons on the front lawn of the hotel and laughed ourselves silly! Hearing Ernest's final words to me, I remembered that wonderful vacation and thought, "What would I do with wall-to-wall carpeting now?"

Who is someone you never saw again? And what I mean is, someone you knew or someone you just saw for a moment, someone you remember but never saw again.

Well, at my age, I've lost many friends. But someone else in particular comes to mind. We used to have an activities coordinator here. Jenna. She planned really fun things. Comedians to come in and perform for us old bats. Visits to lesser known museums like a ceramics museum just down the road that I never knew existed. She arranged for UCLA and Long Beach State professors to give lectures here. Come to think of it, she's the one who started the "Walker Waltz." I learned to play Rummikub because Jenna sometimes stayed after work to play with me. It's become one of my favorite pastimes. Jenna was real with me. "How ya doing today, kid?" she'd always say. "Filled up your Depends yet?"

I loved it. Too many people treat us old people like we're fragile china or something, ya? Anyway, Jenna got another job. We have a new activities coordinator now. But he's not as good.

What's your life motto?

Oh, well, my sister Manuela and I always say, have a lot of faith. And if that doesn't work, have a lot of mimosas.

Thanks to Alejandra for sharing her story with us. Join me next time to hear one long-haul trucker's surprising hobby. Hint: it involves a hook. And I'm not talking about a fishing hook.

CHAPTER FOUR

"**Y**ou quit your fucking *job*?" Jeff replied when I informed him of my plan. We met as freshmen at UCLA and he knew me, maybe even loved me, better than anyone.

"Uh huh," I said, annoyed that my ex-husband still had the ability to make me feel sheepish. I still couldn't believe it myself, though, what I'd done. Had Marcus the librarian felt this astonished when he quit selling industrial carpet?

Once the idea sprouted in my brain, it was as if it was already decided, like the way that first inkling of "maybe I won't go to the gym today" results in an afternoon on the couch. Once thought, it was done. Imagining weeks or months of solitude, peppered with interviews with new people, became something that energized and calmed, thrilled and terrified me. Some kind of tornado funneled me right out of my existence. It was like I was…flung.

"Isn't your company looking for buyers? Wasn't that the big payoff you've been waiting for?"

"Uh huh." I squeezed my eyes shut.

What had I done?

Jeff's reaction echoed that of my friend Jill, whose only words for me were, "Wow, I could *never* do that." I had no idea whether I could either.

"Do you think maybe you're, I don't know, running away from home? I mean, your mom just died. Don't you want life to settle down before such a big decision?"

What was keeping me in Santa Monica anyway? My son was in college in Texas. Jeff and I would stay connected whether we saw each other in person or not. Scottie and I hadn't lived in the same state in more than thirty years. Of course, I had my friends in LA, those friends who'd attended my mother's memorial. They were friends to grab coffee with, to join me for a movie. But they weren't like Scottie, the kinds of friends I saw on TV or in movies — there was no one in LA for whom I'd safeguard a mortal lie, anyone I'd ask to fish out a wayward diaphragm like in Sex and the City. Yet on the road, I'd know *no one*.

"Running away from home? Really, Jeff? I'm trying to…I'm trying to *understand* home. What is it for me now? My mother is gone. Alex is gone to college. You're gone with Milt."

"I'm never gone from you."

They say you marry someone else's family, which is true. How lucky I'd been to marry into Jeff's. They were so normal, bordering on boring, and I was all in. The stable insurance business his parents ran together. The ranch-style house. The sturdy American cars. I felt badly that Jeff had inherited my family, my dead dad, volatile mother, my disinterested brother.

But I'd take the expression one step further. You also marry someone else's childhood. Jeff married mine, complete with cruel critiques and love that had to be earned. And maybe, as my new research was suggesting, he'd even married my ancestors. And I'd married his. What I discovered only after many years was that Jeff's childhood had been one of tamping down. His inclinations had been suspected and therefore suppressed. It was like when Scottie's parents discovered she was a leftie and then forced her to only write with her right hand. It worked, but only for pens. Everything else — from turning doorknobs to punching in a phone number — she still did with her left hand. "Things were different then," both Scottie's and Jeff's parents would say later about their choices, which by today's standards seemed unduly harsh.

When Jeff told me that he'd fallen in love with Milt, his physical therapist, the man who'd been assigned to strengthen his quads after ACL surgery, we laid in bed, clutching each other, weeping. It was surreal to be clinging for support to the person who was responsible for my distress. Little did he know that mixed in with shock and sadness — especially for Alex — I cried out of shame. Because even though my marriage had been a loving one, I was strangely relieved to be released from it. He didn't know that I'd long wondered how it was possible to be both happily married and also deeply unfulfilled, even lonely. I'd privately pondered what life would be like without him, about who I'd be with a different life partner or no partner at all. Blindsided, relieved, I was also, of all things, a little jealous. Jeff was courageous in a way that I never could be.

"And I'm never gone from *you*," I finally said on the phone then. "But you're growing old with someone else now."

"Ouch."

"You know what I mean."

Hot sea air drifted into the kitchen from an open window and I moved toward it to breathe it in.

"I've been wondering for awhile how I can take Peeps to the next level," I added. "Now I can interview people from all over. Coal miners in Wyoming, teachers in…I don't know…Minnesota, women's clinic doctors in Mississippi, famous authors living…wherever…Seattle, Atlanta."

"You've told Alex?" he asked.

"I did."

"And?"

"He loves the idea."

"Of course."

We both knew our son, a new adult with an octogenarian's wisdom. "He only required that Austin be on the itinerary."

"Easy ask," Jeff said, with a half laugh. "Okay, so you quit your job. You're following the Yellow Brick Road in an RV. How are you going to, you know, support yourself?"

The question bloomed with subtext. Even a decent divorce like ours was expensive. Jeff paid me alimony and, probably due to guilt, was exceedingly diligent about the checks. Every few weeks, he delivered them in person, along with biscotti from our favorite Westwood bakery. I brewed Earl Grey and we chatted, mostly about our boy, just like we've always done. It's a strange and kind of beautiful ritual. In the divorce settlement I paid him a dollar for our Spruce Street house, now worth triple what we paid for it twenty years ago.

When Alex was in high school, I started working for my friend Dana, who published a weekly newsletter for attorneys, a widely read staple in the legal profession. I spent twenty hours a week writing for and editing it. Dana's end game was for the newsletter to be purchased by a publishing conglomerate. She'd been approached a few times but was holding out for the magic offer. If Dana played her cards right, she wouldn't have to work again once the newsletter was sold. Part of my salary was paid in equity so I, too, had much to gain. But I'd just thrown away a stable income and the chance for a huge upside by quitting. When I'd called Dana to resign, she'd seemed oddly unmoved, which was a blow to my already precarious ego.

"I have money saved," I said to Jeff.

"I trust you," he said with an exhale. "But...I'll miss you."

Obsessive vehicle research kept me up many late nights. I'd lie in bed weighing pros and cons of the dozens of options. Convinced there was a distinct right and wrong choice, I wanted to make sure I landed on the correct side. I quickly eliminated the option of a custom van like the one I'd seen on the street in Santa Monica. They were too pricey and I needed more than an outdoor shower hose and a compost toilet that slid under a kitchen counter.

I went to two RV lots in Simi Valley. I left the first one within thirty minutes because the showroom manager kept putting his hands on my shoulders as we maneuvered through different units. At the second showroom, I headed right for the first woman I spotted wearing the blue corporate t-shirt.

Before we toured a single rig, Sharon ran through the options.

"A towable unit will be cheaper. And you can unhitch and use your car to get around town once you've parked the RV," she explained. "The downside is you have to re-hitch whenever you want to get going out of town again."

"Mmm, not sure that'll work. I don't plan on staying more than a day or two — maybe even less — in each location." And the truth was, I wanted to be able to depart — *to escape*, really — on a moment's notice without having to hook everything back up, something I was already insecure about my ability to do.

She guided me to a twenty-four-foot drivable Class C with a gas engine.

"Big enough for a proper bathroom and small enough to park on the streets of even the most populous cities," Sharon said. "And you don't need a special license to drive."

Something about its compactness appealed to me. It was my antidote to the fear of the wide open spaces I was about to venture into alone. Shrinking my surroundings, it seemed, would enable me to drive off towards that Big Life I coveted.

I settled on a Ceres Prime built on a Ford chassis cab. It was brand new but last year's model so I got a discount. Sharon had a fancier model for the same price, but it was used. "I'll take the new one," I said. "I once saw a toenail clipping on the floor of a hotel room and I've never been the same."

I drew on my home equity line to buy it. Money would be tight, and I needed to be frugal on the road. But I knew that some people, families even, lived in motor homes full time because they had to. I knew how lucky I was to be able to choose to take the journey. My spine tingled as I initialed "MGN" at the bottom of every page of the purchase agreement.

"Last decision: exterior color," Sharon said as she collated the paperwork.

"I like the color of the demo," I said. "That sandy beige?"

"You said you're doing this drive alone?"

I nodded, unsure what that had to do with vehicle color.

"Let me recommend this one," she said, flipping through a large binder and then spinning it towards me. "Midnight Sparkle."

"I don't know," I hesitated. "It's kind of…masculine."

"That's the idea. You *want* it to appear masculine. Otherwise someone might presume the situation to be exactly what it is: a vulnerable, middle-aged woman traveling alone."

An old-fashioned paper map came "free" with the RV. The morning after making my purchase I unfolded it on my dining room table and stood over it for thirty minutes at a stretch just looking. Santa Fe, St. Louis, St. Paul. Those might be stops along the way but my definitive destination would be Syracuse, New York: 2,700 miles from my home and hometown of Los Angeles to the hometown of my mother. There, I'd see my uncle Oscar, my mother's remaining living sibling. I'd always loved him but hadn't seen him in years. I'd never talked with him about my mother, how she treated me. And she never told me much about how they'd grown up. My bedside research about epigenetics raised questions about how her early life impacted my own.

Just as I was about to fold up the map, Alex FaceTimed me.

"Hang on," he said after I answered. I got a view of his dorm carpet as he carried the phone across the hall.

"Dude," I heard him say, "what's that site again? The one you used when you drove here from Boston at the end of the summer?"

I heard a muffled response and then Alex say, "Thanks, man," before putting his face back in front of the camera for me to see. "Mom, check out iTravel. A guy on my floor used it when he brought his car out here this semester. It gives you routes, places to eat. It's all user-driven. No pun intended."

I spent the next hours on iTravel and then marked my definitive route on the paper map with a brand new yellow highlighter. The path was unorthodox, traveling up and down — or, rather, down and up — and east-ward. It looked like a yellow echocardiogram of the country, which struck me as an apt metaphor. I felt, after all, that somehow the health of my heart depended on this trip.

Water factored into my route as I vowed never to stray more than thirty miles from a water source, be it an ocean, lake, river or sound. Even though I rarely dipped even a toe into the Pacific, I felt a strange security living a few hundred yards from it. And so when I stared at the map on my table, I zeroed in on irregular blue splotches and zig-zaggy blue lines. The size and length didn't matter. I just needed to be near it.

I also sought patches of green. Jeff and I had never been an out-doorsy couple, but now I wanted to explore nature. One of the most inter-esting Peeps interviews I'd done was with a Pepperdine professor who studied *shinrin-yoku*, the Japanese concept of forest bathing, or using time in nature to induce health benefits like reduced blood pressure, and to treat grief and depression. I planned to test it out.

Next on my list was whittling down my belongings. I cracked open plastic storage containers I filled with my brown comforter, khaki shorts and other items that weren't meant for RV life or for late fall and winter weather in the South, Midwest and East. I tossed tons. A stack of Blue Books from UCLA. (For years after graduating, I was certain someone would claim I hadn't really completed all my credits so I held onto those Blue Books as proof.) The size six swimsuit from my Maui honeymoon that I'd kept just in case the "one stomach flu away from my ideal weight" notion was true. (It's not.)

In addition to purging my possessions, I cleaned and cleaned. The chlorine smell of Clorox wipes became intoxicating. I'd always felt an odd satisfaction from wiping down my kitchen counters every morning whether they needed it or not. But this was next level. I emptied my bedroom closet and, on my hands and knees, I dug deep into the corners of the hardwood floor, sweeping orphan grains of sand towards me. I rarely went to the beach but somehow living in Santa Monica meant sand infiltrated everything.

In a long and shallow plastic bin that slid neatly into the RV's underbelly storage, I packed items to bring on my trip: the heavy hiking shoes I'd bought on a whim, *Transgenerational Transmission of Environmental Information,* a framed journal entry that Alex had written in kindergarten using his "best guess spelling" that never failed to make me laugh. ("Ay lyke schol. Sum problms. Tu much paypr waystid on arplaynes.") A bottle of Viagra that Jeff left in our medicine cabinet when he moved out. Some condoms I found in Alex's dresser when I packed up his room. Suffice it to say I was open to dating both older and younger men along the way.

My kneecaps ached from wiping floors and my hips hurt from going up and down the kitchen stepstool to gather glasses and vases from upper cabinets. So I took a break. Scottie had recently extolled the virtues of compression socks so I slid on my new pair before sinking onto the couch with my computer.

I created a new file: On the Road Peeps Sources. If I was going to elevate my podcast while traveling east toward my uncle, I needed to find people to interview. I dropped into that file names, numbers and email addresses after scouring old messages I'd received with out-of-area sources who'd been recommended but were previously inaccessible because they were too far away. And I posted on the old Peeps blog a call for new sources country-wide, with a note that the most urgent need was for sources in California's Central Valley, where I'd be headed first. Finally, I wrote to a few college friends and colleagues from Dana's newsletter asking for source ideas. It was unnerving, putting myself out there. I was shy about the show.

I poured myself an eighth of a glass of Chardonnay and returned to the couch.

"Snark alert," Scottie texted a few minutes later. "Have u seen Paige Harger's new profile pic — yikes!"

"Call me," I wrote back. "Got news." It was time to tell my best friend what I'd done.

"That," she said after I filled her in, "is mother fucking bad ass."

"I wouldn't go that far," I replied, though I was relieved to have not just her approval but her enthusiasm, which helped patch over Jeff's financial concerns.

"You're a shero!"

"Would you fuck off already?" I said. Truth be told, *Scottie* was my hero. Gorgeous, with long legs and thick, wavy hair that required no coloring even at our age, she was also whip smart, a scientist whose job had something to do with identifying biomarkers for obscure medical conditions. A bit of a troublemaker too, it was Scottie who introduced me to Bud Light in ninth grade. She now lived in Connecticut and we spoke or texted once or twice a week. Topics had shifted in recent years from fifty percent

British royal family gossip, thirty percent stories about our kids, twenty percent snarky comments about high school friends' Facebook posts ("Lara Greer looks like a drag queen!") to ninety percent perimenopause.

"I always thought it would be me who picked up and left. My current fantasy is Iceland," she said.

"You always did love the cold."

"How are you doing without, you know, your mom?"

Scottie knew there were no easy answers. Once when I slept over at her house, Scottie's parents returned home tipsy after a dinner party. Her mom, who'd known me forever, sat with us in the kitchen as we gossiped about various romances among our friends. Slurring, Scottie's mom revealed, "Every time I saw your parents, Meggie — in the grocery store, at a preschool event — they were bickering. *Every* time. And it struck me because your father seemed so…gentle when he was by himself. An odd match. She's so…prickly. Anyway," she said, swinging her sequined handbag over her shoulder and heading upstairs to join her husband, leaving me and Scottie speechless in her wake, "your mom is lucky your dad stayed with her."

"You know," I said on the phone to Scottie, "a lot of mixed emotions."

"I get it. Your trip will be a great distraction. When do you leave?"

"Soon," I said. "Soon."

At my next therapy session with Melinda, I told her about my plan, how I'd use the next few months to see where Peeps could go and, by visiting my uncle Oscar, to uncover familial roots of behaviors that I'd long wanted to understand.

"Then," I explained, "I'll seamlessly return to my old life here."

"Uh huh," she said, her tone dubious.

"I mean," I continued, "I leased my house, but I can live in the RV in my own driveway, if I want." It's what I'd been telling myself.

"Of course," she replied, in her sing-songy way. "But I don't think you'll need to turn around."

"But what if I don't—"

"But what if you do," she interrupted.

"You didn't even hear what I was going to say!" Surely, some of my *what-ifs* were legit.

"It doesn't matter," she said. "It'll be wonderful for you to experiment."

"Experiment with what?"

"With not knowing what will happen."

"But…." I didn't even know what my next objection was.

"Just keep driving," Melinda said.

"And if—"

Melinda leaned towards me, her strawberry blond hair swaying as she spoke. "Just. Keep. Driving."

I delayed telling Brad as long as I could. We met up at a cafe just off Venice Boulevard that featured oat milk cappuccinos in bamboo mugs and Bossa Nova covers of Prince and The Police tunes emanating from the speakers. I explained that I'd be gone for at least the next few months.

"Wow," he said, his expression registering first surprise and then disappointment, which flattered me. "When are you leaving?"

"A couple of days."

"*Days?* How long have you been planning this?"

"Not long. Sort of spur-of-the-moment."

"Whoa. I know I haven't known you long but you strike me as a distinctly non-spur-of-the-moment kind of gal."

"I'm sorry," I said, covering his hand with mine. "I feel like I'm leaving something good. Like walking away from a freshly baked chocolate cake without taking a bite."

"I'll take that as a compliment," he said, though he wasn't smiling. "I just thought we had something starting here."

"We did," I said. "I mean, we do!"

"I don't mean to be dramatic," Brad said. "I just need to process. Did you sell your house?"

I shook my head. "Found a renter, a friend of a friend of Jeff's. I want Alex to have his home to return to for summer break. The renter is a guy named Kenneth, a flight attendant based at LAX. He negotiated a rent that was less than I wanted but his friend-of-a-friend status gives me—"

"—a measure of security."

"Exactly," I said. "And I'm hoping he'll inflict less wear and tear given that his job actually requires being *away* from home."

"You've really got it all figured out."

If you think that, I thought, *then you really do hardly know me.* "Just seems that way," I said.

Brad leaned forward and kissed me on the lips, sending lightening bolts down my arms. I felt like a teenager.

"Wanna spend the night tonight? Before you leave...."

"I do," I said. "I really do. But...I don't think it's a good—"

He waved his hand between us. "You're right."

What was I doing? Maybe sleeping with Brad was just what I needed. On the other hand, great sex with a handsome man would only sow more doubt about leaving.

"I *will* come back," I said, squeezing his fingers. Then I quickly added, "But I don't expect you to, you know, wait for me or anything."

"I know."

I exhaled, wondering if the opportunity cost of this trip was a relationship with a man who was, perhaps, the Ernest to my Alejandra.

CHAPTER FIVE

When I interviewed Alejandra in Long Beach, I asked — as I did of every source — if she might refer me to other potential podcast guests. She led me to Kelly, who'd been her caregiver for a few months after Alejandra had back surgery. I interviewed Kelly in Encino, my last LA interview before launching my RV Peeps tour.

When I asked Kelly about who she'd never seen again, she spoke of a former work colleague who years before had accompanied her to an animal shelter to adopt a cat. They were only work acquaintances but the woman had several cats herself and offered to go with Kelly, a cat newbie. While Kelly was drawn to the teeniest of kittens, her friend found one in a corner cage who simply did not stop purring. Kelly had wanted a colorful kitten, a calico or tuxedo cat. But the cat her friend discovered was an ordinary five-month-old tabby, much larger than the teeniest, cutest kittens.

"Please," Kelly's friend insisted, "just hold this one."

Within moments, Kelly's heart burst open, she recalled. And as she told me the story — continuing on to say that the coworker moved away and Kelly lost touch with her — that very tabby cat, now sixteen and the solid rock in Kelly's life, which had otherwise been peppered with abandonment and addiction, sat on the chair across from me in Kelly's studio apartment. I could hear him purring from six feet away. And whenever I glanced at him, he slowly blinked back at me. When Kelly told me about her life motto — "One hour at a time" — the cat hopped up behind me and began kneading his paws into my scalp. Kelly called it "making biscuits."

I'd never had a pet before, unless you counted the big orange feral Tom cat that adopted me when I was fifteen. I've never told *anyone* about Tom, not even Jeff.

Growing up, I lived off one of Los Angeles's many canyons and from our small back yard we often spotted coyotes and even wildcats in the distance. One afternoon I was outside listening to my Walkman, practicing dance moves from a music video, when Tom — that's what I eventually named him — moseyed up to me after jumping a small hedge. We weren't a pet family. My mother claimed to be allergic, though looking back she likely just needed a handy excuse for not allowing pets. But Scottie's family had three cats, one of whom loved me, so I was familiar enough with felines. Collarless — and therefore likely feral — Tom was unafraid, a people-loving cat. With music still blaring through my foam-covered ear phones, I stood motionless as he walked between my legs, rubbing his saliva on my bare calves. I knelt down and cautiously scratched the top of his head. He purred for five straight minutes before hopping back over the hedge toward the canyon. From then on, he returned often, maybe two or three times a week. I spent more time outside, listening to music or sorting out trigonometry problems on sheets of binder paper that faded in the sunshine, hoping that Tom would visit. I couldn't leave food out for him because that would attract raccoons and bees. But I did buy a package of cat treats and slipped him pieces whenever he came.

And he came several times a week for nearly two years. We didn't vacation much but I did go to summer and winter camps. When I was gone, I feared Tom would get discouraged — or sad — when I was absent and stop visiting altogether. But without fail, the day after I returned home, he'd appear and never seemed to hold a grudge. He accepted my extra treats with his usual purrs and saliva markings and our routine quickly reestablished. As my senior year approached, I worried about what would happen to Tom when I really went away — to college. I'd never told anyone, not even Scottie, about my relationship with Tom. It felt so symbiotic as to be almost magical. I didn't want to spoil it by trying to explain it. But I did start thinking about how I could make my departure to college easier on both of us. There was no way I could ask my mother to look after him. She already did the bare minimum in looking after me and my brother.

Then one day I drove up the canyon after school and saw an orange mound in the road. It took all of a half-second for me to understand. Tom had been hit by a car. I swerved to the side of the road and ran to him. He'd been hit but not run over, his body intact. I placed my hand on his belly, which was still and cool. He was gone.

The world spun as I went back to my car and grabbed the sweatshirt I'd thrown in the backseat. I wrapped Tom in it and drove him to a teeny, hidden park alongside the canyon. I didn't know what else to do. We didn't have a vet.

When I'd bought my car used from an upperclassman who was moving out of state for college, it came with an emergency kit. I dug it out from the trunk and looked inside it for the first time. There was no shovel, but I did find a pair of pliers. I cradled Tom in the sweatshirt and found a spot in the corner of the deserted park. With the pliers, I dug a shallow hole and placed him in it, covering him with the sweatshirt and then the dirt I'd loosened.

"Thank you, thank you, thank you," I whispered.

Looking back, I'm not sure what I was thanking him for. Maybe his immediate acceptance of me, his reliability, his giving me a secret and something to look forward to.

I returned home dirty and tear-streaked and was thankful my mother and brother weren't around. I later wondered what was worse: finding him dead on the road or if I'd never known that he died, just wondering why he suddenly stopped visiting. Alex often asked for a pet over the years but I never agreed. I remembered my utter heartbreak when Tom died and didn't want Alex to suffer that. If I was really being honest, it was because I didn't want to experience that kind of despondency ever again.

But the morning after I interviewed Kelly, I found myself somewhere I'd never been, even though it was less than two miles from my house: the West Side Animal Shelter.

I'd spent hours making my RV not just a mode of transportation but a comfortable home. In addition to plushy pillows and double-duty device chargers, I also needed scaffolding, something to root me even more to the RV, which I'd begun to think of as Irv. ("RV" - "Irv." Bonus that the name Irv conjured to me someone safe and reliable, like an avuncular, wise physician.) Caring for a pet would force structure on a trip that was, aside from my plotted echocardiogram route, utterly structureless. And adopting a pet meant I wouldn't really, truly be alone as I drove away from home.

I expected the clank of metal cages and the stench of animal feces, but West Side Animal Shelter was so California posh it was almost embarrassing. I thought of the dozens of homeless encampments beneath the 10 freeway overpass not three hundred yards from where the dogs and cats awaited adoptions in roomy glass homes complete with heated floors and blankets donated by an upscale department store. It was brightly lit and cheerful. Bizarrely, I felt underdressed.

The stiff handle of the cardboard crate I'd bought the day before dug pleasantly into my palm as I walked slowly down the first aisle. Though I was in unfamiliar surroundings making a decision that could impact the next fifteen to twenty years of my life if the longevity of Kelly's cat was any indication, I felt calm, a sensation that was unsettling because I was so unaccustomed to it. I tended to muscle my way through life, expending untold energy beating back uncertainty and worst-case-scenarios at every turn. That I didn't feel that way in the shelter about to select a companion to accompany me on a crazy road trip felt like some kind of sign, a thumbs up from the universe.

I passed two enclosures with litters of kittens darting from end to end. I grew exhausted just watching them. I continued walking. In the fifth enclosure of that first aisle, I came upon a small but fully grown cat. She sat majestically in the corner, seemingly content to simply observe the action taking place outside her glass home. I read the sheet on the clipboard hanging on her door.

"Spayed female. Approximately 1 year old. Found with collar but no tag in a meadow in Encino. Origin unknown. Owner claim period expired." According to the paperwork, she'd been at the shelter just under a week.

My heart pulsing in my ears, I opened the door and stepped inside. From a distance, she looked ordinary but up close, she was stunning. She was grey with white and black stripes that spanned the length of her spine. Her eyes were a dark blue. I lowered myself to the floor in the corner opposite her. Within moments, she began purring. I spoke to her gently, telling her about Tom and Peeps and the RV I'd nicknamed Irv.

"Are you interested?" I whispered. At that, she stood up and stretched, elongating her magnificent stripes, and then walked over to me and placed a paw gently on my knee. She continued to purr.

It was settled. I wanted to take this gorgeous creature with me. On my podcast adventure, to my Uncle Oscar's house in Syracuse, everywhere I went the rest of my life.

I stood outside her enclosure and called down the aisle to the volunteer on duty. I didn't want to leave my station and risk someone else adopting her. With a blue Sharpie, the volunteer made a note on the paper hanging on the clipboard and took my cardboard crate.

"I live in a really small, um, space," I cautiously revealed to the volunteer, who wore a dark green apron with large pockets. For the sake of my future companion, I felt compelled to be honest, but feared the shelter worker would put the kibosh on this whole thing. "Like a studio, a *very small* studio. Will she be okay with that?"

The woman jutted her chin towards the four-by-four enclosure I'd just exited. "Have you seen where she's been living since she got here? *Happily* living, I might add? She just needs love and plenty of enrichment activities. Toys, hide-and-seek games. We'll give you a handout on that downstairs. She'll be fine. I'll get her inspected, packed up and ready to go. Meet you at the front desk," she said.

I nodded, hoping the tears forming in the corners of my eyes would not accidentally escape down my cheeks. I wasn't a crier but I knew in my bones I'd always remember that moment. The volunteer noticed. "She's a very sweet cat," she continued. "I wonder what her history is, how she spent a whole year before winding up here."

For years, Jeff had a colleague named Dorothy who peppered her speech with Yiddish words. Through her I learned how evocative the language was for precisely conveying certain concepts. Mensch. Schlep. I'd always been grateful for Dorothy because the precision of these words made me a better communicator. She taught me that "beshert" means destiny or inevitable or preordained. I couldn't help but think of Dorothy then because it felt like beshert that this friendly, affectionate cat would become my companion as I launched my odyssey. I'd purchased an RV, but adopting that cat was what enabled me to drive away. The signing of pet adoption papers felt like the definitive no-turning-back moment. My heart raced. Was I setting myself up for years of love that would certainly lead to the unique kind of heartbreak the loss of a pet brings, the same piercing sadness I experienced burying Tom with my bare hands?

The front desk clerk punched my information into a computer, printed out a surprising number of forms to sign, and handed me a silver folder labeled Caring for Your Feline. The volunteer appeared from a side door and placed the carrier on the counter next to me. Over the whizzing of the printers, ringing phones and the tune playing through the ceiling speakers, I could hear my new cat purring.

"What are you going to name her?" the volunteer asked, as I signed Megan Gale Newlin on the final form.

Without glancing up, I replied, "Dotty."

The volunteer peered into the box through the air holes. "Dotty?" she said. "With all those *stripes*?"

I looked up, realizing and then relishing that my name choice would be confusing and therefore an automatic conversation starter with anyone who met her.

"Dotty," I confirmed with a smile. "Short for Dorothy."

I spent my last night in LA and my first night in the RV with Dotty in my Spruce Street driveway. I'd miss my little seaside cottage, a small one-story built in the late forties with three bedrooms, a sun room and a teeny backyard. It wasn't chic like Laura's, but it was where I'd raised my son, spent my life's most meaningful years. I thought of the thump of his toddler feet on the hard wood as he ran, never walked, from room to room. The spot on the counter where he'd sit as I prepared toast or oatmeal, looking out the window to the ocean a quarter mile away, narrating what he saw. Seagulls, surfers, fog burning off in the morning sun right before our eyes.

"Knock, knock," Jeff yelled outside the RV in the morning.

I peeled the curtain back and waved. I'd been up early, making final preparations to Irv and to my house for Kenneth the renter. I opened the door and invited him into my new home.

"Whoa," he said.

I stood with my hands on my hips and glanced around, proud of my new digs. Irv was small, in a good way. I remember once reading about animal behavior expert Temple Grandin, who loved — no, needed — the feeling of diving under couch cushions and having her cousin sit on top of her. That's how Irv made me feel. I'd be traveling with just my most favorite things, my world compact, metaphorically smushed between the cushions. It reminded me of the summer before Alex's senior year of high school when he spent countless weeks redoing his bedroom, culling through old Lego sets and Dodgers and Lakers posters, stuffed animals and too-small T-shirts, making way for vinyl records and collectible comic books he kept pristinely in plastic sleeves. He pared his room down to just his most prized possessions so that he barely had to leave that space. And that's exactly what happened. He spent the bulk of his senior year with friends or alone in that room, listening to music, reading comic books and working on college applications. Though his desire for isolation hurt my feelings a little, I now understood the allure.

"Want a tour?" I asked.

I started with the enormous windshield and two swiveling captain's chairs, complete with heated and cooling seats, cup holders and retractable tables for work or dining. We walked two steps into the kitchen with its two-burner stove, half-sized oven and convection microwave.

"I like these," he said, referring to the counters, a pretty tan and chocolate brown marble. "And these," he said, swiping his palm on the cabinets, a sunny pine.

"They stay closed on the road with magnets," I said, demonstrating. "And this fridge," which I opened to show my stock of eggs, yogurt and almond milk, "looks small, but it holds more than a week's worth of food."

I showed him the dinette for eating and working. "This converts into an extra bed. I'm hoping Alex will stay here with me a night or two. And this TV swivels so you can watch from either the dinette or the captain's chair."

"Nice touch," he said, pointing to the small plants I'd hung above the kitchen sink. "I'm dying to see the bathroom." I remembered that's what I wanted to see when I met the man in the van.

"Over here," I said, guiding him two more steps in. "It's got a shower over a tub. And see? Glass shower doors rather than a curtain. Counter space isn't great but see the skylight? And the toilet's porcelain, not plastic."

"No need to convince me."

Maybe I was trying to convince myself.

"Here's the closet." I pointed to the hanging clothes bar and then opened some of the drawers. "It came with this handheld vacuum that charges in here. From what I'm reading, this small vacuum is going to be in constant use."

"Should I have taken my shoes off?" Jeff asked.

"No, no, you're good." Though I planned to wear shoes inside as little as possible.

"And that's the bedroom?"

"Well, 'room' is a generous description. But it's behind an actual door," I said, while opening it, "which was one of my requirements. I'll be fine working at the kitchen table, but I don't want to feel like I'm sleeping in the kitchen."

Jeff stepped inside and gasped. "And who is *that*?"

"That," I said, "is Dotty, my new roommate. We met yesterday and are already getting along great." She'd slept next to me in the bed and had already used the litter box three times.

"Wow," he said, keeping his distance from my new pet, "you're definitely not the person I married."

"That makes two of us."

"Ha. Touché." He turned to face me. "You still sure about all this?"

No. "I am."

"Okay, then. I came by to say goodbye, but also to give you this." He pulled a slim black box from the inside pocket of his jacket and handed it to me. "I didn't have time to wrap it."

I flipped it over to the top, which featured a photo of something that looked like a weapon.

"A *gun*? Jesus, Jeff." We both despised guns so much that Alex wasn't even allowed to play with water guns as a kid.

"What? No," Jeff said, grabbing the box back. He pointed to the product name. "It's the 'Taser-ator.'"

"A taser gun. Only slightly better," I said, both touched at his desire to protect me and insulted that he thought I needed this protection.

"The taser was Milt's idea. We want you to be safe," he said, grabbing my hand and placing the box back in my palm. "You matter to me, Meggie."

"I'm going to be fine." *Was I?*

He made his way towards the RV exit. Once outside, he pointed to my house. "It's all still here — we're all still here — if you change your mind."

Thank you for joining me for episode twenty-five of Peeps, celebrating the world in a grain of sand. Though younger than me, Maya is who I want to be when I grow up. First off, she's stunning, with shiny black hair, a glowing complexion and confident posture. Her voice, as you'll hear, is deep and melodious. She's straightforward and no-nonsense, not once taking her chocolate brown eyes from mine as we spoke. We met in her downtown Los Angeles office.

Good morning, Maya. We're two of seven billion people. Can you tell me what's it like to be you?

I work in the fertility industry. Unlike in the early years, now when a patient has in vitro fertilization, usually only one viable embryo needs to be implanted. So what that means is when a patient decides the family is complete, there are many...leftover embryos. And they're stuck in a kind of limbo, you know?

What do you mean, "limbo"?

Well, sometimes they're abandoned by people who stop paying storage fees and can't be found. Some couples can't bring themselves to donate the extra embryos to science. Even when a patient has decided her family is complete, disposing of embryos brings a different kind of, you know, finality than for families who conceive on their own. Still, the empirical fact remains that something needs to be done with these embryos. Not surprisingly, everyone — doctors, clinics — is afraid to act. No one wants to get sued. I head the ethics committee for my company. I'm charged with figuring out how we should proceed in these cases. I work alongside academics, clergy, bioethicists, physicians, social workers, psychologists and, of course, lawyers. It's demanding. Demanding and fascinating.

Tell me something about yourself or your background.

Mmm, well, something about me: I'm a longtime opera lover. I went to my first, Rigoletto, when I was a student at Howard University. My roommate was an opera buff. She dragged me kicking and screaming. I only agreed because the Kennedy Center gave a student discount. I figured for ten bucks, at least I could, you know, say I'd been to the opera. Turned out, I loved it. I was legit hooked. I joined Howard University's opera club. Attended performances of Carmen and Le Nozze di Figaro. After graduation, I was broke so I had to settle for CDs for awhile. But once I started making money, opera was where I splurged. Now I've got season tickets to the LA Opera. And once a year I meet my old roommate in New York to attend a performance at Lincoln Center. Last year, I took an online course in eighteenth-century operas.

Maya, what's a physical object you'd take with you into the afterlife if you could?

Easy. My copy of The Joy of Cooking. I picked it up at a garage sale back in my twenties. I was just learning how to cook then. The book had some handwriting in it, which I loved. My favorite is on the eggplant parmesan recipe: "Everyone liked this but Timmy." I've added my own notes after years of trial and error. Adapted the recipes to be just right for me. It's, I don't know, like an unconventional record of my adulthood. So, yeah, I'd take that.

What's one thing you do every day?

Every day I knit four rows on what I call my "weather scarf." I alternate the colors based on the day's weather. For example, the one I'm working on now has stripes of gray (overcast), blue (rain), red (hot) and pink (temperate). I keep knitting all year, which makes it scarf length by

December. Then I start a new one, shifting the color choices. I love the nonsensical, nonuniform stripes. I don't wear scarves much here in LA but I always wear my weather scarves when I go to New York.

Maya, what was a pivot moment in your life?

Well, something that comes to mind: I always knew my job had a human element, that it was not just abstract or science-based. But it really hit me a few years ago. My company was contacted by a woman whose brother had died a couple of years before. He'd been young, like thirty-six. The woman received a DNA kit for her birthday and almost as soon as her results went online, she was contacted by a young man. Turned out, he was her biological nephew. That's when she learned that her deceased brother had been a prolific sperm donor in his late teens. She tracked down where he'd donated and that's how she got to us. She wanted to know whether we still had any of his sperm. If so, she wanted it. Wanted to create more nieces and nephews. Wanted, like, pieces of her brother.

What happened?

Perhaps I shouldn't have started this story since it's outside my ethical bounds to finish it. Sorry. The point is this: I truly understood then that the work I do is not just medical or scientific or theoretical. It's personal.

Who is someone you never saw again?

Like someone who died?

**Maybe but not necessarily. Like someone who you knew —
or briefly spotted — who you remember and think about,
but don't know what ever became of them.**

Huh. Well, for a few years, I had to be in Silicon Valley one or two days a week for my job. Kind of a pain but also kind of awesome. Had my favorite hotel, got to know the staff there. Even got to know some of the ground crews at the Burbank and San Jose airports. Anyway, I usually flew back to LA on Friday afternoons. Every single week, I was on the same flight as this woman and her daughter. The woman was a petite, real skinny Minnie. Her daughter, about eight, was like a mini version of her. Always well-behaved, the little girl drew or read on the short flight. Every single week I wondered: what the heck was bringing them to LA? It couldn't have been for work because the woman brought her daughter, who was school-aged. Was she divorced or widowed and visiting a boyfriend? Grandparents? She'd recognize me too. We'd smile and nod at each other. But we never spoke. Never once talked about why we were always on that same flight every single week. I suppose in my case, it was obvious: single woman, work slacks, briefcase, and all. Eventually, I no longer needed to be in Silicon Valley. I never saw that pair again. I think about them every once in awhile. That little girl would be in her twenties now.

Maya, what's your life motto?

Oh, I don't buy into all that stuff. I just live my life.

No sayings or words of wisdom?

Okay, actually, not sure this is a motto, per se. But I often hear in my head this instruction my parents used to tell us all the time growing up: just because someone else doesn't show class, doesn't mean that you shouldn't. Or, as my brother says: don't be a dick.

My thanks to Maya. I've got some other fascinating Peeps lined up. I hope you'll join me to hear their stories in upcoming shows.

CHAPTER SIX

I pulled away from Spruce Street with Dotty perched happily on a yellow cat bed I'd placed on the passenger seat, a shade of sunny yellow that would have fit right into Laura's beautifully appointed Marina del Rey home. That first day, I drove more than two hundred miles to Fresno to meet with a Superior Court judge who moonlighted as a Little League referee, the first of about five interviews — including an orthopedist to the ski stars in Incline Village and a frozen yogurt shop owner — I lined up in advance. I committed to have at least that many sources in the queue as I made my way toward New York.

Driving north from Fresno, passing vast agricultural land, I was struck by the golden hues of the changing autumn leaves. The greens — everything from fern to teal to olive — seemed to glow, and the sky was a royal blue. Near Stockton, I contemplated a spontaneous digression to Yosemite but reminded myself that sticking to a plan was essential, particularly in the first days. I had to get as far away from Santa Monica as I could because otherwise it would be too easy to ditch the whole plan. I'd rented out my house to Kenneth, but deep down I knew I could still return, living in the RV with Dotty and simply resuming my old life. So I continued northeast towards Truckee, a small town just outside Lake Tahoe, where I planned to dump sewage for the first time.

Late afternoon, I pulled into a gas station in Auburn, about ninety minutes from Truckee. I was on strict orders from my son not to let Irv get below half a tank, a tip he'd read about while perusing iTravel on my behalf.

"Where you headed?" asked a woman at the gas pump next to mine as she gave Irv an admiring once-over. No fewer than five small faces peered out at me from the windows of her mini van. It was a question I'd already gotten a dozen times even though I'd only been on the road a couple of days.

"Right now? Tahoe." I maneuvered my new gas tank with a bit of smugness. Irv was a guzzler so in my first days I'd already gassed up several times and had gotten the process down by then. Truth be told, though, I was dreading my first sewage dump.

The woman regarded me wistfully as her mini van shimmied with all the activity inside. "And after that?"

"I've got a route that goes up and down through the U.S. My ultimate destination is upstate New York — Syracuse, to be exact — where I'll see my uncle," I explained.

I didn't tell her I hoped seeing Uncle Oscar in the flesh, looking him in the eye as I asked about my mother, seeking insight into her past. And that, in turn, could make me finally understand why she'd treated me with such disdain. Which might then help me stop moving through life under a constant barrage of "what if" thoughts. If I could *explain* the origin of my fear, then perhaps I could undo it all. I was grateful my uncle, in his late eighties, still had his wits and agreed to meet with me.

The mini van woman pressed on. "And what happens after Syracuse?"

The gas pump clicked and shook in my hand indicating that Irv's tank was full. I was relieved at the timing. No one — not even Jeff, Alex or Scottie — had asked me that. Despite all my preparation, planning, packing and cleaning, my own negligence was kind of stunning: I simply hadn't thought past Syracuse.

"Um, I...don't know yet," I confessed.

Would I stay awhile in Syracuse, where my mother grew up? Would I drive south and visit Scottie? Would I spend time in Austin to be near Alex? Would I make a bee line for the safety of my home on Spruce Street in Santa Monica? What would I do with Peeps?

The woman glanced inside her minivan, still wriggling with the chaos of her kids inside. Then she looked back at me. "Lucky you."

I knew why she said it, why it seemed glamorous to her. With a car full of kids, she knew exactly what she'd be doing for the next fifteen to twenty years. But I wanted to tell her that the unknown was as disconcerting as the monotony of the predictable.

I fingered the business cards in my pocket, the ones featuring Peeps. Melinda had encouraged me to hand them out with abandon, to practice touting my show. I'd ordered a box of five hundred. I'd handed out three. This was the perfect opportunity to share. The woman already seemed interested in what I was doing. But her gas pump clicked off and I lost my nerve.

We waved as we got back into our vehicles. On the passenger seat, Dotty rolled on her back, besotted with a stuffy in the shape of a carrot I'd given her back in Santa Monica, her playfulness distracting me then from my discomfort over where, when and how my journey would *really* end.

Already, Dotty and I had a routine. When I slept, she rested at my feet on the bed. When I worked, she sat, much the way a colleague would, opposite me at the dinette, usually grooming her paws. I'd already begun referring to that as her beauty time. And she really was beautiful. I'd studied her richly hued stripes, which traveled in perfectly proportioned, color-coordinated darts down the length of her spine. And when I drove, she was in one of three places: playing on her carpeted kitten tree, sitting demurely in her yellow bed on the passenger seat, or perched on the driver's seat head rest with her warm paws on my shoulders, her whiskers grazing my cheeks.

My elation at successfully maneuvering Irv along my most treacherous route yet, Highway 80 with its mountainous switchbacks, vanished as I arrived at the sewage dump on Bear Meadow Highway in Truckee. I'd been dreading this first dump ever since I bought Irv and I'd hitched my hopes on making it through with the help of some fellow RV'ing good samaritan who'd take pity on me and show me the ropes. Unlike the hair at my part, or, to be frank, in my nether regions, my eyelashes were not yet grey and, feminist though I was, I wasn't above batting them if doing so would make some dude feel like a hero by assisting me with this unpleasant but necessary task.

Once, in my late thirties, I had to rush Jeff to the hospital when he felt tight-chested and inordinately winded while yanking weeds in our small back yard. The doctors discovered a blocked artery, which turned out to be easily fixed and, for him, a blessing in disguise. It inspired him to become a vegetarian and embark on a new exercise program that included daily swims and occasional jogging, which was good for his heart, though bad for his ACL, which led to his need for a physical therapist — enter Milt. While *he* pledged to get healthy and fit, *I* silently pledged to become more self-sufficient — just in case. I began adjusting the thermostat myself, researching mutual funds, fixing loose cabinet doors and troubleshooting our Internet router. If something were to happen to Jeff, I didn't want to be saddled with my own incompetence in addition to crippling grief. But like most resolutions that emerge after a health scare, my determination faded. Before long, I was back to calling Jeff, even after he'd moved in with Milt, to change the batteries in the really high smoke detector.

The autumn sky was growing darker and the Truckee sewage dump was deserted. Hoping that silence would somehow help me spot my unwitting savior, I lowered the volume of Purple Rain, my soundtrack as I'd passed the 6,000-foot Donner Summit just fifteen minutes before. I pulled up to the side of the building and was about to get out when I saw the sign handwritten on a piece of torn cardboard: PUMP BROKEN.

Shit.

Should I ditch the stop in Tahoe and bolt to the next place on my list?

But that would undoubtedly take me off course for the night. Alex and Jeff had made me promise that I'd arrive at all overnight parking places before dark so I could make sure it was populated and secure. My rigorous planning had left me — at least for that night — with limited options.

I glanced down at Irv's sewage meter. Full. Definitely full.

I realized then how alone I really was.

Was I even fit for this trip?

Just then, another vehicle arrived and I grew hopeful that perhaps I could problem-solve with another RV'er, perhaps a nice family. But as it pulled up alongside me, heavy metal blared from an old van, dented and rusted. Two men in the front seats motioned for me to roll down my window, which I did, the scent of Sierra pine hitting my nose.

"Busted, huh?" the passenger said jutting his chin toward the pump, then turned to his driver and laughed sharply.

A door slammed shut. The driver walked around the front of his RV towards mine. Dotty jumped from my headrest to the floor with a loud thud and I hopped two inches into the air at the sudden noise. My nose inhaled barely an ounce of air as the man came towards me. He was right out of central casting: overweight, red flannel shirt, a hunter type. Scottie and I always insisted that hunting was the sport of those with miniature penises. I smelled alcohol and tobacco as he approached. I rolled my window back up so it was open only an inch. A foot away from my window, he hiked up his pants, revealing the metal handle of a hunting knife tucked into the interior pocket of his jacket.

What was I thinking?

No one would mess with the man in the van I'd met in Santa Monica — he was huge and twenty-five years younger than me.

My brain flashed to everything I could be doing instead of being at an abandoned sewage pump station at the northeast edge of California. I could be on a date with Brad, perhaps launching my life's greatest romance.

My ears rang so loudly from panic that I couldn't even hear what the man inches from me was saying. Breath held, I pressed Irv's ignition button.

Nothing.

Both men cackled manically. The driver reached towards me through the cracked window, the tips of his fingers hanging inside my home, his nails long and dirty, like a witch's claw.

"What's your rush?" he slurred, so close I could see his nose hairs. "Let's hang."

My mind spun to the taser Jeff had gifted me. It remained unopened in its package, tossed in Irv's underbelly storage.

Idiot.

The passenger got out and similarly approached my window. "Don't want comp'ny?" he said, elbowing his driver. "Lady must not be in her right mind. We might have to insist."

Start, Irv, start!

Sweat collected on my upper lip. I realized then that my foot had been on the accelerator rather than the brake. My legs trembled but I managed to shift my foot to the left and finally the RV started up. I lurched out of the parking lot, narrowly missing getting sideswiped by a passing BMW, a horn blaring in its wake. In my large side mirror, I saw the men doubled over laughing as I drove off. Feeling equally relieved and incompetent, I swiped the sweat from my upper lip with the back of my wrist and expelled large puffs of air to slow my heart rate.

I pulled into a crowded gas station a few miles later, still shaking. My phone had a weak signal but I was able to Google the closest Wal-Mart. I decided I'd pee and wash up in the store and then continue to the lake in the morning. Hopefully someone at the RV park there would direct me to another pump. And I vowed not to take another sip of anything liquid until I'd successfully emptied Irv's completely full sewage tank.

I arrived at Wal-Mart, feeling a mix of dejection and resourcefulness. There were six other motor homes there and I parked next to the furthest one. A knock on my door sounded the moment I shut off the ignition. I gasped and clutched my heart, still unnerved by the men I'd managed to get away from. Through the small window on the door, a woman with a gray-haired bob waved.

"Sorry to scare you," she mouthed.

I clamped my eyes shut and expelled air. I got up, legs unsteady, and clicked open the door.

"Hi, there," said the woman, whose face featured a roadmap of deep grooves. "I'm Pam. We're all about to fire up a barbecue. We'll make some room on the grill if you'd like to cook something."

I stuck my head further out the door and saw a gathering of about eleven people. A circle of camping chairs. Beers and wine glasses in hands. Shrieks of three children surrounding a man holding a bag of marshmallows. A cool breeze blew against my face.

"Oh, no thank you," I said, wrapping my arms around myself, palms tucked under my armpits.

"Ya sure? If you don't have food, you can get stuff inside," she said, pointing her thumb backwards towards Wal-Mart. "Or we probably have extras. Randall?" She turned and yelled to her left. "We got enough for this new neighbor?" A pause. "Yeah, if you like chicken apple sausage, we got plenty."

I looked again at the crowd, the children, probably ten years younger than Alex, pawing for s'mores. I glanced back at Pam, who was probably ten years older than me. I felt out of place, a new wave of misgivings cloaking me like a blanket.

"That's so nice," I said. "I appreciate the invitation. I've been driving a lot today and I think…." *I want to be alone, to isolate myself from people, both good and bad.* "I just need to pop into the store and call it a night."

"Suit yourself," she said, not unkindly. "You change your mind, let us know."

In the Wal-Mart rest room, I peed and dabbed my armpits with damp paper towels, wondering if I should have been more social and accepted the nice offer. But I ate dinner in my parked RV, staying close to the store in case I needed to use the bathroom one last time before going to sleep. I also decided it was a good time for 5-4-3-2-1.

I see Dotty's whiskers twitching as she sleeps.

I hear the clang of the spoon in the pot as I stir soup.

I feel the bottom of my yoga pants stretching against my calves.

My phone dinged with a text, suspending my practice. As always, I hoped it was Alex. I missed him intensely, but when he left for college in August, I forced myself to let him reach out to me more than I to him so that he could launch his adult life without his mom breathing down his neck from afar. It was a struggle simply because I *liked* him so much. The text wasn't from Alex, but from Brad.

"How's the trip so far?" he wrote.

I smiled, amazed that he hadn't just written me off since there were a grand total of zero dates on tap in our immediate future. I contemplated a reply that would be informative, casual and sexy. But as I drafted it in my head, another text came in.

"What's that Woody Allen film where Cate Blanchett goes from gorgeous Manhattan socialite to homeless nut muttering to herself on a park bench despite her cocktail of antidepressants?" From Scottie.

"Blue something?" I replied, testing my ever-decreasing memory skills. I remembered that film with a particular brand of horror that can only come from seeing pieces of yourself in a character's downfall. I'd watched that movie years ago with my favorite moms from Alex's preschool and, at drinks afterwards, we all — *all* — confessed to being on Lexapro. If I'd had the energy at the time, I might have examined why every single one of those bright, well-loved women was on anti-anxiety meds. But who knew what lurked behind the curtain of others' lives? Did they know my husband was gay — I certainly didn't — or that my every decision was guided by fear?

"Yes, Blue something," she wrote back. "I'M HER."

I wanted to return to the text chain with Brad, maybe even call him. But Scottie sent a rapid series of short texts, documenting ways she was feeling off her rocker: wild mood swings with pockets of utter fury, debilitating insomnia, the inability to remember basic words like freezer, garage and the name of her first born.

"U are not crazy," I replied. "U are perimenopausal."

I felt confident in my amateur diagnosis since my doctor had cited perimenopause as the reason I was having nightmares involving hatchets and arson and why I referred to everyday objects as "thingies."

"Ah, fuck me," Scottie wrote. "Wait, I take it back," she added. "FUCK WOODY ALLEN. Fucking pedophile probably made that Blue-whatever film precisely to sow terror in the minds of middle-aged women. As if we didn't have enough to deal with without the patriarchy aggravating our menopausal rage. Ha-ha. Soon-Yi was born in '70s. Joke'll soon be on him!"

I was still thinking more about how to reply to Brad when he texted again: "Heading into the gym. Hope trip is good!"

I replied to Scottie with the LOL emoji, though between missing out on an exchange with Brad and recalling how quickly and realistically a perfectly normal woman devolved into insanity in that film, I felt more unease than amusement.

I'm so happy to welcome you to episode thirty-one of Peeps, the interview show that celebrates that the world can be found in a grain of sand.

It's odd to me that I met Aaron in a dive bar in Coalville, Utah, of all places. With his fine clothes, salt and pepper goatee and erudite manner, he'd look more at home in a Vienna cafe or perusing Rembrandts at the Louvre. But much about Aaron surprised me. Take a listen.

Of seven billion people on this planet, what's it like to be you right now?

Ah, my passion is African-American quilts. I'm a collector. I discovered them purely by chance at a flea market. I was actually on the hunt for an antique end table. That was about fifteen years ago. Soon I became obsessed. Quit my job to learn more about these unique textiles, their origins.

What are they like, exactly?

Oh, full of bold shapes and colors and asymmetry. Usually made from scraps of old clothing. Sometimes even tobacco and sugar sacks. I've met with professors and sellers and traced the tradition to West Africa and through slave ships. Many designs feature a weaving quality, a technique descended from textiles made by African men. I could go on and on. They're beautiful, though. I've driven back and forth through the South several times to add to my collection. Got nearly two thousand quilts now. All hand-made. I built a climate-controlled room in my house to store and display them. Now professors come to me to see what I've got.

They sound fascinating. What a neat hobby. And what can you tell me about your background, about yourself?

My sister is Shayna Goodman.

Wait—

Yes, that Shayna Goodman, star of stage and screen. Winner of a Tony and an Oscar. Face on magazine covers. She of two million Instagram followers. Shayna is two years younger than me. Sometimes people have no idea about this until I've known them for years. Other times people — strangers, even — take one look at me and ask if I'm related to her.

Now that you mention it...holy cow.

Yup. When we were growing up, people used to ask our parents how it was possible they had identical twins of different ages and genders!

What's that like, being the sibling of, like, a huge celebrity?

One reason I don't always volunteer that information is that people often assume I'm rich. Or that I can help them somehow. I've had "friends" disappear as soon as they realize that's not the case. Most of the time it's fun, though. Shayna and I are very close. Especially now that our parents are gone. She's taken me to award shows. Flown me to visit her on set in Ireland and on Martha's Vineyard. Whenever she's on location, she finds flea markets on her day off. Wears sunglasses and a ball cap, and searches for quilts for me. Really, though, one thing people don't understand is how hard it is to be famous. It informs everything in her life. She told me recently that she now hesitates before doing a good deed. She doesn't want it to look like she's doing something just for the PR value. Can you imagine?

Huh. No, I can't, actually. Aaron, what physical object would you take into the afterlife?

A ceramic mug my sister made in third grade. I keep pens in it.

Tell me one thing you do every day.

I write one haiku poem every night before going to bed. It's usually about anything, about nothing. Sometimes it's about something I saw on TV. Sometimes it's about some ache or pain I've got going on. Sometimes it's about nature or some intense emotion I'm feeling.

How cool! Willing to share a couple?

Ha! I should have realized you'd ask that before revealing my habit! Okay, well, I've never shared these with anyone. Really, no one. But why the hell not? Let me pull out my iPad. Let's see….

Baked potato is

A bit of a sad dinner

But also yummy

Blue jay visits me

On my deck today. Is he

The same from Tuesday?

One more.

My dad used to say

"It's a two-trip world." Today

My brand new watch broke.

Aaron, can you tell me: what was your life's pivot moment?

Not sure what you mean by "pivot moment."

Well, was there a time in your life when something shifted? A moment or a longer period that changed things for you? Even a little bit?

Okay, so one was when I was about twelve. My parents took us to this resort area near the Gulf, in Texas. An artsy little town with small shops and galleries and things. One store had these beautiful crafts and folksy art pieces. I saw a series of collages. On beautiful, textured paper. Featured everything from tin foil to newsprint to actual leaves to watercolors to gold hand lettering. Striking to me, really striking. And this…I don't know… this wave of inspiration and creativity flooded my body. I remember thinking, "I will do that!" The whole rest of the trip, I fantasized about the collages I'd create once I got home. I imagined I'd get rich selling my beautiful creations. After the vacation, I purchased a bunch of supplies. Metallic pens, textured papers, artist-grade glues. Even some frames for my future masterpieces! I spread everything out on the kitchen table and made about three collages. They were awful. I mean, just trust me. Awful. And I knew it. They looked like a kindergartener made them. Nothing like the lovely pieces I'd seen in that little Gulf town. In frustration, I threw away all the supplies.

And how did that change you?

Well, it was the first time I felt the effect of art, of creativity in my body. When I felt it again, with the African-American quilts, I knew better than to try to start quilting myself. I'd be a collector. And that's what I did.

Aaron, who is someone you never saw again?

What do you mean?

Well, is there anyone you met or saw or interacted with that you never saw again but still think about?

Okay, got it. Yes. When I was in elementary school, tether ball was a big pastime during recess. I literally broke several fingers playing. Even got a concussion when the rusty, wobbly pole finally gave way and toppled over. Onto my head. Anyway, I grew up in this fancy neighborhood outside of Dallas. An incredibly cliquey community. You know the kind, right? One girl — very pretty but quiet, not one of the popular kids — was playing tetherball against a popular guy. Kind of a douche but he was popular. You know the type, I'm sure. I was on deck, observing their game, waiting my turn. They had a close call and argued about it. But it had been quite clear to me that the girl's play was good. They asked me, the observer, to make the call. The ultimate determination. The girl's play was good, as I just said. But her opponent was popular and she was not. I was weak and afraid. I called her out. The girl — I think her name was Cathy — stared at me wide-eyed. She was not out and she knew it. Worse, she knew that I knew it. That I straight-up lied just to stay in the good graces of a douche-y popular kid. She stomped away with angry tears. That was probably, what, forty-five years ago? A freakin' recess tether ball game. But I'm still so ashamed whenever I think about it. Can't even believe I'm telling y'all. I wish I could apologize. Tell her how my weakness in that moment still haunts me. I wish I'd had the strength to say what I really saw.

What's your life motto?

I read a lot of self-help kind of books. So I have a lot. One of my favorites: The grass is always greener where you water it.

As always, I'd like to thank today's guest. Aaron, it was a pleasure talking with you.

Someone collects pennies *only* from 1968? Learn more next time on Peeps.

CHAPTER SEVEN

At the edge of Boulder's Calkins Lake, the late October breeze welcomed me to Colorado's Rocky Mountains. The lake looked as clear as the air felt traveling to my lungs and its surface reflected the yellows and oranges of the leaves on the trees that surrounded it. Sailboats glided across the waveless water. A crow flew low above me and I felt my distance from the sea most acutely then. With its riptides and undertow, the Pacific frightened me. But the smaller patches of blue on my road map were like beacons. Sources of water like Calkins Lake were an antidote to unease. I wasn't always able to park overnight alongside lakes or rivers, but I visited them whenever I could and I'd often combine these waterside visits with meditation, which was another one of Melinda's prescriptions. Meditation was an uncomfortable, fidgety experience with my mind free-associating instead of zeroing in on my breaths. From the bench where I planted myself at Calkins Lake, I could see Dotty perched on Irv's dashboard gazing at me through the windshield. I gave her an index finger wave and she tapped the window with her paw in reply and then settled in for perhaps her tenth nap of the day, though it was still early enough that the nearby hikers weren't even pulling lunches out of their backpacks yet.

Exposure to the elements — whether it was the enveloping sun in Nevada or the Utah wind so blustery it blew hair straight out of my pony tail — had become nourishing. In those early days after driving away from my life, being outdoors was a balm, a medicine of sorts. Sometimes I'd just sit on a camping chair outside Irv for forty-five minutes at a stretch. The practice was new to me, ironic considering that for years I'd lived at a coastline that people came from all over the world to experience. The air in Colorado was different from any place I've ever been, and not just because oxygen is sparse. Colorado's air penetrates the skin, deep into organs.

Two teenagers walked by me at Calkins Lake, one carrying an old-fashioned boom box not unlike the one I had in high school that I used to tape songs off the radio, always capturing the DJ's voice talking over the opening notes. I did my best to tune out what the teenagers were playing. In recent years, I had to be selective about the music I listened to — no Taylor Swift, no Hamilton, not even my beloved Barbra Streisand-Barry Gibb duets — because music and lyrics lodged in my head, sometimes for *weeks*. Melinda explained that was "clinical rumination," a symptom of anxiety. I was so prone to ear worms that I even selected vague and unmemorable music for the Peeps podcast intro and outro just to protect my own self.

The bench was worn and wobbly. If my body moved too much, one of the green planks shifted and I tilted off balance. So after waving to Dotty, I closed my eyes, sat still and measured my breathing.

Two men sat on the bench next to mine. I went from guessing how long I'd been meditating to actively eavesdropping on their conversation, which was peppered with "bro" and "dude" and "like." I grew certain that I could describe those two men even though my eyes were closed. They sounded like the kind of young men I hoped Alex would not become: too self-aware, too self-centered, too self-involved. One was probably shaved headed, the other likely had gel products on subscription delivery from

Amazon. They were probably wearing expensive athletic gear and perhaps even had custom-built bikes leaned against the bench.

A dog brushed against my legs and a woman yelled, "Sorry!"

When I opened my eyes to nod to her, I took the opportunity to peek at the men. I was right about the hair — on both counts. But wrong about everything else.

The bald guy clutched a straw sun hat in his hands and was berating himself. "Why was I so stupid?"

In my few years working on Peeps, I uncovered themes of the human condition. One of the most prominent was that many people struggle with *getting over* things. For one person, it might be the premature death of a parent. For another, it might be getting fired from a job. For someone else, it might be that long ago romance that didn't work out. Clinging to past regrets or disappointments was so common I considered making it one of my standard interview questions, as in "what have you not been able to let go of?" But I assumed it would too easily steer the interviewee to a negative place. So I left it out. Yet that clinging, that inability to let go, like I was hearing then — it was still a theme I observed often.

At a back table in a Starbucks just outside the CU Boulder campus, I waited for a neuroscience professor, my next interview. I preferred to meet sources in their natural habitats so I could gather telling details to include in my intros. One of my favorite interviews was with a handyman on site in Calabasas. I observed the remarkable precision required to install a corner soap dish in a brand new shower. Watching him drill into just-laid tile gave me an appreciation for his skill, which I was able to convey to the audience because I'd witnessed it with my own eyes.

In the case of this professor, I wanted to observe what was hung on his office walls, how he interacted with colleagues and students. But he insisted we meet off campus. With anyone else, I might have protested more, claiming my mic wouldn't pick up clear audio amidst the bustle of a coffee shop. But I'd been especially excited about interviewing this particular man, having read about his work in the appendix of *Transgenerational Transmission of Environmental Information*. Yet I was apprehensive too, as apprehensive about what I might learn as if I'd followed through with getting a reading from the future teller in Marina del Rey. Two ends of a spectrum.

After I clicked off my recording equipment, I hoped to grill him about the brain's processing of fear. Was my approach to life something I could shrink, expand or maneuver through using exercises like 5-4-3-2-1? Or was it an immutable result of my DNA just like my eye color or my final position on a growth chart? And what, dear God, about my mother?

My mother left Syracuse for California three days after she turned eighteen. She wanted to be a television actress, in the vein of Eve Arden, Audrey Meadows and Shelley Fabares. She was beautiful — long legs, full features — but for one thing: a mole. About a half inch under her left eye, it was large and oblong. She spent her entire adolescence begging to have it removed. Eventually my grandparents took her to a plastic surgeon, who explained that not only would removal leave a scar more unsightly than the mole itself, but it was too close to her eye, embedded in too-thin skin. My mother was told explicitly, sometimes harshly, in audition after audition that viewers wouldn't be able to look past it, no matter how strong her performance. It was in the late fifties, long before Cindy Crawford, mole and all, became a supermodel, long before mainstream acceptance of unusual faces.

Shut out of her dream, my mother refused to return to New York, instead taking a clerical job, which, she never failed to remind us, she hated. She met my father at that job, and continued working after I was born and after my dad died of a heart attack in his early thirties.

At the Starbucks table, my phone buzzed.

"Can I call U?" Jeff wrote.

"Abt 2 do an interview," I typed back. "Everything OK?" *Alex?*

"Need UR advice. Work-related. Call me when it's convenient."

Jeff often joked that I missed my calling as a therapist. Even after our marriage, he consulted me whenever work or personal situations got sticky, flattering me by frequently reporting back that I'd given him "spot-on" advice. Fortunately, he'd not asked me for relationship advice once he began seeing Milt. I didn't mind helping him — he continued to be there for me too — but that's where I drew the line.

"Hello there," a man said as he slid into the chair across from me. Wearing khakis and a navy flannel button-down, he had a kind face with a complexion that suggested he'd been freckled as a kid.

"Uh, hello, Professor—"

He held out his hand. "Brian. Call me Brian."

"How'd you know it was me?" With Alex's help, I'd taken great care tending to my digital footprint, using only animated bitmojis for profile photos on every social media outlet.

He nodded toward the pile of equipment. "Dead giveaway."

"Right! Can I get you a latte or something before we start?" I asked, hoping he'd decline so I wouldn't have to edit out slurps and swallows from the audio. Similar to the overly repetitive "uh" or "like," mouth noises can irritate listeners. It was my job, a tedious one at that, to remove them. Plus, I didn't have the funds to treat every source to coffee. Lattes were one of my regular splurges back home in Santa Monica, but I was now paying for gas and overnight parking fees. And since I quit my job with Dana, I had no steady income other than the alimony I received from Jeff, which had diminished by nearly half once Alex went to college. I was now brewing drip.

"Nope, I'm good," Brian said. "Before we get started, though, can I ask *you* a few questions?"

"Uh, sure." This was unusual. Sources tended to love diving right in to talk about themselves. I glanced at the time on my computer even though I had nowhere else to be.

"I listened to a couple of episodes of your show. In preparation for this," he said, pointing to my laptop. "The first questions — what's it like to be you, what's your background — why start so vague?"

Few people asked about my methodology. "Well," I said, "a subject might tell me about growing up on a farm or emigrating from El Salvador. Another person might dive into their academic history. It's *how* they choose to answer, not just the answer itself, that's revealing."

"Makes sense. And the question about taking something with you after you die. You must have heard some weird stuff."

"That's true. I've heard: 'my grandmother's mah jongg set so we can play together again' and 'the roll-top desk I got for my bar mitzvah.' One guy said, 'My appendix, which is soaking in formaldehyde in a jar in my garage — just in case.'"

"The scientist in me would like to set that guy straight," Brian laughed. "And what brings you to Boulder, of all places you could interview people?"

I didn't want to reveal — yet, anyway — that *he* himself, his research was what drew me here. Instead, I told Brian about driving to see my uncle, with a stop soon in Texas to visit my son.

"I drove across country once," he said, picking up my pen and twirling it. "When I was twenty-two. On a single day, I got no fewer than three speeding tickets, each in a different state." He paused and looked down at the pen in his hands. "I felt awful. I thought, 'I should be arrested!'"

I reached forward to turn on my mic. But he tapped my hand with the pen. "Wait," he said, "finish telling me about your trip."

Was Brian the neuroscientist flirting with me? I was out of practice with this kind of banter.

My hesitation must have been apparent because he added, "Just curious is all. I'm a nerdy professor immersed in academic journals and clinical trials. I don't get out of my lab much. Even this run-of-the-mill Starbucks is interesting to me. A solo RV road trip is...beyond. So far so good?"

"Aside from a close call with my sewage tank, pretty good."

"Lonely?"

Flirting?

"Actually," I said, picturing Dotty back in the RV, "not so far." I gently reclaimed my pen and used it to point to him. "I'm sure you've got much more important things to get back to. Should we begin?"

"It's curious that you created a whole podcast to ask people questions but you don't seem to like answering them."

I gazed up at the far corner of the ceiling. Now *that* was a Melinda-level insight. I'd long attributed my propensity to ask questions to my genuine interest in people. But maybe it was also a defense mechanism. My mother had never been interested in my life, so why would anyone else be?

"Just ignore me. I'm no shrink," Brian said. "Like I said, I don't get out much. Let's go ahead and start."

I nodded without comment, relieved to return the spotlight to him. But I made a mental note to think more about what he said before my next session with Melinda. And I vowed to express even more appreciation to my sources. Thanks to Brian's observation, I realized that answering personal questions was not necessarily as comfortable as I presumed.

During the interview, Brian described his area of neurological study, which was synesthesia, a condition in which sensory or cognitive pathways cross in an unrelated way. For example, a synesthete might associate colors with certain musical notes or "see" numbers or months of the year in a mental map of sorts, he explained. It's a harmless, even enviable condition that tends, he said, to run in families.

I turned off my mic. "Are there other, unexpected things, similar to synesthesia, that are inherited?"

"Such as?"

"Like, um…."

How to explain what was driving my personal research? I flashed to a day in my childhood, when I was about eleven, when I returned from school to discover that my bike, which was always leaned against the side of our house, wasn't there. I went inside to ask my mother where it was. She was watching TV.

"I gave it away," she said without looking up.

"To *who*?" I asked in disbelief.

"Don't *whine*, for God's sake, Meggie. I don't know." She aimed the remote at the screen, switching between Jenny Jones and Geraldo. "There was some charity pick-up on the street this morning so I gathered some junk we didn't need and left it out for them to take. There's too much stuff around here."

I felt the breath leave my chest. I rode that bike nearly every afternoon. She had to know that. My tires were probably still muddy from the ride to Scottie's house the very day before, evidence of my use.

"But—"

"You don't want to give things *to charity*?"

In my room, I kicked the bed frame, my face hot. No tears came. What use would crying be? This wasn't the first time she'd done this. A year before, I was awakened one morning by the sound of men hauling our piano out the front door.

"What are you doing?" I'd asked my mother that day, convinced I was still dreaming. I loved goofing around on the piano. I'd even used recent birthday money from my uncle to buy Annie the Musical sheet music.

"I'm redecorating the living room."

That small piano could have fit anywhere, even my own bedroom. But my mother didn't care what mattered to me or maybe she did and giving my things away was her particular brand of gratuitous cruelty.

When my mother received her pancreatic cancer diagnosis not long after my own divorce, I wondered whether she deserved more compassion. It couldn't have been easy for her — dashed dreams, young widowhood, two small children to raise alone. After Jeff came out, I got a first-hand view of sudden single parenthood. But unlike my mother, I never took life's unfairness out on Alex. Unlike my mother, I never flaked out on parent-teacher conferences, leaving my child embarrassed at his parent's disinterest. Unlike my mother, I never disappeared for twenty hours at a stretch, overnight no less, demanding my child "stop being so dramatic" for sobbing in relief upon her return. I never yelled at Alex my mother's frequent refrain of "I didn't sign up for this!" whenever we did something to exasperate her. If anything, finding myself alone in middle age made the pain of my mother's parenting even more acute.

"Earth to Megan Newlin." Brian the professor leaned forward with a grin.

"Sorry," I said, shaking my head to dislodge memories. It was the second time that day that I'd thought of my childhood bike. At the last moment before leaving Santa Monica, I'd thrown my hardly used road bike onto Irv's back. When I returned to the RV from Calkins Lake that morning, I'd given the bike a good tug to make sure it was still securely attached. I hadn't yet ridden it on the trip, but I was glad to have it.

"You were asking about genetic inheritance...."

"Right. So can personality traits" — *like cruelty*, I thought — "be inherited just like eye color?"

As a newborn, Alex screamed incessantly, one day so much that I had to sit in the backyard for two and a half hours while he wailed in his crib, afraid of what I'd do if I got any closer. When he was nine, I yelled at him to "get the fuck out of the car" when we arrived to his tutoring appointment with a minute to spare because of an accident on Sepulveda. He'd known that I was obsessive about being on time and he'd known that we were on the verge of being late, yet he'd taken off his shoes during the drive. "Get out of the car, goddamn it. Shoes on later." I frightened myself sometimes. Even though Alex sweetly told me often that I was "the best Meggie-mom" — his nickname for me — the memory stung.

"Your question is actually right on the cusp of some interesting science that many of my colleagues are examining," he said, picking up my pen again. "One woman out of the University of Montana is studying how baby rodents respond when their mother is removed from the cage for a few minutes and then returned. If the mother's licking and grooming behavior is different after that absence, it induces a permanent change in the baby rat's stress response. But more importantly," here, he paused, "it may determine the way that baby rat's *own offspring* respond to stress."

I was getting used to living in tight quarters. Though my knees still knocked against the frame when I made my bed and my elbows banged against the sides of the shower, my biceps were growing stronger every time I lifted my mattress to access the underbed storage. And I'd quickly learned tricks like keeping windows closed at all times because in an RV, dust doesn't just get into your car, it gets into your *house*, coating all belongings.

I was learning to be frugal with water too. It was beyond even the drought-level conservation I'd adopted as a native Californian. This was next level: washing dishes with a half-cup of water, taking a ninety-second shower, filling my water bottle at cafes.

The small space had advantages too. I vacuumed the entire floor with the hand-held in three minutes flat. And I discovered multiple uses for objects. Oatmeal made in a cast-iron pan, for example, is delicious.

But when you live in an RV, there's no ability to stock up, so frequent trips to the store were required. After meeting with Brian, I drove two miles to Target to get essentials: paper goods, frozen meals, vitamins and lotion. Sometimes I treated myself to People magazine or random items from the dollar bins. That day, there were pretty notepads with a paisley pattern on clearance. Keeping most of my notes on my phone and laptop, I didn't need them. But I thought of Aaron, how the beautiful African-American quilts brought him joy, and placed three of the notepads in my basket.

I walked through the parking lot, bags hanging from my elbow pits. The sky was dusk purple. From a distance, I saw a bright red grocery cart resting perpendicular to Irv's door. When I reached the cart, I gingerly pulled it backwards, revealing the first blemish, a three-inch horizontal scratch, on my home.

Inside, I unpacked my Target bag and plopped into the dinette booth with my laptop. I messaged three potential sources that Brian the professor had referred me to. And I answered emails, including one from a potential source I'd written who declined to be interviewed, an infrequent but still frustrating occurrence. Then I did some research about an online pharmacy I'd never heard of that had reached out about sponsoring five Peeps episodes.

An email arrived from Nathan. "Greetings from Tokyo!" he wrote in the subject line. "Big news — I just learned I got a second scholarship for next year!"

I sometimes wondered what my father would make of his two grandsons, born long after he died, both terrific young men, studious and earnest. I had no memories of my dad, other than a vague sense of his mild-mannered presence. My mother took little pride in her grandsons' accomplishments — or ours, which is probably why my brother didn't aspire to much beyond making a basic living, one just robust enough to support his pot habit. I tried to impress her by being good. Yet she treated me with the same indifference, the same annoyance bordering on hostility, no matter how I performed. She arrived so late to my college graduation that she missed my walk across the stage.

"So now *I'm* to blame for traffic on the 10 freeway?" she hissed.

I wrote Nathan back with congratulations, I fed Dotty and heated up a Lean Cuisine that I ended up tossing after four bites, the meal unsuccessful at disrupting uncomfortable memories I wasn't in the mood to relive.

Thanks to blackout shades that came with my motor home, I was able to make Irv dark no matter where I parked at night, whether it was a Wal-Mart lot, an RV park, or a small-town commercial street. But the nighttime noise was something else. Everywhere I went, the sounds were different so I couldn't adapt to them like I did with the rhythmic ocean tides that came with my Spruce Street house. My first night in Utah, for example, I unwittingly parked under the Salt Lake City flight path so jetliner noises kept waking me. In other locations, it was city sounds: horns blaring, partiers partying, sirens. Other places it was dead quiet, which was equally unnerving. I woke on more than one occasion certain that someone was trying to break into the RV. What helped most at night was Dotty. Her steady breathing steadied mine, her purrs a pleasing white noise machine.

After my interview with Brian, I was tired but not sleepy. And I was eager to continue my journey. So I broke one of my cardinal rules: not traveling in the dark. I retracted the large windshield shade, turned on the ignition and followed the yellow signs to the highway heading south.

CHAPTER EIGHT

C rossing the border into Texas brought an excitement rivaling a
kid's on a June night before the state fair. It had been more than
eight weeks since Alex left LA for college and I couldn't wait to see
him on both his turf of UT Austin and mine, the RV, and introduce him
to Dotty. Hours before our appointed meet-up time, I parked Irv next to
a massive truck with antlers affixed to the back of the cab and stickers of
sexy cartoon women provocatively holding guns. I felt far from California.

What was familiar, sadly, were the under-freeway tents and tarps,
sleeping bags and blankets. And from my new next door neighbor at the
RV park, I discovered that no fewer than seventeen vehicles lived there full
time. When I looked around, it was easy to spot which ones they were. The
rigs were older, not well maintained. Yet again, I took note of my fortune.
Money was tight but Irv — cozy and brand new — was my choice. And on
top of that I had a real house to return to.

Alex was in class until the afternoon so I decided to translate my
gratitude into action, something Jeff, one of the most generous people I'd
known, had taught me. I headed to a nearby market and bought a handful

of gift certificates and drove back to the freeway underpass where I handed them to the individuals living in tents.

Then I cleaned the RV, dumped Dotty's litter box, and tucked away my podcasting equipment. I hoped Alex might forego his dorm for a night to stay with me. I'd give him my bed and sleep on the dinette-turned-bed, and I also hoped he'd indulge me with his signature morning hugs. He'd always been the most affectionate little boy, even during those years when he was obstinate and exhausting. Even in high school, he'd sit right next to me on the couch while we watched West Wing reruns or YouTube videos of old Stevie Wonder performances.

I left Dotty with a catnip toy I'd picked up on a pit stop in Fort Worth and walked a few blocks to a hipster neighborhood that was home to a shack selling hot donuts where we planned to meet. I sat on a cement bench. Excitement put me there twenty minutes early so I decided to do 5-4-3-2-1.

It was one of the cognitive practices Melinda recommended that I actually enjoyed. Pinpointing sounds was always the hardest for me. It's easy to see things. You can even dissect one thing you see, as in *I see my dashboard, I see the number 85 on my dashboard's screen.* And for things I feel, I could, if necessary, manipulate it, as in *I feel my arm swinging as I walk.* Sounds, though, weren't always in my control. Sometimes I'd feel grateful for honks as I turned onto La Cienega. When I got desperate, I'd cough and count that as a sound. But I tried to stay true to the spirit of the exercise, especially because my need to control my environment was, Melinda insisted, something I needed to tame. A side benefit of this cognitive exercise was that it made me a better writer for Peeps intros. Instead of noting, *I see a brick on the ground,* I'd say *I see a chipped, abandoned brick on the rain-drenched sidewalk.* Or *I hear the crackling of a campfire shooting skyward like a funeral pyre.* Same for meditation. When I'm fidgety, I say to myself, *Still. Still, like a flag on a windless day.*

There, at the donut stand in Austin, I noted…

I see a recycling bin full of kombucha bottles. I see a heap of used napkins in a compost bin.

I hear tiny birds chatting in a tree above me.

I feel my heart beating with eagerness.

And then I saw him. Watching Alex walk towards me filled me with both a pleasant high that, were I the kind of person who was into drugs, probably resembled the effects of top-of-the-line marijuana, and also a profound disbelief. He was eight inches taller than me and soon to turn nineteen, that magnificent age at which discerning adults could still see in his face the child he'd once been and savvy young women could detect the full-blown man he'd soon become.

"Meggie-Mom."

I had to reach way up to clutch his face, which was rough with facial hair.

"How," I said, standing on my tip-toes to pet the top of his head the way I used to when he was little, "did you get so grown up?" His hair was dark, thick and wavy.

"It happens," he said, with a shy shrug.

He pulled from his backpack a large manila envelope. "Your mail," he said.

Before I left Santa Monica, Jeff agreed to gather mail collected from my renter Kenneth and send the most urgent items to a few stops along my route, the first being this stop at Alex's. Just a few weeks in, money was already tight and I wished some sort of miracle money would appear in the stack. When I spotted a reimbursement check from my health insurance company, I grew hopeful but it turned out to be a grand total of ten dollars. Also in that first batch was a summons for jury duty in Santa Monica. I entered a reminder into my phone to request a deferral. I would not be summoned home — I was just getting started.

We spent the afternoon walking and eating our way through Austin, the highlight being the fried avocado taco at Torchy's. In the early evening, we grabbed decaf cold brews and headed to the banks of Lady Bird Lake to see the bats. At that point in late autumn, our chances of seeing them depart from underneath the Congress Avenue Bridge at sunset were slim. But it didn't matter. The air was still thick and warm at that hour and I was eager to sit and relax. Alex had the foresight to bring a picnic blanket he'd scrunched into his backpack, but I still had a tough time getting comfortable. I could feel the blood settling in my glutes after hours on my feet. I wished I'd worn my compression socks. But the dampness of the grass seeped through the blanket and the coolness felt nice. We snapped a golden hour selfie and texted it to Jeff. Alex posted it on Instagram.

While we waited for the bats, I filled him in on Peeps, and he told me about his classes, his upcoming visit with Jeff and Milt, and Sophie, a girl he'd met in Art History who he was taking to the upcoming fraternity formal. Although he'd grown a little more private through the years, Alex's chattiness was one of my favorite things about him. When he was in high school, fellow moms of boys would complain about how their sons never talked to them, never told them anything. That wasn't the case with Alex.

"So are you, you know, glad you did this?" he asked, laying sideways on the grass, his elbow bent, head resting in his hand.

I flashed to that moment of driving away from Spruce Street with a new pet in tow. The man with the hunting knife at the busted sewage pump. The breathtaking Rockies and the brisk Colorado air. Brian the professor's thoughts about epigenetics. Tunes from the seventies and eighties I revisited for the first time in years, singing along as I traveled mile upon mile, nearly fifteen hundred so far.

"It's only been a few weeks. But so far, I'm gonna say yes."

"Tell me more about your itinerary," he said.

I pulled out my phone and with my finger traced my up-and-down route on a map.

"Being careful?"

There was a turning point in my life and his — about three years ago — when he was old and large enough to be the one to protect me rather than the other way around. I'd noticed it theoretically before it happened in actuality, when a man harassed me in Grand Central Station while we were on vacation. Alex returned from the bathroom and simply stepped between me and the man, who quickly darted away.

"I upgraded the RV with an alarm system."

"Good," he said, shifting his position to sit back upright. "What do you plan to do in Syracuse?"

"See Uncle Oscar."

"Is that dude even alive? He didn't come to the memorial service, according to Dad."

"He's eighty-eight, almost eighty-nine. I wouldn't have expected him to travel all that way for a forty-five minute service." *Believe me, I might not have attended myself if I didn't have to.*

"Why are you seeing him?"

"I want to learn more about your grandmother, our ancestors."

"Can't you just call him?"

"I want to talk to him in person. One thing that's become even more clear to me since shifting Peeps from a blog to a podcast: nothing substitutes for an in-person conversation. Body language, facial expressions, you know."

He shrugged.

"Why do you seem surprised that I want to see him?" I asked.

"I mean, you've never spent much time with that side of the family. I barely know them."

"I did when I was growing up. And I've been doing a lot of reading."

He made a swirling motion with his hand as if to say, "Continue."

111

"Well, you know I've been trying to address some of my...tendencies," I said.

"So you want to learn why the world feels like a scary place."

"How'd you get so smart?"

His thick eyebrows drew together. "What difference would it make, learning about your relatives? Instead of learning why you're fearful, wouldn't your energy be better spent just working on *being* less scared?"

"You sound like your father," I said. "Let me put it this way: interviewing people for Peeps...there's something to be said for asking questions, for exploring who we are, for understanding ourselves. More than one source has gotten in touch with me after an interview and told me that the experience of being asked the seven questions helped clarify who they are, their relationships, their pasts, how they move through the world."

"Well, I hope the effort is worth it then. Hope he gives you what you're looking for."

We waited more than an hour but the bats never appeared. As other onlookers got up and left, we stayed on the grass and watched a few YouTube videos of the bats from earlier that summer, just to get the feel. We committed to return to the lake during my next visit, scheduled for April. Then we hopped in a cab for dinner at the Broken Spoke, a Texas dance hall institution.

"Austin is a great place for carnivores *and* veg-heads," Alex explained with his mouth full of barbecued brisket, his first meat on the day's packed food tour of the city.

Thirty feet from our table, a classic southern band, complete with fiddle, banjo and steel guitar, played country music, a genre we both loved. We watched couples dance, the regulars and the tourists.

"You can tell the difference by their cowboy boots," he said, aiming his chin towards the scuffed dance floor, which was sprinkled with hay, giving the place a sweet, woody smell.

"How so?"

"Take a look," he said. Everyone, men and women, wore cowboy boots. "Brand new, it's a tourist. Scuffed? A local."

We tapped our toes and ate cheese fries and chatted. I jotted down in the notes section of my phone interview subjects that Alex suggested, including a UT professor who'd spent ten years studying Lyme disease and wound up contracting that very disease herself while vacationing in Maine.

I felt a tap on my shoulder and turned to face a short man with a long mustache. He wore 501s and a brown flannel shirt. A local — his boots were scuffed.

"Join me for a dance?" the man asked with an outstretched palm.

Alex smiled and looked down in his lap, struggling, I could see, not to laugh. I was a terrible dancer, something he teased me about. Not only was I uncoordinated, I once even threw my neck out trying to make him laugh by playing air guitar.

"Uh, thank you, no." I smiled.

The man stayed put. "Awww, please?"

"No, really, thank you. I'm an awful dancer."

"That's okay!" he said. "I can show you…." He reached his hand two inches closer.

"Thanks, man. We're visiting," Alex explained, waving a hand between us. "Have a great night."

The man walked away.

"I'm afraid I hurt his feelings," I said.

"No need to be hella afraid all the time," Alex said, his tone serious.

"I'm working on it. Which is why I want to see Uncle Oscar in Syracuse."

"You don't need to go digging up the past to move forward. You can be who you are, just without fear."

He sounded then so much like Jeff, who spent years insisting that I should simply *instruct* myself to not be afraid of things. The riptides in the Pacific. Identity theft. Illness.

"Perhaps," I said, feeling chided. "But for now, this is my plan."

I both loved and hated that Alex's opinion mattered so much to me. His wisdom made me proud, but my own dependence on it sometimes annoyed me. I wondered if he and Jeff — and even Milt — had bonded by shaking their collective heads over this trip of mine. Do we ever get over wanting approval from the people we love?

Back in the RV, I showed Alex around. The top of his head nearly reached Irv's ceiling, and we had to side-step around each other as I pointed out features of my home on the road. I introduced him to Dotty, who drooled on his index finger as he scratched her under her chin.

"She likes you," I said.

"Cool cat. I'm glad she's keeping you company."

"She is. Speaking of that, I was hoping maybe you'd stay here tonight? Kind of like a mother-son slumber party? Like that time we 'camped' in a tent in the backyard as a dry run for your sixth-grade camping trip."

"That sounds fun, but I promised Sophie I'd pop by later tonight."

I glanced at the clock on the microwave. It was nearly ten-thirty. I was ready to curl up for the night. He was just getting started. Just like when I saw Nathan in Santa Monica, I realized how old I really was.

"Okay," I said, trying to keep my expression neutral even though I'd been looking forward to spending more time with my boy. It felt like I'd lost a contest I was sure I was going to win. *I'd come all this way. My own mother never made an effort with me. Couldn't he just spend* one night *with his mom?*

"Meet me for breakfast in the dining commons?" he said, diffusing my disappointment with his invitation.

"It's a date." I had a mid-day interview with a woman who ran canasta tournaments throughout Texas. After that, I was supposed to head due east. *But maybe I could stay?*

"Love you, Meggie-Mom," he said, warming me with a hug before stepping out of the RV into the dense Austin air.

What I'd lacked in my parents, I'd way made up for in my child. If the Universe had offered me a deal at the outset — "your father will die before you can know him, your mother will fail to meet your emotional needs, but you will have a boy who will challenge you and love you and exceed all your dreams of parenting" — I'd have taken that deal. Alex could never erase the scars of my childhood. He could not undo my mother's short fuse, her dismissiveness. He couldn't mute her voice that still played in my head, the one that admonished me to "stop overreacting," her "I didn't sign up for this!" mantra, the huffs and eye rolling that conveyed that being my parent was a burden. Yet the joy Alex brought me, even as he was pulling away from me, stepping head first into his own grown-up life, buffed those scars, transforming them from an angry purple to a fading pale pink. For his sake, as much as my own, I needed to move on, to continue east.

I locked Irv and got ready for bed, no longer as sleepy as I'd been a few minutes before. I felt grateful and, at the same time, lonesome. If I were back home in Santa Monica, I could reach out to a friend to grab a late night cup of coffee or catch a movie. But I'd removed myself from everything and everyone I knew. I'd given up the accessibility of the familiar.

I considered texting Brad. He *had* encouraged me to keep in touch. *Maybe he'd come meet me?*

But he'd probably been snatched up by some other lucky divorcee by now. I might have captured his interest initially, but I probably wasn't special enough for him to wait for. I remembered Alejandra and her Ernest.

Would anyone keep a log of what they wanted to tell me after I die?

I could practically hear Melinda's voice: it was unhealthy, not to mention disempowering, to turn to a man I barely knew to heal the damage that my mother and probably Jeff had inflicted. To distract myself, I opened my computer and responded to emails from podcast listeners, a task that was taking up more time because the volume had increased lately. Some listeners wrote to tell me about how a particular episode resonated with them, some wrote with suggestions for future interviewees or volunteered to be interviewed themselves. One writer insisted the interviews couldn't be real. Then I wrote and recorded a short show promo and uploaded it to a podcasting community website, an advertising tactic I read about in the Pod Path newsletter.

I finally closed my laptop and began my nighttime routine, checking the locks, activating the alarm, programming the coffee maker, cleaning errant cat litter from the floor. Then I joined Dotty in the bed, and read *Transgenerational Transmission of Environmental Information* until consciousness slipped away.

Welcome to Peeps, the podcast that highlights the world in a grain of sand. It's episode thirty-nine. I can hardly believe it.

Nancy is in her late twenties, with wispy blond hair and the quietest, most soothing voice and speech cadence of anyone I've ever met. She speaks so softly you may even need to turn up the volume on your listening device. Sipping sweet tea in the garden of her Beaumont, Texas bungalow, complete with purple coneflowers and a Black Willow tree, I told Nancy she could make a fortune producing ASMR videos for YouTube. But her soft, palliative manner belied the horror of what she'd endured in recent years.

Thanks for meeting with me. You're one among seven billion — what's it like to be you right now?

Where to start? I dated a man — let's call him "Guy" — for about a year. The ideal boyfriend at first. Attentive, affectionate. I felt so lucky, like it was finally my time. We moved in together pretty quickly. Then he, um, transformed. Grew possessive and abusive within weeks. First verbally, then physically. After about a month of that, I ended the relationship. But he didn't. When he lived here, he'd installed technology all around. "The Internet of things" is what it's called. Some I knew about. But others I didn't. After I kicked him out, he began using all these things to harass me.

Can you explain?

Definitely. Because I want people to know about this. It's why I agreed to talk to you. Here's an example: we had a digital lock at the front door. He changed the entry code remotely every single day so I couldn't get into my own house. And in the middle of the night, the doorbell would ring.

But no one would be there. He did that remotely too. We had Internet-connected lights, speakers, thermostat. Even the icebox. He'd turn lights on, blare music at three in the morning. He'd heat the house an ungodly amount when it was hot, shut off the heat completely when it was cold. The technology — it was a tool for revenge and control. To scare, confuse, intimidate me. I went to the police. But they doubted what I told them, saw me as the crazy one. I mean, how could I prove the doorbell rang at midnight and that my crazy ex had done it from afar? I sought legal assistance from a friend of a friend. But there's zero language in the restraining order form for these digital tools. My social life died. I was scared to go out. I shut off all devices, and became, like, even more isolated.

Nancy, that's just...I'm sorry you went through that.

Yeah, it wasn't easy. But, you know, here I am.

Indeed. Here you are. Let's move on. Tell me something about yourself, your background.

I do part-time bookkeeping for physicians and dentists. A job I mostly do from home, especially now. But my real dream is to become a gardener. Maybe I will someday.

Nancy, what's one object you'd take with you into the afterlife?

Uh, my laptop? It has everything. Documents, photos, videos. I don't have money to get a new one. Never let it out of my sight.

What's one thing you do every day?

Get outside. If I didn't force myself to step outdoors, I'd become a true hermit. A few months ago, I learned about a website where you can exchange postcards with strangers. You send one and then you get one and then you send one to someone different and then you get one from someone different. It's a whole algorithm. Anyway, I registered. Now I send a few postcards a week. Mostly because it forces me to walk three blocks to the mailbox. And it connects me to the outside world. Yesterday I received a postcard from someone in Buenos Aires.

Tell me the pivot moment in your life.

Well, I've heard that it takes most victims of physical abuse seven incidents before leaving. For me, it was one. One time of Guy grabbing and twisting my wrist, shoving me against the wall. But leaving him wasn't the ticket to my life getting better. It was the ticket to things getting worse, to all the harassment. One day, he came banging on my front door. He screamed that I was a whore, a stupid slut. By then I'd removed the digital lock there. Had an old-fashioned deadbolt. But he had a crowbar and bashed in the skinny window on the side of the front door, reached his hand around for the deadbolt. I was terrified. My whole body quaked as I barricaded myself inside the powder room. When he couldn't get the front door open, he left, yelling about how he'd come back and kill me. But here's the crazy thing: the entire incident was caught on the doorbell camera that he'd installed to spy on my comings and goings. So that's when he was finally arrested and I got some relief. He's behind bars, but I'm still afraid of him. He hurt me from far away before. And he struck a plea deal with the DA so he's getting out in a few months.

I'm sorry, Nancy. It's awful to feel unsafe. I'd like to ask you now: Who is someone you never saw again?

You mean, like an old friend or something?

Anyone. An acquaintance, a friend, a relative.

Well, before I met Guy, I did a little online dating. I went on one date with a man who had these, like, facial tics or something. A lot of blinking at first. But then it moved to his cheeks and his mouth. His face was constant motion. I'd been excited about meeting him because our profiles aligned precisely and we'd had several great text exchanges. He was a doctor. Graduated from Harvard! Even before I observed the tics I was disappointed in his looks when I walked into the coffee shop where we planned to meet. He was short and pudgy. Awful to admit, so shallow of me. But physical attraction is a thing, right? Anyway, I couldn't even concentrate on our conversation. I was so, you know, distracted by his tics. Probably had Tourette's or something?

Then what happened?

So it was my personal policy then to only meet online dates for coffee. No drinks, no dinner. I always wanted to be able to exit quickly if it didn't go well. I mean, how long does it take to drink a cup of coffee? But I barely made it that long with this guy. Barely twenty minutes. I was kinda, um, angry that he hadn't warned me what to expect. I mean, maybe if he'd told me he had a physical difference, I could have prepared myself. Maybe even looked past it. But I was, like, more angry at myself. Ashamed that I couldn't ignore his differences, couldn't give him the fair chance he deserved. I made a big show of finishing my latte. Then claimed a headache and left. I did actually have a bit of a headache because of those two strands of anger — at him, at myself. Needless to say, I never saw him again. But

I can't help but wonder if what happened later with Guy was my punishment. For dismissing that tic man so readily. For being so superficial. That was years ago now. I really hope he found a nice woman.

What's your life motto?

Well, my grandmother used to say, No grit, no pearl. I guess I kind of live by that.

Peeps would be nothing without brave people like Nancy.

What's it like to be a university professor *and* autistic? Tune in next time to find out.

CHAPTER NINE

Naked and freezing on my first morning in western Louisiana, I turned on my shower and nothing came out. The water spout emitted a groan as I twisted the handle. That was it. As always, my day had been planned to a tee but somehow, I'd have to add "find an RV repair shop" to my agenda. I'm not a fan of the unexpected.

My mother's refrain — "I didn't sign up for this!" — played on loop in my head as I wiped my arm pits with baby wipes. I drove through towns with names like Benton and Bossier City looking for a shop. My pump was under warranty but the one shop I could find within a hundred miles of where I was didn't carry the brand I needed. So I had no choice but to purchase an extra fancy electric pump.

"That'll be four hundred," the woman at the service desk said with the prolonged vowels so characteristic of the south.

"But I was told the pump is one-fifty," I said, confused.

"Labor," she said, her eyes fixed the stack of papers she was paging through using fingers with bitten down nails.

I handed over my credit card, which, between gas, dinners out and maintenance costs, had seen a lot of action in the last weeks.

I should have insisted on higher rent from Kenneth.

In the shop's waiting room, I poured myself watery coffee from a carafe on a tray next to the television, which blared a daytime game show. I sank into a torn fake leather couch that reminded me of the crummy chairs in the shoe store back in Santa Monica. I removed my computer from my bag and wrote to my old boss Dana asking if she had any freelance assignments for the legal newsletter to send my way. I preferred to spend my time scheduling, conducting and producing Peeps interviews rather than write about dry goings-on in the legal profession. But this trip was costing more than I expected. I needed money. I tried not to think about the income I'd given up had I stayed on as editor at Dana's company. At least I still had some of the ownership shares she'd paid me before.

After writing Dana, I Googled "ways to monetize a podcast" and scanned articles about advertising, something I'd previously given only a passing thought to. A half hour later, Irv was still being worked on and I'd registered Peeps with services that match advertisers with shows. And Dana emailed me back.

"So sorry," she wrote, adding a sad face emoji. "I've got nothing. The last potential buyer just bailed because the Legal Sentinel out of Chicago just launched its own newsletter. I can't compete. So now I'm looking to sell the company for parts. In the meantime, I'm cutting original reporting in favor of wire stories."

I inhaled, my neck craned towards the popcorn ceiling. Not only could she not help me with earning extra cash, but the equity I'd built up in Dana's company was now likely worthless. I felt awful for Dana, who'd devoted her professional life to that newsletter. I wrote her back with thanks and my condolences, adding my own sad face emoji, which couldn't quite convey the financial stress I was feeling.

When the water pump installation was done, I *should* have settled into the nearest Wal-Mart parking lot and sent messages to the few other editors I knew who might be in the position to toss me an assignment or two. That would have been the wise thing to do.

Instead, I went gambling.

I don't have many *traditional* vices. I'm not a big drinker. And even though my tightly wound constitution might actually benefit from an occasional joint, I'd always been terrified of drugs, maybe because of what I'd observed of my brother. I'd picture myself on a bad trip with no way to undo it, being forced instead to ride it out. *No. Way.* But every once in awhile, I liked to gamble. I ended up in Nevada maybe once a decade so I didn't have many opportunities to try my luck. But I was in Louisiana, where gambling is legal. So when I passed a casino after driving away from the RV repair shop, I spoke a word to Dotty that she'd never heard before: "Detour!"

Bayou Belle was a casino cliché: smoky, crowded even on a Wednesday afternoon, and depressing. On my way to the blackjack table, I passed unsmiling women shoving plastic buckets under the slot machine chutes, collecting their winnings joylessly. Taking a seat at a table, I promised myself that I'd stay only until I spent or won a hundred bucks. On the third hand, I split my fives and hit on both fifteens, drawing a seven and an eight. Just twenty minutes after entering Bayou Belle, I was out a hundred bucks. Ignoring my vow, I stayed two more hours and lost more.

"'Kay, folks," the dealer said. "Y'all are gonna have to find a new table. I'm on break."

Thank God, I thought, grateful to be forced from the seat I might otherwise have spent the whole day in. The man next to me began organizing his pile of chips.

"Hey," I said to the dealer, trying to salvage something good from the day. "Any chance you'd be interested in being interviewed for a podcast?" I gave him my Peeps elevator pitch.

"Nah," he said. "My parents think I'm in nursing school."

I nodded and stood to retrieve my bag hanging from the back of my chair.

"Hey," the man next to me said. "If it's a card dealer you're interested in, my sister used to work here. For years. Now she's home. Three kids. She'd probably talk to you. She's always looking for a distraction."

I excited Bayou Belle with a new interview lined up, a headache from all the smoke and a nagging feeling that my trip was a bad idea, making me do things I never would otherwise.

A thirty-four-year-old mom of three, Carrie, the sister of the man at the blackjack table, was what I'd call a harried beauty, a description I ended up using for the title of the episode. All honey-haired and perfectly proportioned faces, her three children swirled around her lower legs like dervishes.

"C'mon, y'all," she sighed while herding them onto the couch for a snack and a movie while I set up my recording equipment in her kitchen, which smelled of detergent and something bitter, which I finally identified as fish food once I spotted the small tank on her counter.

"It's only nine-thirty, and I'm already so tired," she said under her breath. "Tired" sounded like *taared*. To me, she said, "This morning was a morning I'd like to forget. I hope it doesn't leave scars on my son."

I was poised to launch into my standard questions, to steer Carrie towards her time as a card dealer. Grateful as I was for this new interview opportunity that had resulted from my ill-fated stop at Bayou Belle, I had other interviews to get to and a long stretch of driving towards an important stop in Kansas City. But an interviewer's intuition was emerging in me as I was meeting so many more of my sources in person rather than over the phone. I sensed that what Carrie was saying about her life now would be more resonant than anything she could reveal about working in a casino. And were I to interrupt her with the formality of an official question, the magic would disappear. So without asking anything, I hit record and let her talk. Later, with her permission, I'd splice in my "What's it like to be you?" question.

"I'm an introvert," she continued. "Every single day, I'm, like, pushed to my limits. Constant noise, uncontrolled volume levels," she put her hands in front of her face, the way infants do when they're overtired. "Nonstop requests and demands. I feel, like, maxed out beyond what I can handle."

"Once," I recalled to Carrie, squirming as I remembered it, "my son kicked me in the shin when I announced it was time to leave a preschool birthday party. Driving home, I called him a little shit. Sixteen years later, it still makes me bristle to think of it. Even now, with my son in college, whenever I hear a condemning reference to Alec Baldwin's infamous voicemail to his daughter, I have this oddball urge to surrender to the police."

Carrie snorted a laugh through tears.

As joyful as parenting could be, it was also relentless, with no relief, no breather in sight. Endless lunches to make, dishwashers to empty, shoes to buy for rapidly growing feet, birthday parties to purchase gifts for, dentist appointments to schedule. There's that saying that youth is wasted on the young. But there needs to be an addendum, a supplement. Something like "parenthood is wasted on the parents." Because when I finally wasn't too exhausted to make chocolate chip cookies or propose a spontaneous outing to the miniature golf course, it was too late. Alex was a teenager no longer interested in hanging out with me. Now he was in college. I'd always be his mother, of course. But the *meat* of parenting? It had passed. I was oddly envious of Carrie, as exhausted as she seemed. She was in the thick of it, the hardest part. But she was still in it.

"Your son is *not* scarred for life," I said, reaching across the kitchen table and tapping my hand on her elbow. "Just like my son wasn't."

Her lip quivered. "I have…anger issues," she replied. "No idea why. I have a good—," she looked around her kitchen as if to prove her point. "— a good life. But when I'm depleted, I'm just full of anger. This morning I yelled. I was aggressive, slamming doors. I frightened my own children. I'm ashamed, embarrassed."

This, I thought, *this is why I do this podcast.*

"Thank you for sharing." My words would be edited out later, not to be part of the episode. But I needed to say them and she needed to hear them. "What you're saying, your honesty…it resonates. I have an old friend, her name is Dorothy. She taught me the meaning of the word 'mitzvah.' It means a good deed. But it's really more than that. It's an act of empathy, of kindness. You've done a mitzvah by talking with me. You will help someone, probably many more, feel less alone."

I settled into an RV park on the east side of New Orleans, not far from Frenchmen Street, which, according to Scottie, who went to Tulane University, was where the locals went to hear live music.

When I'd left Carrie's house, she gifted me two dozen homemade cookies. I'd already eaten six on the drive and it was time to remove them from my reach. I knocked on my RV neighbor's door, something that still felt odd though it was the custom on the road. A man, maybe mid-thirties, opened the door. I explained the excess of treats and held out the cookies, still pleasantly arranged on the sturdy paper plate despite my earlier binge.

"Who's that?" a woman peeked over the man's shoulder. "Justin!" she said, "invite her in already!"

Though I kept most neighborly visits outdoor only, I was always eager to peer into other motor homes when I was in the mood. The man beckoned me inside and I gazed around. Theirs was a true home, complete with twinkly lights strung in the kitchen, hand-knit blankets in modern colors tossed over the small couch, a baked potato bar being set up on the counter and two kids playing cards at the table, each given half of one of the cookies I'd brought. "It's almost dinner," the woman said to them.

We chatted for a few minutes and I learned the family was living on the road full time, homeschooling and earning their livings as Instagram influencers. Perhaps it was even their #vanlife photos and videos that had inspired the man in the van back in Santa Monica. I'd have to ask him when I interviewed him on his return from Mexico.

"Join us for dinner?" the man asked as he used tongs to grasp two more potatoes from the microwave.

For once, I was tempted to linger with neighbors longer than just a few minutes. I wanted to learn about homeschooling, about where to buy those twinkly lights, about how they monetized their social media.

"That's kind of you," I said. "But my best friend told me not to miss live music while I'm here in NOLA. So I'm going to do that. I'd invite you to join *me* but…." I nodded to the kids.

"Yup," the man laughed. "Maybe we'll join you in a few years."

I returned to Irv to finish getting dressed. After a cuddle session with Dotty, I removed cat hair from my shirt with a tape roller, and walked a mile to Frenchmen. It felt good to move my body after the long drive from Carrie's house.

At the edge of Esplanade Avenue, I could hear the faintest trumpet sounds from the clubs. The air was peppered with the scent of boiling crawfish and corn as no fewer than four families were cooking in their front yards, relishing what had to be the last weeks of outdoor cooking on that November evening. Alex was a longtime jazz enthusiast so through osmosis I'd acquired an appreciation of the genre. But I was no sophisticated connoisseur, so I just walked into the first club on the row, a place called Sweet Augusta.

"Table for one."

I wasn't an adventurous eater — unless kale and quinoa counted, which it didn't when you were from California — but I'd pledged to try as many local foods on this trip as I could. I ordered gumbo and Sweet Augusta's signature Creole Bloody Mary.

At one end of Sweet Augusta, there was a small stage, elevated up two stairs from the dining room floor. One band wrapped its set just as I was seated. In the relative quiet that followed, I heard my phone ding with a text.

"Dude," Scottie wrote, "First hot flash ever. Hooolllllllyyy crap."

I'd had night sweats for years and had taken to piling Jeff's under-shirts, which I'd swiped in the divorce, at the end of the bed so when I woke drenched in the middle of the night, I could whip one shirt off, replacing it with the next from the stack. But I'd never had a proper hot flash.

"Go," I wrote back.

"Thought I was having a heart attack," Scottie texted. "In 2 seconds, my whole body was overcome w/ raging heat. Like, 200 degrees! If I was a little cartoon man w/ a sombrero on a Mexican restaurant menu, I'd be the one in dark red indicating Very Spicy. & the nausea! It overtook me. Srsly thought I was dying. I laid down on the tile floor of my kitchen. 2 minutes later, I was FINE, back up chopping vegetables for dinner!!"

Partly amused, partly horrified, I shuddered, then tapped out my reply: "Just think of them as 'power surges,'" and added a link to a black cohosh supplement that had suspiciously been appearing in my Facebook feed lately.

When my drink arrived, the next band took the stage, a trio of piano, sax and drums. The drummer came out last carrying a mini set of cymbals that looked like they were made of tin, and he sat down at the kit. My age or perhaps a little younger, the drummer was the band leader, introduc-ing the pieces and describing their inspiration. They played a few songs I recognized: St. James Infirmary and Corcovado and then launched into a few originals. The music had a Latin feel, with occasional ragtime notes. My food arrived but I could hardly eat despite my hunger. That guy, with the tin cymbals he brought together dramatically and with the joy of a young boy, had me riveted.

My history with men had highs and lows. When I was in eighth grade, I was curvy, hormonal, and covered in acne. When I look back at photos of myself from that time, vulnerability vibrates through the frame. One afternoon my mom told me that a boy across the street, a year older who went to a Catholic high school, liked me but wouldn't date me unless I cut my hair, which for years I'd been wearing long past my shoulders. Shocked that he'd told such a thing to my mother but also intrigued, I went that weekend to Supercuts and requested a bob, absolutely the wrong look for my wavy hair and small face.

The next time I saw the boy I said, "My mom told me you wanted me to get my hair cut." He looked at me like I was from outer space.

"Who are you?"

I darted away, holding in tears until I crossed the threshold of my front door. I told my mother what happened.

"No boy is going to really like you until that acne is gone," she said.

From the den, Leith yelled, "And your new haircut is lame!" My mother didn't rebuke him.

As I got older, sex had become *more* mystifying to me than when I discovered it as a late teen. In my middle-aged opinion, sex is complicated. Sometimes it's like a dance — an unrehearsed dance, a metaphor I borrow from my favorite Barbra Streisand song. That's the way it had been with one particular guy in high school, the person with whom I'd developed my "Night Moves," to use another musical analogy. Absolutely nothing was awkward with him. In fact, that was probably when I felt the sexiest in my life. And to this day, that boy from high school remains the best kisser I'd ever kissed. *Think* about that for a minute: I was seventeen and had no idea that was the *pinnacle* of kissing for me. I'd presumed it was merely a *preview* of what the rest of my life had in store.

I wish I'd savored it.

If it's not like an unrehearsed dance, sex can be clumsy or clinical, an unspoken "You touch me here, I touch you there." Like connecting to AOL with a nineties-era dial-up, even if, in the end, it's satisfying. That's how it had mostly been with Jeff. In the final years of our marriage, sex had been transactional. Perhaps his homosexuality should have been more apparent to me. Once, during foreplay, he said, "I forgot to tell you, today I found the perfect drop-leaf table for the living room." At the time it made me laugh. Looking back, not so much.

During sex, people share an unbelievably intimate moment, complete with an exchange of fluids, raw facial expressions and noises. When you really think about it, sex is weird. So when both Jeff and Scottie encouraged me to try dating apps to meet someone, I said *no way*. I didn't want to reveal or observe that kind of private moment with anyone new. I wasn't sure I ever would. Maybe that's why it had been easier than it should have been to leave LA after the promising first few dates with Brad.

That said, everyone once in awhile, I just...wanted it. That's how I felt at Sweet Augusta on Frenchmen Street. Seeing the drummer with his miniature tin cymbals, his biceps stretching his t-shirt sleeves, his grey hair gelled a bit at the top. It was clear he was doing what he loved. It was sexy. He smiled at me from the stage and I felt myself redden the way, perhaps, that Scottie had during her first hot flash. Even before Jeff left me, I had long since stopped feeling sexy. I may have been at one time, maybe back in high school with the Night Moves guy, but no more.

Case in point: a few months before leaving Santa Monica, I was roaming through Brentwood Country Mart after dropping something off at the little shopping center's quaint old-fashioned post office. I walked into Homestead Salads, which was part market, part restaurant, and there was Jennifer Garner having lunch. While pretending to examine jars of olive tapenade in the market, I observed her. She was even prettier than she appeared on screen, with luminous skin and hair that looked like it didn't have — or need — any styling. In contrast, my hair was dirty under the baseball cap I was wearing not only to hide the fact that I needed a shampoo but also to hide the greys sprouting from my part that wouldn't get fixed until I had time to draw over them with a brown Sharpie, a between-appointments trick Scottie had taught me.

I gawked for a few minutes, then walked across the Country Mart's courtyard to the restroom. I piled two toilet seat covers, as was my custom, onto the toilet, one of those high ones intended for wheelchair users. Thank God I was in a single-use bathroom because something about the height of that toilet, the two paper covers and my very full bladder made my pee shoot forward rather than down. My underwear and yoga pants, lowered to my calves, were instantly soaked with warm, ammonia-scented urine. Being eco-friendly California, the bathroom had air dryers instead of paper towels so I had to use wads of toilet paper that instantly shredded as I attempted to sop up the golden dampness from the white tile floor. This would have felt far less humiliating if I hadn't just been observing gorgeous Jennifer Garner. She was barely younger than me but I was certain — *certain* — this pee situation would *never* have happened to her. Out there in Homestead Salads, she seemed so radiant and fresh. I felt…disgusting. It was a sad, weird turning point for me. My sexy years, I understood in that moment, were gone.

In that New Orleans jazz club, though, with my Bloody Mary and the surging jazz, something was reignited. The drummer continued to eye me from the stage. Attention from a hot drummer? It felt like I was living a Big Life. In my head, I was already crafting the text I'd send to Scottie.

After his set, he came over to my table and I felt…sexy. Unlike the clueless seventeen year old I'd once been, I was determined, this time, to savor it. *This time*, I understood it was fleeting.

"Jimmy," he said, extending his hand, which was large and unexpectedly soft. "May I?"

I swept my hand to the empty chair, palm up, as if to say, "Be my guest."

We watched three songs by the next band, Jimmy bumping his knee against mine under the table to the beat. That was it: a drink, a man's attention and suddenly I wanted my base need fulfilled. It was like I'd been on the verge of starvation and didn't even know it until someone offered me a bowl of Southern grits.

"Wanna git out of here?" Jimmy said with a wink, which I found both corny and alluring.

I nodded. I had no idea where he wanted to go.

Jimmy said a quick goodbye to his band mates and steered me to a late-night cafe a block away.

"No live music here," he explained before ordering two Irish coffees "N'awlins style," which meant they had a hint of chicory. "Quiet enough for you to tell me about yourself." The flattery, the attention was exhilarating. "From New Orleans?" he asked.

Sipping my drink, I shook my head. "California."

"Never been to Cali myself." He didn't have to tell me that because absolutely no one truly familiar with California referred to it as "Cali."

"You from here?" I asked.

"Baton Rouge. Still live there actually. Come here for gigs a few times a month. What brings you to NOLA?"

I told Jimmy about Santa Monica, about Peeps, about the RV.

"Just you?" he said. "By yourself?"

"All by myself."

"Can't say I know of a single Southern lady who'd do such a thing."

His tone was ambiguous or maybe I was having a hard time reading him because his thick biceps and the scent of sandalwood in his cologne were distracting. Was he complimenting or judging me?

Before I could decide, he leaned over and kissed me, a gentle, soft kiss, the kind that lingers, the kind, like Brad's, that makes you want more.

We left our drinks unfinished and walked to the RV, Jimmy pointing out remnants of Katrina all those years later. We weren't far from the Ninth Ward so abandoned homes, businesses and even a school were still on display. When we passed an overcrowded homeless camp in a small park, with about a dozen people warming their hands over a barbecue pit, I saw Jimmy surreptitiously pop a pill into his mouth. I recognized those little blue pills — Jeff had been taking Viagra for years. I didn't mind Jimmy's presumption. It reduced the awkwardness of uncertainty. Thank God I'd taken a few minutes that afternoon to tweeze my chin hairs.

At the threshold of the RV, I hesitated. Absolutely no one had been inside Irv except me, Jeff and Alex. Did I want to let a complete stranger into what had become my home, my own very cozy place?

I pretended to fumble with my keys as I evaluated. The RV had become my sanctuary. Did I want someone else's energy inside? Probably not. But I hadn't had sex in a long time. I should have slept with Brad before I left. Here was another chance. If I didn't take it, would I regret that too?

"Got it," I said, and slid the key into the lock.

In the end, sex with Jimmy was somewhere in between an unrehearsed dance and a decidedly clinical encounter. He interlaced his hands on top of my head as he thrust himself inside me, probably decreasing my already shrinking height by a few millimeters. Had no woman instructed him never to do that? It seemed too much trouble for me to explain how uncomfortable, how demeaning that was. I silently shook my head free of his grasp. Jimmy kept his eyes squeezed shut and I understood that he was probably imagining someone else beneath him. I wasn't thinking about him either. Who had fantasies about their *actual* partner anyway? That night, I thought of Lin-Manuel Miranda and felt satiated.

The first indication that Jimmy was actually kind of an ass occurred immediately after the sex, when he let out a noisy, smelly fart. In my bed.

"Did you just…?"

He laughed uproariously and unselfconsciously. "Just pretend it's one of your own."

I felt myself hovering between the old me and a new me. For the sake of the other person, the old me would grit my teeth but still sputter a laugh that sounded authentic to anyone who didn't know me well. (Alex called it my DPP — "disinterested polite phone" — laugh.) With Jimmy, I gritted my teeth and remained silent.

"Hey, can I get some water?" he said, whipping the sheets off so forcefully that I, too, was left uncovered. I yanked them back over my body. He was already opening cabinets searching for cups. He looked so large there in my tiny kitchen, reminding me how compact my life had become. Dotty paced the counter. Her being up there wasn't my favorite thing about having a cat but she spent half the day grooming herself and I wiped the counters clean several times a day so I put up with it. Jimmy bent his forearm and in one fell swoop shoved her off the counter. In that instant, I confirmed that Jimmy was one of those attractive, magnetic men who is decidedly not nice once the thin veneer disappeared.

I sprung of bed and grabbed the cup from his hand.

"Time for you to go," I said in a calm, measured tone, which took effort as my vulnerability truly hit me then.

I thought of Nancy, who'd never quite regained her life even though her abusive ex-boyfriend was behind bars. I thought of the disgusting men at the sewage dump back in Truckee. Now my taser was unpackaged and nearby in a small, hollow space near the foot of my bed. I calculated it would take less than five seconds to grab and discharge it.

Jimmy regarded me, seeming to evaluate whether he could get one more lay out of the situation. Or maybe he was evaluating something else, something more sinister. Eventually, though, he nodded, grabbed his jacket and left wordlessly. I was half relieved and half insulted.

I locked Irv, turned on the alarm, and sat on my bed contemplating the night. My sheets were twisted and the scent of our encounter — and maybe that disgusting fart — lingered. Though it was a dreaded task that took fifteen minutes given that the bed butted right up against the walls, I changed all my bedding and plunged it into the depths of my laundry bag. Going to a laundromat had not been in the plan for tomorrow, but, as with the detour to replace my water pump, I'd squeeze it in.

Sweating from the effort of changing the sheets, I sat on the floor, petting Dotty, who began purring as soon as I'd shut the door behind Jimmy. I was desperate to become the person I'd long fantasized being — not passive, not settling and, most importantly, not afraid. Was the night I'd just had in New Orleans a step forward or a step back? I thought about what I was willing to sacrifice to move forward with my quest. As I gathered Dotty in my arms and settled back into my clean bed, I realized that it was not my dignity and it was definitely not my cat. Yes, a need had been fulfilled. But I wasn't sure it was worth it.

Would Syracuse be the same?

Less than forty-eight hours later, I was in an urgent care clinic in Fayetteville, Arkansas, peeing into a cup, wincing from the burn.

"Is there any bacteria?" I asked an extremely humorless nurse practitioner with a rectangular face who was typing my lab results into a laptop.

"Loaded," she replied flatly, pulling a prescription pad from her pocket. Wordlessly, she handed me a scrip for antibiotics — another unexpected expense — shut her computer and made her way to the door.

"I haven't had a UTI since college," I said, my voice unnaturally high, as I recalled the UCLA health clinic nurse who'd instructed me to be sure to always urinate before and after sex. I was a grown woman but still felt ashamed at what I'd done — I wasn't sure I could even tell Scottie about Jimmy or this infection. "Rookie move, right?" I added, trying, inexplicably, to establish some sort of rapport with this unfriendly RN before she left the room. But other than getting her to finally look directly at me, expressionless, I failed.

CHAPTER TEN

A few minutes after I parked in the Kansas City RV lot, a neighbor across the aisle knocked on my door.

"Name's Carol," said the woman, who was stout and looked to be in her sixties. "Been here about ten days. So that makes me the resident KC guru."

I introduced myself. "I'll be here just a couple of days," I said. "But always nice to know the expert."

"Barbecue, book stores, bars, I'm dialed in so let me know if you need recs." Carol, I could tell immediately, was one of those no nonsense, tell-it-like-it-is people I loved.

"What brings you to the road?" I asked.

"I live in New Jersey. Have my whole life. But the past few years I've spent winters RV'ing between my son in Atlanta and my daughter in Arizona."

"Sounds like you're a pro."

"I like to think so. How 'bout you?"

I told her about Peeps.

"Where you headed after KC?"

I pointed up and diagonally.

"Oh, I got someone for you, for your show." Carol described her friend, an aesthetician in Ohio.

"I'll reach out to her this afternoon. Thank you," I said, as I punched her friend's contact information into my phone.

"My pleasure." She turned to leave.

"Wait!" I held up a finger, darted to a box I kept at my makeshift desk at the dinette and returned to Carol in the doorway. "This is a little awkward for me but if you're willing to pass these along to anyone you meet who might, you know, be maybe interested in being a guest…." I handed her a small stack of my Peeps business cards.

"Not awkward at all," Carol said, palming the cards. "Gives me an excuse to strike up conversations — not that not having an excuse has stopped me before!"

The next morning, with the aid of a small reading lamp, I applied mascara and light foundation to cover the mud-colored age spots emerging on my cheeks. To conserve water, I used my own saliva rather than water from Irv's tank to blot out errant bits of makeup. I'd taken to sleeping in most mornings but my cousin Derrick asked if we could meet for breakfast before he went to work. I didn't mind because there was almost nothing I loved more than breakfast in a restaurant. Since I was a kid, breakfast out — even at the crummy Denny's in Culver City my mother took us to once or twice a year — felt luxurious. In the RV, I'd been eating cold cereal so I was looking forward to a stack of buttermilk pancakes, which I'd decided on ordering after perusing the Winstead's menu online the night before meeting my cousin.

Typically, I didn't get too dressed up for interviews, preferring to wear varying versions of an innocuous black pants-black shirt combo. But breakfast with Derrick wasn't that. I hadn't seen my cousin in close to fifteen years, the last time being when he toured Pepperdine University with his oldest daughter. Derrick's father was my mother's brother and we saw much more of each other as kids when we congregated with extended family, including our mutual Uncle Oscar and his family, in Syracuse. Those were the happy memories of my childhood. On those trips, I was not so much with my mother and brother as among them.

Nine years older than me and the oldest cousin in the group of seven of us, Derrick was the ringleader during those family gatherings when our days were filled with barbecues, made up games, swimming and spontaneous disco parties. Those yearly visits made me feel that our extended family was pretty normal, even if my nuclear one wasn't so hot. Derrick was the kind of kid who pushed boundaries. He cursed in front of the adults, he repeatedly hit the "open door" button in an elevator while it was moving, which scared the crap out of me. As my mother said often, "Derrick's got a bit of the devil in him." But he was beloved among the cousins. He was handsome and fun, charming and sneaky. One time I got to bring Scottie on one of our Syracuse vacations and she wound up with a huge crush on Derrick, following him around instead of hanging out with me. We'd all been certain that he'd live a glamorous life in Manhattan or Buenos Aires or London making a living as an actor, a lawyer or even a kept man to a much older woman. In other words, Derrick had been destined for a Big Life. So it shocked the whole family when he became an insurance adjustor in Kansas City.

I dressed in cropped skinny jeans and a baby blue gingham button-down. I smothered Dotty's face with kisses and then settled her onto the kitten tree with its view out the side window before stepping out of the RV.

"You look niiiiiice."

I glanced over my shoulder to see Carol scrambling eggs on her outdoor stove.

"You must use a lot of butter," I said, inhaling dramatically and rubbing my belly. "Those smell delicious."

"Butter is, indeed, the secret to irresistible eggs," Carol said. "Want some?"

"I do. But I'm actually on my way to breakfast. With my cousin. He lives here." I felt boastful, even though Carol had no idea how much I revered Derrick as a child.

"Maybe tomorrow then." She switched the spatula from her right hand to her left and saluted me.

I continued down the aisle. Near the park exit, I saw Andrew, a man I'd crossed paths with three times along my route — once in Utah, once in Oklahoma and now here in Missouri. He was like a beacon. Seeing him always made me feel like I was on the right path. He was tossing duffle bags into the underside of his motor home, a small class A he'd bought used.

"I thought you were staying here for several days," I said.

He wiped the hair from his brow and put his hands on his hips. "I was. But I'm done."

"With Missouri?"

"With everything. With this trip."

"What do you mean?" I'd never gotten Andrew's story — where he was going or why.

He zipped another duffle and hauled it into the storage space. "I'm tired. I just…I just want to go home."

I pulled my torso back and upright. "Really?" I wanted to know more. How long had he been on the road? What destination was he foregoing? What would he do with his RV? But I had to meet Derrick.

"I'm sorry to hear that," I said. "I'll miss bumping into you."

"Yup," he said. "Good luck."

I walked out of the park, wondering why Andrew's abandonment of the RV life felt like a personal affront. It wasn't logical. I thought of Maya, the opera lover I interviewed in LA. She'd long wondered about the mother and daughter who she was on the same flight with every week. Like Maya and that pair, I'd probably never see Andrew again.

From the RV park, I walked along Brush Creek on my way to Winstead's, which was a KC institution, according to Derrick. As I'd plunged deeper into the center of the country, water was harder to come by. With its concrete borders, Brush Creek was no Pacific Ocean. But at that point, I welcomed whatever streams and ponds I could find. Biting wind nipped my exposed ankles and cheeks. It was that time of year, that part of the country.

I walked swiftly, eager to get out of the cold and, more importantly, to see Derrick. I was halfway through *Transgenerational Transmission of Environmental Information*, and was convinced that a conversation with Derrick would be like discovering a puzzle piece that had slipped between the couch cushions. I expected to depart Kansas City with a new understanding, perhaps not of everything about our ancestors but of at least how to uncover more from Uncle Oscar in Syracuse.

I walked along McGee Street with my arms crossed, hands tucked tightly under my armpits, and distracted myself from the chill with 5-4-3-2-1.

I see bluebirds whistling as they hop telephone wires...

I see a red pick-up truck that makes me think of that Taylor Swift song...

I hear the beeps of the crosswalk countdown...

I feel emerging sun rays on my scalp...

"Meggie!"

I whipped around and stared into the face of someone I didn't know. A short older man without a hair on his head trotted bow-legged toward me.

"Meggie," he said flatly, extending his hand. "Glad you found it."

I was confused. The man used my childhood nickname as if he knew me but extended his hand as if he didn't. I plastered a smile on my face and accepted the cool handshake while inspecting his face. In my mind, Derrick was handsome and vibrant, with broad shoulders and shiny blue eyes. This bald and paunchy guy was distinctly middle aged, bordering on senior citizen. Amidst the wrinkles and sallow skin, though, were Derrick's eyes, hidden behind metal framed glasses. My good-looking, charismatic older cousin was not what I expected. Worse, he greeted me with a handshake not an embrace.

"Meg?"

"Yes, uh, sorry!" I said, trying to hide my surprise by widening my face into an overly intense smile. "Haven't had my coffee yet! Great to see you." I hoped he couldn't smell on my breath the Starbucks I'd brewed in the RV earlier.

Winstead's was clean and old-timey, with an aqua blue and pink interior and the sweet, meaty smell of bacon frying.

"Oh," Derrick said, handing me an envelope he pulled from his coat pocket once we sat down. "For you. Jeff sent it care of my house."

I peeked inside and saw Jeff had wrapped tissue paper around a small stack of twenty-dollar bills. A handwritten note read: "Remember, you can come home any time. In the meantime, have some fun. On me!"

The feminist in me cringed. I didn't need my ex-husband's permission to do anything. But I was also relieved. I needed any extra money I could come by. None of my editor friends had any work to send my way and my podcast hosting service had just raised its monthly fee.

"So!" I began, probably too excitedly. I could almost hear Alex say, "Calm the F down, Mom."

A server arrived before I could launch into my litany of questions. I ordered bacon and pancakes. Derrick asked for plain oatmeal.

I began again. "What's life like now for my favorite cousin?"

Jeez, I chastised myself, *he's not your podcast guest.* Derrick told me about life in Missouri, explaining how the Midwest both does and does not deserve its hokey reputation. I observed and heard a lot behind his words, which he spoke slowly. And though he peppered his comments with smiles, they struck me as strained.

"Derrick, is, um, everything…okay?"

"Sure. I mean, for the most part," he said, looking down at his oatmeal, which he stirred slowly. "I've been dealing with…I've got some muscle weakness. Some other things too. Hard to work sometimes. I'm looking into disability retirement."

I thought of all the times he'd organized the cousins into human pyramids or dodge ball.

"I'm sorry. Do you have a diagnosis? Anything to treat it?" As usual, I was probably probing inappropriately. Asking too many questions was an occupational hazard of mine. On my second date with Brad, he started calling me "Burn" because I was giving him "the third degree." But Derrick was family.

He sipped his coffee, waved his hand and shrugged. Reluctantly, I took the cue to let it die.

"How's Claire? Your girls?" I asked, shifting topics.

"Claire's battling breast cancer. Second time in eight years," he said with all the emotion of an impartial newscaster. His oldest daughter, he reported, was finishing her final year of graduate school and the other was living at home, in recovery for an opioid addiction that started after ankle surgery required when she slipped on a sidewalk.

"The universe is fucked up," he said with an intensity that provided the first glimpse of the Derrick I remembered, now buried deep within this very ordinary middle-aged man. "Stumble on the sidewalk? End up an addict," he concluded with a half laugh.

As he spoke, I noticed he pronounced his L's like Y's so "left" sounded like "yeft." His family update explained his changed appearance, his distant demeanor, and I experienced a surge of self-recrimination.

So your mother was mean, I chided myself. *Calm down, already.*

"I'm really sorry you've been dealing with all of this," I said. "And I'm sorry I haven't been in closer touch in recent years."

Derrick twisted his expression as if to say, *I wasn't expecting you to be.*

Switching focus, I asked about our other cousins.

He brought his coffee mug to his nose, took a sniff, then sipped. "Melissa has fibromyalgia. Ben got divorced again — third time, I think? Haven't heard from Lisa or Ron."

I'd come to Kansas City, to Derrick hoping to disprove the theory I'd been studying. According to *Transgenerational Transmission of Environmental Information*, as early as age six, we may unknowingly adopt our parents' behaviors, their responses. They get imprinted into our subconscious, becoming our own operating instructions. When emotional needs aren't met in childhood, when kids are marginalized, ignored, scapegoated or even targeted, it's like a disease or a mutation that can then actually be inherited by descendants. Derrick's dad and my mother were siblings. I expected him to be just like he was forty years ago: lighthearted and dynamic. But that wasn't the case — for him, for Leith, or apparently for others of our generation.

"What do you know about Pop-Pop and Granny?" I pressed.

I didn't remember much about the grandparents we shared, who were ancient and frail during those childhood visits to Syracuse. The rare times my mother spoke of her parents, she implied that he'd "whacked" her and she'd "gone off the deep end" in her fifties. Did Derrick's dad and my mother grow up with put-downs and dismissals, criticisms and nastiness? Did our grandmother pretend not to hear a word her kids said the way my mother pretended not to hear me? Did Derrick's father treat him the way my mother treated me?

With each of my questions, the air oozed from Derrick like a busted soccer ball. He claimed not to know the answers. He didn't ask what brought me to Kansas City. He knew nothing about Peeps or the RV trip. The bill arrived, and Derrick didn't object when I reached for it. Though I needed the credit card float, I snagged a few twenties from the envelope Jeff sent because Derrick seemed antsy to leave, throwing his coat over his shoulders as soon as the server brought the check.

Outside Winstead's, I threw my arms around my cousin, ignoring his stiff, unaffected demeanor. He wasn't the man I remembered or expected, but he was my family. Plus, my probing questions clearly made him uncomfortable and I wanted to atone for that somehow. Like small kindnesses, embraces were almost never a bad idea.

Before he pulled away, I felt the tiniest squeeze from Derrick. I smiled at him, and his sadness seemed very close to the surface. No wonder: sick wife, sick daughter, sick himself.

"Thanks for meeting with me, cousin," I said. "I hope things start looking up soon."

His cheeks rose in a smile, but his lips remained pursed together. "Say hi to Alex and Jeff," Derrick called back as he walked away. He didn't even know Jeff and I were no longer together.

Seeing Derrick had been a lighthouse marker for my trip, a destination as important as my reunion with Alex in Austin and my final stop in Syracuse. I sought insight I could synthesize into my research about epigenetics, information that would prepare me for my conversation with Uncle Oscar. But rather than insight, I got evasion and an uncomfortable reminder of just how old we really were.

Walking back to Irv near Brush Creek, I nearly got run over crossing against the light on Brookside Boulevard because my confusion and disappointment made me spacey. I could hear Melinda tell me to do 5-4-3-2-1 just like I could hear my mother order me to get hold of myself.

I see a driver tossing a cigarette butt out the window...

I hear the honking of a horn...

I feel dampness in my armpits...

I'd planned to stay in Kansas City at least another day, maybe two. I'd hoped to visit again with Derrick, maybe even see Claire and their girls. But clearly he had no interest. So there was nothing left for me. I was better off starting my trek up to Chicago. Maybe I'd find some new sources along the way.

Eleven hours later, seventy miles southwest of the Windy City, I was heating up a frozen lasagna when my brother called, usually a bi-annual event. I definitely wasn't expecting a call so soon after we'd just seen each other at our mother's funeral. After a curt hello, he informed me that Cousin Derrick had shot himself that afternoon.

Instantly freezing cold and also unbearably hot, I sunk to the floor. Shaking violently, my teeth clanged together uncontrollably.

"I just saw him this morning."

"Claire said no casseroles, no flowers. She's in a chemo cycle so the memorial won't happen for at least several weeks," Leith said.

I forced myself to suck in oxygen. "This morning, he looked so...old. And seemed so different from how I remembered him. When was the last time you saw him?" Was he bow-legged and pronouncing his L's as Y's? I wanted to ask. Or had he been the charismatic cousin we all followed like the Pied Piper back in the seventies?

"Don't remember." I could hear that familiar whistley inhale. He was getting stoned.

"Did he leave a note? Anything?" *Had our breakfast that very morning triggered something? Is that why Claire had called Leith with this awful news instead of me?*

"Mmm, don't know," he said with a substantial exhale. I could practically smell that skunk smell of his weed.

We hung up and I wailed, overcome with devastation and the burden of responsibility.

Had my probing that morning caused Derrick pain, so much pain that he couldn't go on? Was he already planning his death while he ate his oatmeal and I'd missed signs?

I felt selfish, stupid and very, very sad. I didn't know who to call, how to unload. I considered starting Irv back up and driving right back to Kansas City. But I feared my presence would cause more pain. Maybe Derrick had told his family about our breakfast that morning, my questions about our ancestors. Maybe they believed, as I was starting to, that I pushed him to end his life just hours later.

I heard a tap-tap-tap-tap on Irv's roof, the first rain I'd encountered on the trip. Initially, the rhythm soothed me as I tried to piece together the day. The raindrops on the window enchanted Dotty and she hopped onto the dashboard and ran back and forth across it, trying to catch them through the glass. Her exuberance startled me out of my shock.

My bike.

Tossing it onto Irv's back had been a last-minute decision right before I drove away from Santa Monica. Maybe it had something to do with the fact that my mom had once given my bike away. Securely attaching it to the back of the RV had taken nearly thirty minutes and more arm strength than I actually had. Now it was unprotected from the elements of early winter in Illinois.

I lifted one of the dinette seats, under which I kept emergency supplies: transistor radio, freeze-dried food, first-aid kit, all things I was used to maintaining in earthquake country. I also had a big plastic tarp just in case. I spent my whole existence in just-in-case mode: What if a window broke? What if the roof leaked? What if the toilet backed up and over-flowed? I grabbed the tarp, shoved my feet into Crocs and dashed outside. The bike was already quite wet and rain pelted the asphalt, making it difficult to distinguish raindrops from my tears. It was the first time I'd cried in many months. I unfurled the tarp with a snap, accidentally getting both sides wet in the process. I hurriedly flung it over the top of the bike at the precise moment the wind picked up, blowing the tarp sideways out of my hands and against the side of a neighboring RV.

Shit.

I peeled it off the vehicle, which apparently had been quite dusty because my hands were suddenly sludgy with mud as I tried to reopen the tarp against the whipping wind. After several tries, I was able to lay it back over the bike. It was too short and too narrow to cover the whole thing, but it was better than nothing. The wind blew again and I held it in place. I stood spread eagle with my arms cascading over the tarped bike, the rain soaking my back and calves, wondering how I'd secure it.

What am I even doing here? I'm not cut out for this.

Then I remembered Nancy's motto, the one that enabled her to claw her way out of a psychologically abusive relationship: No grit, no pearl.

Finally I noticed the four rubber bands around my wrists, which I'd slipped there after removing them from the rolled-up tarp. With the rubber bands, I secured the tarp the best I could to the handle bars and the pedals. It wasn't perfect, but it would do until I could purchase a proper bike cover. I ducked my head and ran around to the side of the RV only to discover I'd locked myself out.

Fuck.

Who was I to think I could live this life?

I crawled on the asphalt underneath Irv to retrieve the hide-a-key I'd planted there back in Santa Monica — just in case. Pebbles dug into my kneecaps and I whacked my head on the foot runner as I slid back out.

I was desperate for someone to assure me that it was all going to be okay, that I hadn't taken my life wildly off course only to fail miserably. But I was alone. I remember once asking my mother if she was going to die young just like my father had. I was obsessed at the time with Shirley Temple movies, which I watched on TV on Sunday mornings, all of which seemed to feature the child star as an orphan. The prospect terrified me, as it would any young child with only one living parent, even one she didn't like. I was afraid of losing family ties, no matter how frayed or fragile. When I posed the question to my mother, she shrugged and said, "I don't know. Sometimes I think dealing with you and your brother is going to kill me."

This is a fun one, Peeps. It's episode forty-two and my guest today cracked me up with her candid answer to one question, in particular. As always, the world in a grain of sand....

Fera is pink-haired and hoodie-clad, a grandmother in her mid-sixties. She's gained notoriety in an arena typically reserved for young men, even boys. We chatted over beers in a retro arcade in Rockford, Illinois, where I learned that she recently appeared on the cover of Edge Magazine.

Hi Fera. There are seven billion people in the world. What's it like to be you right now?

You're speaking to a video game champion! I've won virtual and IRL competitions in League of Legends and FIFA. SilverMama is my user name. I love that I'm a woman — a senior citizen — beating young men. One of my gamer friends recently introduced me to drone racing. A new and fun challenge. I've got my first competition in a few weeks. We'll see where that goes.

Tell me something about you, your background.

In my past life — quote, unquote — I was a lawyer. Hated it. Boring and soulless. Consisted mostly of word processing, ridiculous paperwork and shuffling money from one undeserving entity to another. I worked at a large downtown Chicago firm. It was all the worst things about the profession: patriarchal and hierarchical. Its nickname was Mussolini, Hitler, Stalin, and Reagan, a play on the firm's initials. MHS&R was positively littered with middle-aged men who'd clearly been, you know, losers in high school. Now lording their power — or their perceived power, I should say — over anyone they viewed to be beneath them. Secretaries, court reporters, young associates, particularly young women associates. I quit the day after my maternity leave ended. Yes, I took my full maternity leave and then quit. That, my friend, is real power.

If you could, what object would you bring along to the afterlife?

I know I should say my kids' baby books or something sentimental like that, right? I love my kids, don't get me wrong. But my prized possession, the thing I'd most like to take with me after I die is the very first trophy I earned in a World of Warcraft competition. I've won more since then, but that first one is like, you know, an emblem. It signifies how unexpectedly wonderful my life became after a difficult time.

What is one thing you do every day?

Masturbate. I'm done with dating. Don't need a partner. I'm old, but my body still has needs!

Well, then.... Fera, what was a pivot moment in your life?

When I got divorced, my kids were teenagers. The first Mother's Day after we split, my ex took my kids out of town for a family wedding. Total BS. It was the wedding of his third cousin or something like that. Some relative he barely knew. But he wanted to take my kids there precisely because it was Mother's Day weekend. He wanted me to be alone, to suffer. My own parents were gone by then. I wasn't close to other relatives. I had friends but they were busy with their own families that weekend. It was awful. I was lonely and consumed by resentment.

What'd you do?

I spent the day overeating and watching bad TV. It was the days before streaming TV — nothing good was on Sundays. Then I vowed never to get into that kind of situation again. I sought out new friends. Googled "how to meet new friends in middle age." Tried three-on-three basketball at the community center. Tried walking clubs. Tried volunteering. Some reason, those friendships never stuck. I was so frustrated I even considered going back to work at a law firm just to be exposed to new people. That's desperate. Meanwhile, after my ex moved out, my son would sometimes ask me to play video games with him, something he'd previously only done with his dad. I discovered I was pretty good at it! I started playing when my son was at school. So I could improve, so he'd want to keep playing with me. When he left for college, I didn't stop. I joined a local gamers club. Now I've got all these young friends! They think I'm a crack up. These days, I'm invited all over the place. Thanksgiving, New Year's Eve. Everything turned around once I found that community.

Who'd you never see again? Someone you knew or didn't, someone you wonder about?

Oh, I'll tell you someone I wonder about. For awhile, I went to hot yoga classes. You know, those classes where they crank up the temp to about a thousand degrees and you sweat profusely? It was right around the time in my life when my joints were snap-crackle-and-popping. Something about the combination of the heat and the stretching helped me. And there was a woman who went to the same class.

Tell me about her.

Twenty-ish. Big boobs. She was quite advanced at yoga, able to do backbends, inversions, the kinds of poses where I could only get through the first step of the teacher's instructions. This one day we were doing dancer, a standing balancing posture. She kept falling out of the pose. And each time, she'd make these exaggerated facial expressions of frustration and then sigh loudly. Her mat was smack in the center of the room. Everyone watched her out of the corner of their eyes. She'd attempt the pose, fall out and then make those expressions and grunts. Like she was trying to convey a message. Like, "I can normally do this pose!" Like she knew everyone was watching her. Like she had an audience in this stupid fucking yoga class. I mean, come on. Her ego was so — what's the word? — antithetical to the whole yoga philosophy. You know, detachment to outcomes and all that. I wanted to shake her by the shoulders, insist, "Let it go, kid. Let it go." "It" being the ego, the self-consciousness, the performance of it all. But I didn't. A few days later, I injured my wrist — video game perils! — and stopped going to yoga. Never saw her again.

What's your motto for life?

Well, I don't know about that but here's some advice, something I've shared with my daughter. I told you I'm done with men. But between my ex and the jerks I observed in the law firm, they all had something in common. So my advice: never trust a man who doesn't like coffee.

Thank you, Fera. Is it any wonder I love doing this show? I hope you enjoy listening as much as I enjoy talking with everyday peeps.

CHAPTER ELEVEN

In the morning, I discovered a note tucked under my windshield wiper. The paper was wet with rain, but the words were still legible.

"I'm on your left. I can tell you where to get a bike cover. J"

My neighbor in the RV lot turned out to be Judy, a traveling nurse with a supermodel's height and a thick Brooklyn accent. She told me how she'd work a few weeks in one location, usually covering for permanent nurses who were on leave, and, when the job ended or she simply tired of the location, she'd move on, using an app to find her next gig. Her fluid agenda reminded me of the man in the van I met back in Santa Monica.

"I've been in Illinois for three weeks. There's a sporting goods store about six miles that way," she said flinging her arm, "with a whole section just for motor home accessories. Got my own bike cover there, as a matter of fact. They even sell some that come with padlocks."

I had the urge to bury my head into Judy's amble bosom, as I recalled Fera's experience in finding community and belonging in the unlikeliest of places. "This is really helpful," I said, my voice catching.

"Just ignore the automatic rifle aisle," Judy quipped as I left.

After stopping at the sporting goods store, I called Scottie.

"What's up, Wonder Woman?" she asked.

"Shut up." Although Scottie was invariably supportive of me, I've never been comfortable with explicit praise — from her or anyone else. Maybe because my mother never gave me the opportunity to practice.

"Okay, if not Wonder Woman then Amelia Earhart or...," Scottie said. "Forget it, I can tell from your voice something's up."

I filled in her on Derrick, how yesterday we'd had breakfast and today, his body was in a morgue.

"Jesus," she said.

I plugged my index fingers into the corners of my eyes to staunch the tears.

"This is the same cousin I had a crush on back when we were teens?" she said.

"Yup."

"Oh my God."

We were silent for a few moments.

"Meggie, are you okay? This is a lot. Between your mom and now this...."

I thought of Andrew packing up his RV yesterday back in Kansas City. Maybe he'd been a beacon once again. Maybe his abandonment of RV life was a sign that I, too, needed to pack up and go back to my regular life.

"Meggie?"

"I'm here."

"Okay, listen to me. I know what's going through your mind. Please put this awful turn of events aside, just for a sec. What you're doing is the coolest thing you've done ever. I tell all my friends and colleagues about you. You're traveling the country. You're creating something—"

"Just a podcast."

"You're calling your own shots. You're living the life that every woman our age covets, whether they admit it or not." I flashed to Fera, who became a video game champion in her sixties. It was like she was able to live a whole second life.

"I'm scared. And lonely," I admitted. *And sad. Now very, very sad.*

"Meggie, we're all scared. We're all lonely. Every one of us."

What would I do without Scottie? I wondered as my limbs unclenched the slightest bit.

"Hey, I got you, Meg. Keep going, okay?"

I removed my fingers from my eyes and let the tears release. "Okay."

I smelled Chicago before I could see it, the muddy, algae scent of Lake Michigan sliding through my inch-cracked windows. It was different from the salty Pacific Ocean. That, along with the older, compact character of the city, so different from Santa Monica, compounded a feeling of displacement as I made my way towards the city proper. The wildly vertical character of Chicago, its squally skies and the noisy locks separating the lake from the river, its people decked out in scarves and knit hats, made me homesick. Back home, Los Angelenos may have ditched their tank tops for t-shirts as early winter was unfolding, but they were still wearing flip flops, as evidenced by a photo Jeff had sent me of him and Milt in front of a poster for the new JLo movie.

I felt a distinct pull, a desire to return to the familiar, even if the familiar had been unsatisfying enough to inspire me to leave. It was like being at a friend's house as a kid and feeling that peculiar, out-of-place sensation if that family did things different from yours. Like storing glasses in the cupboard rim down instead of upright or, say, holding hands and reciting a solemn grace before dinner. In my case, even eating dinner together as a family was different from how things were done in my house, where my mother simply kept the freezer stocked with microwavable dinners that Leith and I heated up whenever we were hungry. He ate in his room. I ate in front of the TV.

I parked in the city proper, making sure to point Irv's nose to the east so that abandoning my journey would be just that much more work. That's how close Derrick's death brought me to ditching everything. If it wasn't for Scottie. Meditation helped too. I imagined my thoughts of guilt, of defeat as messages in balloons swept away by the wind. And I said over and over in my head, *Don't believe everything you think*, a mantra Melinda had given me.

My duty to Peeps called so I settled at the dinette for work. I was committed to releasing episodes not once but twice a week, a frequency that I hoped would distinguish Peeps from other podcasts that didn't drop new shows as often. It took me at least ninety minutes of editing to produce ten good minutes of audio, which was about the length of each episode. I had to cut long pauses, coughs and sniffs. I tried not to edit out much else, though once I bleeped a racial slur. About a half hour into reviewing the raw audio of an interview with a teacher in central Arkansas, I took a break to check email and discovered a message from the man in the van, the very guy who'd triggered my whole journey.

"Sold My Van!" the subject heading read. I shut my eyes, not sure whether I wanted to read on.

"Hi Ms. Newlin — We met a few months ago in Los Angeles. I showed you my van and you told me about your podcast. I wanted to let you know I never made it down to Mexico. I spent some time in Orange County (learning to surf!) and then parked in San Diego. In SD, I hooked up with some college buddies who recently founded an app that will be disrupting the whole video messaging space. They asked me to come on board as CMO and I said yes. I sold my van and am living on Coronado now, surfing on the weekends. Anyway, when you and I met, we talked about me doing an interview for Peeps. Although I'm not in my van anymore, I'd still love to talk with you about the work we're doing here at the company. I can drive up to LA and give you a demonstration of the app. You could even become a beta user. I'm sure your listeners would love to hear about our—"

I stopped reading, shut off my computer. Just like learning that Andrew had given up RV life in Kansas City, the man in the van's reversal was something I took *personally*. I knew it had nothing to do with me. But imagining him enjoying a vagabond life in Mexico, learning Spanish…it's what I thought of almost every night as I drifted off to sleep in the RV. But that whole time he'd actually been living the tech bro-surfer life a hundred miles from where we met. Now he wanted me to beta test a fucking app? I felt foolish. This man I'd met for ten minutes had inspired the biggest leap I'd ever taken in life. Now I was half way across the country and he was living the corporate life in San Diego.

"Nobody *causes* someone to commit suicide," Alex insisted when I told him about how awful I felt about Derrick, the cousin I'd most idolized as a kid. "He wasn't a teenager being bullied online. He wasn't a Jew atop Masada taking his own life before the Romans could. Shitty timing notwithstanding, nothing you did — *nothing* — caused Derrick to pull that trigger."

"I know," I said, my voice fracturing before I could say more.

"Meggie-Mom, believe me. You always tell me I'm the wisest person you know. So listen to me, okay? What have you got planned for today?"

I sighed. "My first Peeps interview isn't until tomorrow. When I told Scottie I had a free day in Chicago, she suggested an architecture boat tour."

"Great. Do that."

"I'm not really in the mood. And I don't care much about architecture."

"Doesn't matter," my son said. "Go. Okay? You're always saying how much you like to be by water."

Though I was on the road, I was also inside much of the time. I had indeed come to crave the outdoors, and hadn't seen a body of water as big as Lake Michigan in weeks.

"Okay," I relented.

I pulled on my boots, the ones I bought on impulse that day in Santa Monica. I'd only worn them once, back in Boulder, and they were like walking in cardboard boxes, not yet having molded to my feet.

A half hour into the tour, I finally gave up trying to pay attention to the guide's descriptions of the Aon Center and the IBM Building.

Lake Michigan is no Tahoe, I grouched in my head, homesick for California, grieving for my family.

I wanted to go home. I wanted to tap my heels together three times, close my eyes and arrive on the doorstep of my clapboard cottage on Spruce Street. I thought about my normal autumn routines, cycling along the Pacific Coast Highway in Malibu, Thanksgiving bonfires on the beach.

Which was better? The devil I knew — fearful patterns, confusion about my place in the world? Or the devil I didn't know — what I might still find along my route? What I might uncover about my family in Syracuse?

This kind of rumination always led to a particular brand of self-loathing. Sure, my mother never understood me. But I was no cancer patient. I'd not buried a child. Between New Orleans and Kansas City, I interviewed a woman named Kira, a spousal rape survivor. Multiple times a week for thirteen years, Kira's husband forced himself on her with physical power and verbal abuse. He said it was God's will that she obey him, that she should welcome the encounter because other men would find her repulsive. When she finally made her way to a home for domestic violence survivors, Kira learned that he'd deposited the checks she'd earned tutoring middle school students into a secret account he used to pay for online porn so she left that awful marriage with a fraction of the assets she'd always assumed they had.

"It may take years to unearth it," Kira said of her life motto, "but 'Colossal courage is within each of us,' even the meekest, most beaten down. It's how we were made."

I'd left that interview with heavy limbs, a heavy heart. I'd suffered *nothing* like Kira. I'd suffered nothing like people who, say, had to live their entire lives hiding who they really were because they were gay or depressed or atheists. That kind of pain must be unimaginable. I was a blessed middle-aged woman just too caught up in her own damn head.

And then right there on that boat on the Chicago River, a man tended to his adult son, who had short, deformed limbs, an offset jaw and drool dripping. The man smiled at his son as he tucked a blanket under his chin, a gesture so tender and selfless that I had to look away. I hated myself in that moment.

That man had a Big Life. I had a fucking podcast.

I departed the boat and walked nearly two miles, through Streeterville and Old Town, to Jonny B's, a pizza joint one of my RV neighbors suggested. The Cubs were on TVs in the ceiling corners, the cheers and boisterous chatter the perfect soundtrack to accompany my overactive, sticky mind.

Maybe I should ditch the trip *and* the podcast, I thought. I mean, what did Peeps really accomplish, anyway? I could even sell the RV, put Dotty in a carrier and hop on a plane that could deliver me home *within hours.* If I continued east, something in me might actually fracture. When I told this to Melinda during our last session, she replied, as she often did, simply with song lyrics. "Leonard Cohen: 'There's a crack in everything — that's how the light gets in.'"

I sat at a small table in the corner of Jonny B's. The pizza was doughy and thick. I longed for the spicy, thin slices from the Brentwood hole-in-the-wall Alex and I loved. When I finished my second slice, my phone rang with a 650 number. I didn't know anyone in Silicon Valley so I let it ring. When my pizza arrived, I listened to the voicemail.

"Hello, Megan. My name is Kendall Keller. I'm with Pod Path in Palo Alto. I'm calling to let you know that your grant application was very impressive and you've been awarded one of our grants for the coming year. Congratulations. We received several hundred applications for just twenty grants. When you get a moment, please give me a call back and we'll discuss the next steps."

My heart raced, and tears threatened to flow again. Who needed a future teller like the one I considered seeking answers from back in Marina del Rey? Life is full of messages, if you listen.

Outside, I drank in the foggy air at the edge of Lake Michigan, my stomach churning, the abundant basil from the pizza sauce creating a peppery film in my mouth. Loons flew and squawked along the lakefront, and in their songs, I heard another message of sorts. I decided to stay put, to drive neither east nor west but to remain in Chicago — at least through the next day.

CHAPTER TWELVE

"I don't really know how to tell you this," Jeff began when he called me the next morning.

My first thought was Alex. Always Alex.

"Wait," he continued. "Alex is fine."

The man knew me.

"What, what it is?" I asked, sitting up so fast I knocked my head on the small shelf near my bed. A steady whoosh of Illinois winter wind sang outside. A sandy, pungent odor told me Dotty's litter box needed a change.

"Your, um, house."

"Oh God." *Fire. It had to be fire.*

"It's flooded."

"How?" Had Kenneth been irresponsible? Left the bathtub running?

"I was just over there. Appears to be a cracked pipe. Not a crack pipe. A cracked pipe."

"Your bad joke is telling me it's bad."

He sighed. "Bad, Meggie."

"Apparently," Jeff continued, "hundreds of gallons of water can leak out of a pipe crack that's as small as an eighth of an inch. That's a lot of water."

"I showed Kenneth the shut-off valve before he moved in. Didn't he turn it off?"

"He was working, Meg. Gone for two days. Came home to inches of water."

Yesterday's resolve to press on with my journey evaporated. What to do with Irv? With Dotty? "Okay, I've got to get home. I could fly but I need to—"

"Oh, no, you don't," he rebuked.

"You think I should drive?"

"No, no, Meg. Stay right where you are," he said, raising his voice. "I'll handle it for you."

"You'll what? What do you mean?"

"I can oversee the cleanup. And then we'll talk about reconstruction."

I bristled at his marching orders. At the same time, I silently exhaled in relief. Jeff still took care of me, even though I wanted my independence. "I can't ask you to do that."

"You're not asking. I'm insisting. Finish what you started."

"But you're the one who was so appalled I'd left my job with Dana, that I was crossing the country solo."

"I'm still shocked. That doesn't mean I don't support you, what you're doing. I've been listening to your show, Meg. It's really great."

Warmth rose from my chest up my neck as I bashfully lowered my head.

"Thanks." I switched the phone to speaker as I removed the sweats and wool socks I'd been sleeping in and began dressing for the day. I clamped my eyes shut as I dared to ask, "How bad is it, Jeff?"

"Structurally, it's bad. All the flooring, et cetera needs to be replaced. Many walls and some furniture too."

"What's happening now?"

Jeff explained that a demolition company specializing in water damage was already working on the house, thanks to calls he'd made even before reaching me.

"I don't feel right having you handle my problems," I said.

"Please, Meg. I'll do it, at least for the time being. Milt knows a contractor."

I stood in my small motor home bathroom and looked at myself in the mirror, really looked at myself for the first time in many weeks. I was a little heavier, a little paler than I was when I left Santa Monica. But I noticed something else: I looked younger.

"Meggie?"

"Yes, here. Okay, thank you. And thank Milt."

"I will. What you've got to do — and you know I wouldn't wish this on my worst enemy — is you've got to deal with the insurance company."

"Right. I'll get on it. Thank you for helping me. I know you don't have to."

"It's okay. It's my son's house too. Speaking of that, I'll tell Alex."

"Thanks," I said, wiping my face with a damp paper towel, thinking how ironic it was that water was so very precious in the RV but had become disastrous at my home in Santa Monica.

"Oh, and Meg?" he added.

"Yes?"

"Kenneth obviously can't live there now. So...think about that lack of income and, you know, rebuilding costs, as you move forward."

Not only could my renter not live there, but neither could I. My back-up plan, my security was gone. For the very first time, I was homeless.

I did my best to put the flood out of my mind — something that required multiple rounds of 5-4-3-2-1 — before I began the first of the day's two Peeps interviews.

The first was with Zoe, an attractive twenty-three-year-old grad student in psychology. She had precise posture, a fluency in French and an earnest, cheerful manner. She struck me as the kind of person who might put eyelashes on the headlights of a VW Bug. One other thing Zoe was: plump. In our interview in the crowded museum cafe at the Art Institute of Chicago, I learned that she was the lone heavy person in not just an average family but a lean, athletic family. She showed me pictures on her phone of her middle-aged father in a wetsuit carrying a surf board, her older sister — slim as a model — biting a marathon medal between her teeth, and her tanned middle-aged mom alongside tennis buddies.

"As you can see, my face looks just like my mom's and sister's. So there's no question I'm definitely from this family," Zoe said. "I'm just not *of* them in the body sense. I mean, look at my sister's boobs."

While Zoe was, as Scottie would say, "busty," her sister had what I liked to call Bob Seger boobs — "way up, firm and high." After years of pretending to enjoy sports and being on the cusp of overweight status, Zoe finally plunged over that hurdle during her senior year of college despite the fact that she didn't overeat and walked four miles on the treadmill most days. As Zoe grew plumper and bustier, her self-esteem plummeted. Her parents, while loving, made her feel worse, offering to pay for weeks at a weight loss camp, what her mom called a "fat farm."

"Remember that one-hit-wonder from the Nineties: 'I Touch Myself'? My mom loved that song and played it all the time," Zoe whisper-sang to remind me of the playful tune. "Senior year, I'd sing it in my head but I'd change the lyrics: 'I hate myself, I want you to hate me.' It was totally subconscious. I didn't even realize I was doing it until one day, I stopped and really listened to what I was saying over and over in my head. It all struck me then: no wonder I'd been in a string of bad relationships and toxic friendships. I hated myself because of my size — my *natural* size — and I gave others the opportunity to reinforce those feelings. That's when I finally decided to see a counselor on campus."

From that therapist, she learned about diet and fitness culture and got clear about what healthy looked like for her, both physical and emotional health. For her master's thesis in psychology, Zoe was developing a health curriculum for middle schools that focused on counteracting messages kids get from the media.

My conversation with Zoe was what I needed in those awful hours after Derrick took his life, after my home flooded. The human spirit never failed to move me.

After Zoe left, I jotted down impressions I'd use later when crafting the episode intro. I noted Zoe's uplifting demeanor, how she'd managed to turn self-hatred on its head, and at twenty-three, had found her purpose in life, one that helped others no less.

With ninety minutes before my next interview, I packed up my equipment and roamed through the museum. I discovered a small room with a temporary exhibit on flowers, specifically, how different painters — from Renaissance artists to Impressionists to Post-Modernists — interpreted that most ubiquitous of subjects. I sat on a leather bench across from a large, Pop Art painting of a field of red poppies so bright I could almost smell them. Soft classical music piped in from the speakers in the ceiling. It made me want to shut my eyes and curl up on that bench for a nap.

Instead, I left the museum and circled the long city blocks surrounding it to get refreshed before the next interview. I rounded the first corner and the lightest of snowflakes began to fall. This was the first snow I'd seen in a long time, probably since I chaperoned Alex's eighth grade trip to Washington, D.C. I spun around with my palm facing upward, hoping to catch the elusive flakes that melted the instant they hit skin. What surprised me most was how everyone else on the street seemed equally delighted even though this probably signaled the beginning of yet another crushing Illinois winter. But still they stopped, their palms similarly turned skyward, and then continued on, smiling.

I returned to the museum cafe. In the back corner was Leon, my next source. He was unmistakable: six foot six, broad-shouldered, hair in the midst of turning white from blonde. He wore grey wool slacks and a navy V-neck sweater. I could tell he was my source because the one thing I knew about him was that he once played linebacker for the Chicago Bears.

I introduced myself, re-set up my equipment and dove in.

I've always appreciated that notion that what you do every day matters more than what you do once in awhile. It helped relieve my guilt those rare times I'd lose my shit and scream at Alex when he was a kid. So that's where Peeps question four came from: What is one thing you do every day? Some people wash their feet every night before bed. Some people start each day re-watching the video of their baptism. Scottie brushes her hair one hundred times before bed because "that's what Marcia Brady did."

Proving once again that the simplest questions lead to remarkable insights, my conversation with Leon took an unexpected turn when I asked the one thing he did every day. If offered a billion dollars to predict what he would say, I'd be in precisely the same tax bracket I'm in now because I never would have guessed what that hulking, two-time Pro Bowler responded: "Practice calligraphy."

"I was an artistic kid," Leon explained. "Like, super artistic. I spent weekends in elementary school recreating Calder mobiles. I drafted one-panel comics that ended up in local newspapers. I saved my allowance to buy origami paper." Leon grinned. "Because of my stature, my parents had me playing basketball beginning in first grade. In fifth grade, I switched to football. Before I knew it, I was swept up in the high school and college athletics machine."

"Tell me more."

"Fast forward several years. I spent fourteen seasons with the NFL ending right here with the Bears in Chicago."

"What happened after that?"

"So the short answer is that within just a few months, I plunged into a funk. Bordered on clinical depression."

I remained silent. It's what Melinda would have done if Leon was her client.

"I made good money in football," he went on. "But not enough to support my four kids in college *and* plan a secure retirement. I'd majored in classics in college. I figured I didn't need a more 'practical' major because my career would be in sports. Long story short, after football I ended up… wait for it…selling cars."

I raised my eyebrows.

"I actually didn't mind selling cars. Jeez, it's easier on the bones than blocking bodies. I made decent money and enjoyed meeting new people," Leon continued. "But what I did mind was how uninspiring it was. My kids were leaving home. My job was secure but boring. I needed something more. My wife said I should think back to what I loved doing when I was eight. She read somewhere that eight was when one's true essence was revealed. I thought of all the art projects I loved back then. I signed up for classes at our community center. Except for ceramics, I enjoyed them all. But the one that spoke to me the most was calligraphy."

Leon exuded a serenity I knew I could never have perceived in a phone interview. Sitting with him in that cafe, I was reminded how my road trip, while not easy for me, was exactly what Peeps needed.

"You have a…a calmness…about you, Leon. I can't imagine you having the…aggression required of a professional football player."

"I hear that a lot," he said. "It's calligraphy, I tell ya. Something about the precision, the difficulty. Next month I'm heading to Japan for eight days to study with a lettering master there."

Since returning to his childhood passion, Leon enjoyed both his job at the dealership and his empty nest more. "I gotta admit," he said, "for awhile I hid my passion from everyone but my wife. I mean, who thinks someone like me is going to be into quills and brushes? But the more serious I got, I slowly began to tell people, often by presenting them with a calligraphic gift I made. Not one person, even my former teammates, razzed me about it. Now, it's one of my favorite things to spring on people at cocktail parties."

Later, back with Dotty and Irv, I listened to the raw audio of the interviews with Leon and Zoe, taking notes and marking the timing of the best content and toning down ambient noise. Then I drafted and recorded what I hoped were compelling intros. It was the most creative and challenging work. If I don't get that intro pitch perfect, a listener might skip the episode altogether and perhaps never return to the show again.

For Leon's intro, I noted his bravery in extolling a passion for something so against type. It takes great strength, I said, to surrender to who you really are. I realized then that perhaps it was just that — rather than the calligraphy itself — that brought serenity to Leon.

I closed my laptop and glanced over at Dotty, who was elegantly licking her paws and then wiping her face. Her grooming rituals always soothed me. I felt a strong urge to call someone then. Not to text, but to speak to a real human voice, someone who knew me. It was too late to call Scottie on the east coast. Alex was studying for a midterm. I didn't want to bother Jeff, who was already helping so much with my flooded home. I didn't want to admit my loneliness to my Santa Monica friends. So I called Brad. Brad, who might have turned into a full-blown boyfriend had I stayed.

"Hello? Answering for Brad on Brad's phone!"

A woman's voice. *Of course* it was a woman's voice. I came of age in the eighties. I knew a Meg Ryan movie plot twist when I saw one. The woman who answered, whoever she was, was lucky. Brad was a unicorn — a handsome, smart, kind, attentive, *single* middle-aged man.

I hung up. Brad would see my number, of course, so I powered down my phone and leaned back against the dinette booth, pointing my gaze upward. If he left a message, it could wait.

What did I enjoy most at age eight? I wondered.

At that tender age, I worried I'd miss the bus after school and have to sleep on the concrete outside Mr. McGarry's room — that is, if I didn't get kidnapped first. I worried we'd break down while driving on the 405. I worried I'd get arrested for looking more closely than necessary at the neighborhood kid's penis when I changed his diaper while babysitting. I worried endlessly about California's drought of '76, certain that we'd have to store up water we'd have to collect from public bathrooms. During the gas rationing of the Carter Administration, I calculated how many days it would take me to walk to San Diego in case I ever wanted to escape my home life and start over in a new city on my own. When I read about the spraying of insecticides from helicopters to eradicate medflies in Northern California, I didn't eat fresh produce for six months.

That was my life at eight.

At the same time, eight was also precisely when my interest in people emerged. I read obsessively about First Ladies — all the way through Roslyn Carter! — in a collective biography I checked out repeatedly from the school library. I poured over the Guinness Book of World Records. I never cared about the tallest buildings or the fastest cars. I scoured those ultra-thin newsprint pages for entries about *people* — the man with twenty-inch fingernails, the oldest living identical twins, the couple with twenty-two adopted children. It was also when I started reading Dear Abby and obituaries. The little vignettes, the glimpses into people's lives, were like candy to me.

Maybe I became so interested in people because no one seemed all that interested in me growing up.

From my seat at the dinette, I leaned to the left, reaching across my teeny kitchen to snag the Jonny B's leftovers box on the counter. While Dotty kneaded biscuits on my lap and purred, I held the brown box under my chin as I ate and thought more about the day's interviews. I wanted to be more self aware like Zoe. I wanted to surrender like Leon had.

"We're continuing east," I told Dotty, my mouth full.

I showered, grateful my pricey new water pump was still working well. I patted an overpriced moisturizer to my skin, inserted my mouth guard to prevent nighttime teeth grinding and fluffed my comforter and pillows. Since I was waiting to hear from my next interviewee with her address, I checked my messages one last time. An email from an unfamiliar address carried the subject line "Urgent — Your Uncle Oscar."

"Hello. My name is Pam. I'm a nurse at St. Joseph's, a hospital here in Syracuse. Your Uncle Oscar asked me to message you. He says he would have asked his kids to contact you but they just left. He says it's urgent that he reach you. He has had some kind of episode — unclear if it was respiratory, cardiac or neurological. The physicians are conducting tests. The upshot is he lost consciousness in his home. He's coherent now but is having some cognitive difficulties, which may or may not pass. He's being monitored here in the ICU and will be hospitalized for at least the next several days. Your uncle says to tell you he hopes to be well enough to see you in a few weeks as planned. But please check back with either St. Joseph's or your family."

My heart hit the floor.

My mother. Derrick. Was Uncle Oscar next?

I had been so looking forward to seeing my uncle after so many years. He was also the lynchpin of my trip, of my research about epigenetics. What if he didn't make it? What if he was too ill to see me? What if this episode now caused him to remember nothing about my mother, their childhood?

I dashed off a reply to Pam, cc'ing my uncle's personal email address, sending my well wishes. I didn't say that I now planned to get there in a hurry.

Welcome to episode forty-seven of Peeps, the show where we see the world in a grain of sand. This is a hard one, peeps. I even considered not running it. But the human condition is raw and we need to be here for it, for all of it. Harris is a mild-mannered man from Shelbyville, Illinois, who I met while I was out getting some exercise. Harris often closes his eyes for prolonged moments when he speaks. His flawless skin and jet black hair are at odds with his age, which is fifty-eight. We met on a Sunday afternoon at Lake Shelbyville, a beautiful spot with lots of coves and "fingers." We conducted our interview on a bench at the beach and I recorded our conversation with my phone rather than my computer, which I didn't have with me. So you'll hear some background noise, including fishing boats and the shouts of brave souls who bundled up for a winter game of beach volleyball.

Harris, we just met. You're one of seven billion people in the world. What's it like to be you right now?

Well, right now I'm dying.

I—

No, no. Please. You needn't look at me that way.

But—

I'm relieved. For many years, certainly my whole adult life, I've barely maintained the will to live. Never did anything about it, if you know what I mean. Didn't want to hurt my family. About nine months ago, I learned

I've got cancer. I'm not treating it. Just not interested in fighting. I haven't told anyone about my illness or my decision. 'Til now.

I...I don't know what to say. You certainly have the right to make decisions for yourself. I just...I hope your doctors have talked to you about minimizing your...suffering.

Thank you.

Um, okay, Can you tell me more about your background?

After college, I spent a year in law school. I flunked out. Not because I wasn't studying. Because I was studying the wrong things. I'd read these court cases for class, then I just couldn't get them out of my mind. One was about the Tylenol poisonings. Remember those? Back in the early eighties? Are you old enough to remember that? Okay, so you know that several people died because run-of-the-mill Tylenol bottles were laced with poison. This one particular case was especially awful. What happened is: a person died from the poisoning and her funeral took place before the authorities figured everything out. So in their grief, the woman's family members had headaches from crying so much. And all of them took pills from the same tainted bottle. Of course they died too. I can't explain it, but the case, it, like, gutted me. Simply couldn't stop thinking about it when I was supposed to be making study guides for Torts and Property Law. Another case: a woman working in a factory — this was before many workplace safety laws were enacted — bent down to pick up something that she'd dropped on the factory floor. And her long hair got caught in the machine. The woman was scalped to death. I just couldn't, um, bear these stories. I thought about these people constantly. Spent money I didn't have ordering transcripts and other documents from the trials. I'd go to the library — this was way before the Internet — and read everything I could about the survivors of these tragedies. I needed proof that the families were okay. Never found out very much. That's how I ended up becoming a tax preparer for H&R Block. I decided I was better fit to work with numbers. Not people.

Harris, what is a physical object you'd like to bring with you into the afterlife if you could?

Ah, my grandmother's wok. I don't cook with it. But if I put my nose right up to the metal, I can smell faint hints of soy sauce, sesame oil, rice vinegar. Brings me back to being in her kitchen, to being loved. She passed away when I was eleven.

That's lovely. What's one thing you do every day?

Every morning, I eat one cannabis gummy and then watch practical joke videos on YouTube. The combination makes me laugh. And that guarantees I will laugh once every day.

What was a pivot moment in your life?

My father was a hard father to have. When I was on the tennis team in high school, I played all the time. My doubles partner and I were second in the league. One afternoon, I showed my father the callouses on my palms from gripping my racket. I still remember the feeling of his rough fingers as he inspected my blisters. "You're not practicing enough," he said and walked away. In college, I tried to talk to him. Tried to tell him I was feeling sad all the time, feeling uninterested in life. He just sat for a long moment. Then simply said, "I find those feelings to be unproductive." It was then that decided that life, for me, would be about just biding time. I don't blame my father. He did the best he knew to do. But if he'd responded differently in those moments, I may have had a, you know, different life. From then on, though, I understood — no, I accepted — that I was simply to have the life I was having. It released me from having to strive, to seek more.

Who is someone you never saw again?

Well, my father, for one. He died when I was in my thirties.

Anyone else? Someone else you were close to? Someone you wish you could find and say something to?

Oh, yes. So I'll begin my answer by noting that I've never owned a car. I prefer public transportation. People ask me why I choose to wait for buses or trains instead of getting from place to place faster and in my own vehicle. I just shrug. "Because...I'm Harris," I explain. So one time, many years ago, I saw a woman on the bus. She was pretty in a very plain way. No makeup. Nicely proportioned features, nice coloring, a natural kind of beauty. I watched her read a beauty magazine. I wondered about her life. After a few minutes, I got off the bus at my stop and immediately regretted not speaking to her. I should have told her she had no business reading a beauty magazine because she was already lovely. I didn't have any grand ambitions of a relationship or anything like that. But I should have told her what I believed. I've looked for her on every bus I've taken since then.

What is your life motto?

"I'm Harris."

Thank you all for listening to Peeps, for being a witness to pain, to joy — and thank you to Harris. Join me next time for my interview with the sorority girl who's gained notoriety for creating the crossword puzzles in the university newspaper that everyone on campus is obsessed with.

CHAPTER THIRTEEN

It took me a long time to fall asleep. I kept visualizing myself being yanked by the arms in two different directions, and I felt as if I might split in two. Brad had indeed left me a voicemail after my hang up the night before. He didn't explain who'd answered his phone, but he did say that he'd been thinking of me, that he wanted to hear about my trip. And in turn I felt the urge to call him back and spew everything, tell him about all the people I'd met, about what happened to my house. Oh, my house. I wanted to see everything for myself and I wanted to stay far away from it until everything was back to normal. At the same time, Uncle Oscar was sick and I had to get to Syracuse as soon as possible. I was still seven hundred miles away. Finally, though, I drifted off and dreamt of floods and Brad's kisses and summers with my mother's family when I was a child.

In the morning, I lifted myself onto my elbows and groggily looked around. It was unusual for Dotty to not be between my feet on the bed. I made a kissing sound with my lips, which usually got her to drop whatever she was doing and pounce on my lap. But...nothing. I figured she was in the kitchen sink — one of her favorite places to rest — or under the table with a toy I'd bought her on the way home from the Art Institute. I sleepily made my way to the cupboard with the cat food because just opening that cabinet door always brought her running and if not, then certainly the clink of food pellets hitting her little metal bowl would. But again… nothing.

I started to panic. Like, really panic. The kind of panic reserved for moms whose first born has just learned to run-walk and is suddenly nowhere to be found in Target after the mom finally chooses between the two brands of multipurpose cleaner. The kind of panic you feel when the pilot barks into the intercom, "Flight attendants. Take your seats. NOW."

I felt the rough carpet of Dotty's cat tree on my palms as I squatted down to look for her behind it, my knees creaking after the night's inactivity. I heard an impatient "C'mon, c'mon, c'mon" from my own lips as I scurried around Irv searching for my little striped companion. When I felt an unusual chill as I passed the bathroom door, my mantra transformed into "No, no, no, no, no." The night before, I'd texted Scottie to say that I was likely just a couple of weeks behind her in menopause roulette because I was sweating at nearly midnight even though it was thirty-eight degrees outside. When I got up to use the bathroom in the middle of the night, I'd cracked the bathroom window about five inches hoping that a tiny bit of cool air would travel into the bedroom from the one inch gap where the bathroom door met the floor.

I'd. Closed. The. Door.

I must have. But when I approached the bathroom that morning, I discovered the door had not been latched properly and instead swung easily on its hinges. In that millisecond, I realized the five-inch bathroom window opening was just enough for a curious, lithe, eight-pound cat to dart through after hopping onto the bathroom counter.

I felt so sick with dread, I nearly collapsed. Instead, I shoved the bathroom window all the way open and screamed, "DOTTY!"

It was a shriek and a prayer, an apology and a primal desire to undo time, to rewind just a few hours so I could close the bathroom door as firmly as I thought I had. Tears collected in my throat and gushed out of my eyeballs. My spirit felt so weak I could barely stand. Dotty trusted me to keep her safe and I'd let her down. I loved how pleasantly self-contained RV life was, but maybe our motor home was too confining for her. How selfish I'd been. She was probably out there terrified and yelping, wondering where I was.

After returning from my interviews at the Art Institute cafe, I'd moved Irv from an inner city parking lot to one on the eastern outskirts of town, getting just a couple of miles closer to Syracuse, my way of sealing the commitment I'd made to continue east rather than retreat west, to get to my uncle as soon as possible. Now, outside the bathroom window, all I saw was a vast field.

My wild shriek transformed into whispers as I repeated the name of my sweet cat, who'd become more than just a co-pilot or roommate. I relied on her more than anything else during this trip. Whenever I was out of the RV, it was Dotty I looked forward to spending time with upon my return. She was the scaffolding for my otherwise unstructured days. Her paw pats served as affection and encouragement. I loved her clean, dander smell. I loved watching her slim, youthful body play and bathe and sleep. She was my companion, my family. I thought of her out there alone in the field. Was she confused? Terrified? Wondering how I let this happen to her? Did she think I abandoned her? Had she wandered onto the street on the far side of the field? Had someone run her over? I thought of Tom, of driving up that hill as a teenager and spotting his orange body in the road. I sank to the bathroom floor, lifted the toilet lid and threw up.

Leaning against the vanity, I forced myself into problem-solving mode. I stood and looked out the window again. Perhaps there were mice in that field that kept her busy so she'd still be nearby. Maybe she'd jumped out only moments before I woke up. I decided to move the RV to the far end of the field and work my way backwards. If I didn't find her, I'd visit every animal shelter in Chicago. I had several interviews scheduled and a sped-up timeline to get to Syracuse but none of that mattered.

I didn't even have on proper clothes, having tossed everything off during my fit of menopausal heat. I threw on a t-shirt and hopped into the captain's seat. My bare foot felt odd on the accelerator not only because I'd never driven Irv without shoes but because I felt something wispy under my toes. I looked down and there was Dotty, staring into my face and purring. Her collar had gotten caught on the edge of the accelerator pedal, trapping her beneath it.

I hadn't felt such profound relief since getting a "come back in" call from the breast health center after a mammogram, and learning from a follow-up ultrasound that the mass they'd spotted was merely a cyst.

Sobbing with relief, I released Dotty from her makeshift noose, grateful that she hadn't cut off her airway by trying to run. My beautiful little companion hadn't even cried. Instead, she simply waited patiently for me to rescue her.

My God, I loved that cat.

My trip was a revolving string of victories and defeats, a rigorous hike with sharp switchbacks, like my route itself. I observed the ups and the downs as I came upon them, but I just didn't know which way it would end. It was like snapping off the petals of a daisy. "He loves me" or "he loves me not"?

Victory, defeat, victory.

CHAPTER FOURTEEN

"I swear, my uterus is having a Going Out of Business sale."

Scottie's text came in as I parked Irv outside a nondescript house in a nondescript town in southern Michigan.

"Uh, what?" I dictated into my phone as I wiped down the dinette and kitchen counters. I used a spray bottle with water I collected at a water fountain mixed with vinegar and lemon juice. It was something I did constantly. I hadn't realized how quickly small spaces get dusty and dirty. But I didn't mind. The twice-daily ritual soothed me.

Though I needed to get to Uncle Oscar, I detoured off Highway 94 so I could interview Jane, who I'd been dying to meet. Back in the nineties, in one of Northern California's most notorious murders, Jane's sister had strangled a ninth grade classmate who'd ditched her for a more popular group. The case remained unsolved for many months until Jane's sister finally confessed. Jane's parents split up a few years after their daughter went to prison. In an effort to not be damned by association, Jane and her mother changed their first and last names and relocated deep in the Midwest, first in Nebraska and then to southern Michigan.

When Scottie's text pinged, I'd been deep in thought about how to best protect Jane's identity and location while at the same time giving listeners the necessary background and details I committed to in every interview.

"Dude," Scottie replied, "In 12 minutes, I bled through a tampon, a 'super absorbent' pad AND MY PANTS."

I gathered my notebook and recording equipment, unwrapped a new catnip toy for Dotty and then replied with a freaked-out-face emoji, which was all I had time for.

"I'm certain that even if she'd lived to our age," Scottie concluded, "Princess Di would never bleed this much. Same with Princess Kate. & why the F is she Kate & not Cate since she's Catherine?"

I chuckled, stopping for a moment to feel the laughter in my body, something Melinda would applaud. Dotty wriggled on her back, inviting me to rub her belly on my way out the door. I was still so grateful that Dotty was safe with me. In those first days after a leaky pipe nearly ruined my Spruce Street house, when I was endlessly on the phone with Jeff, potential contractors, plumbers and, God help me, the insurance adjustor, it was Dotty who kept me sane. She purred in my lap as I learned that repairs might have to include shoring up the house's foundation. From her favorite perch atop the dinette seat, she kneaded biscuits on my shoulders as I learned that the house would be unlivable for an "as-yet undetermined" period of time because dangerously unhealthy mold was now the biggest problem. When, as I drove from Chicago to Michigan, the insurance adjustor told me that the foundation work would not be covered under my plan, I glanced over at Dotty in her yellow bed in the passenger seat and conspiratorially rolled my eyes. She stretched and yawned as if to say, "Don't I know it, sister."

Now forty, Jane was living a nice life by most standards. She was in a stable marriage to a kind man, had twin daughters in elementary school and a well-paying job as a dental hygienist. Her house was ordinary, with shopping lists, party invitations and dance recital schedules affixed with magnets to the General Electric fridge. Sitting in the living room, I smelled the onions from the soup slow-cooking in her Crockpot. Jane was probably half a foot taller than me, with a high forehead and hair that dusted the tops of her shoulders. She exuded a palpable sadness that others must have wondered about. Although Jane's mother visited her other daughter in prison once a year, Jane had zero communication with her sister and all other extended family except her mother. She went to great lengths to ensure that no one knew her connection to an infamous murderer, even adopting the verbal tics of a native Midwesterner. When I arrived, she asked me, "Jeet?" which I understood as "Did you eat?" only because she held out a plate of muffins. The sole person in Jane's life who knew about her sister's crime was her husband. The only nod to Jane's earlier life was the name she'd give to one of her daughters: Sonoma.

Yet Jane had reached out to me after one of her friends had been a source for an earlier Peeps episode. She offered to speak with me provided I protected her anonymity. The trust she'd placed in me was an obligation I was proud of. Jane was in a one-of-a-kind situation. The murder her sister committed was Jane's background, her what's-it-like-to-be-you, her pivot moment, and her someone she never saw again all wrapped in one. Jane's responses were extremely measured and careful, a communication technique she'd obviously honed after many years meting out words and information. It struck me as profoundly exhausting.

How had she managed to forge a life when others, like my cousin Derrick, found coping too hard? As was always the case with Peeps, Jane's humanity knocked the wind out of me.

"I don't have a life motto," she replied as our interview ended. Her voice was soft, her words slow. "If I had to pick one, I guess it's just 'Be kind.' I mean, do you know how many *millions* of people are incarcerated in this country? Well, guess what: all of them have siblings and parents and children whose lives have been turned upside down. The heinous murder my sister committed had nothing to do with me. Nothing. But it changed *my* life irrevocably. I'll never know what my life, my *one life*, would have been if my fourteen-year-old sister hadn't killed someone. Back in the day, I thought I'd grow up to...."

Jane paused and then waved her hand in front of her face as if to force herself to wipe away a useless fantasy. It looked like a private and long-practiced gesture. "So, anyway, I guess, my motto is just be kind. While not everyone has a secret as big as mine, you never know what someone has been through. Cliché."

"Clichés become clichés usually because the sentiment is true," I replied.

On my way out the door, I hugged Jane extra long. "Thank you for trusting me," I said. I, too, was curious about how Jane's life would have unfolded if her sister hadn't strangled someone. I thought of Harris and how different his outlook on life, his will to live might have been different if his father had been more sensitive, more empathetic. To Jane, who was thriving against the odds, I said, "You should be proud of the life you've created."

After leaving Jane's, I decided to take myself out to breakfast, something I hadn't done since my morning in Kansas City with Derrick. One truism I discovered from life on the road: the smaller the town, the better the diner. Jane recommended a place called Rosie's. I never knew how many diners are named Rosie's until I took a cross-country road trip.

As with all the best diners, the smell of potatoes and grease met me at the front door. This particular place stood out from the others I'd visited for one thing: its pace. Truly Midwestern, the patrons and staff alike were friendly and in absolutely no hurry. I'd heard about this phenomenon. But for the first time, I observed it myself. Even the silverware and pots clanged to a slower tempo. This was a sharp contrast to the hustle of other places in the country, especially Los Angeles, where everyone from

Hollywood producers to metro bus drivers was in a rush. This tiny, slow-paced Michigan diner didn't even take credit cards, let alone Apple Pay.

Treating myself to French toast, I thought about Jane holding all that secret pain. I thought of her progeny — not just her kids but also the descendants who hadn't been born yet. In *Transgenerational Transmission of Environmental Information*, I learned about studies of worms that transmit memories to descendants through epigenetic change to prepare their offspring for environmental conditions, helping ensure survival. Scientists were slowly discovering that memory transmission probably explains why some people, like children and grandchildren of Holocaust survivors, suffer from anxiety, depression and even PTSD even though they themselves had never experienced trauma.

Would Jane's kids and grandkids have abnormal stress hormone profiles because of what she'd been through? For that matter, had Jane's sister killed someone with her bare hands because of some trigger that had been planted in her own gene makeup generations ago? Jane told me she spent untold energy suppressing her own outbursts of anger, at a patient in the dental practice, at bad drivers who cut her off on the road. "I scare myself," she'd confessed. "What if what caused my sister to do what she did is somehow in me too?"

On my way out of Rosie's, I paused in front of a bulletin board near the cashier. It featured notices for tutors and gardeners. I fingered the Peeps business cards in my pocket. I'd begun handing them out with more frequency — to RV'ers in parks and Wal-Mart parking lots. But I'd never pinned one onto a bulletin board in a small town where I knew a grand total of one person. I pulled a card from my pocket and rubbed my index finger along the edges as I debated.

I'd received the Pod Path grant but its continuation depended on a ten percent increase in listeners over the next six months. And the more listeners I got, the more advertising money I received. And the more listeners I got, the more emails I received suggesting new interviewees.

What the hell? I thought as I tacked the card next to a notice about chihuahua puppies available for adoption. *If someone laughs at my card or takes it down, I'll never know.* I was unlikely to ever return to Rosie's in Michigan again. Realizing that, I spun around and took in the place, inhaling the scent of the grill, hearing the lyrics to Carol King's "It's Too Late," one of my mother's favorite songs, playing softly from the speakers, watching the Midwestern crowd slowly eat breakfast in community.

The only downside to diner breakfasts is how stuffed and sleepy I felt afterwards. I had an interview set for early afternoon with a friend of Zoe, the young woman I'd interviewed in Chicago. Her friend worked repairing bikes and, as a side hustle, taught self-hypnosis to chronic pain sufferers. So I needed to combat my desire for a post-diner nap and decided to do so by staying outdoors.

A quick search on my phone revealed a hiking path around a small reservoir not far from the diner. I walked a half mile south, plowing through small town traffic and then through an industrial area. Though they were molding a bit to my feet, my new boots were still stiff, bruising my heels and squishing my pinky toes. More than once I imagined tossing them once and for all over a cliff. I enjoyed the walk, though. While I missed the bustle of Santa Monica, I'd come to appreciate the solitude offered by no-man's-land places like this town in Michigan.

I reached the reservoir and sat on a bench to adjust my shoelaces. It was tempting to glance at my phone, to see if Alex or Scottie had texted or if an upcoming source had gotten back to me about pushing up scheduling given the fragility of Uncle Oscar's health. But I resisted. On Melinda's urging, I was determined to spend bits of each day disengaged from the future and the past.

I closed my eyes and inhaled, the Michigan air frosty and fresh despite the industrial buildings releasing steam nearby. With each exhale, I felt my hip flexors release. The reservoir was all blues and browns, with white clouds reflected in the water. To my right, a woman and a little boy who looked about five walked toward me, clearly having just completed their own loop around the water. They held hands and swung their arms, triggering a twinge in my sternum as I reminisced about my own little boy. He'd been difficult and tiring in those years, but I longed for it nonetheless. I should have enjoyed that time, with all its struggles, rather than wished it away.

"Sometimes when *I'm* scared," the woman said to the boy, pausing after each word like a preschool teacher imparting an important lesson, "I tell myself, 'I'm okay.'"

Without missing a beat, the boy said, "That's not what *I* do."

A door slammed behind me and I spun around. The boy and his mom had entered the public bathroom. I was dying to know what the boy *did* do when he was afraid. And I was even more curious to hear how the mom replied. When I was a child, not one adult ever explained that telling myself "I'm okay" was something I could do. Like when I was six and my brother threw a fork at my face, my mother ordered me to "just relax" since it didn't even hit me. When I cried at school because I didn't have a guest for the early June Father's Day luncheon, the teacher instructed me to avoid the celebration by delivering copies from the ditto machine. No one said, "You're okay."

What if Harris's father had told him he was okay, that his feelings of depression, of hopelessness were human and could be dealt with? Would he have the will to treat his illness instead of letting it ravage his body?

Sitting at the reservoir, I realized that though I still struggled with meditation, I was starting to understand it, to notice that there actually *were* spaces between my whirling thoughts. They were mere milliseconds of space but they were there nonetheless. Melinda insisted that those spaces held the answers that I — that everyone — sought. One thing it had allowed me to do was to get better at what Scottie and I called "reframing." It was corny, kind of pop psychology. But it worked. In Scottie's case, she'd reframed the way she thought about her eighth grader's incompetent math teacher. Instead of a burden, it was a blessing because it enabled Scottie to spend extra quality time with her son, who needed her assistance with algebra problems. In recent days on the road, I'd come to reframe my marriage to Jeff as not a failure but instead as simply a discrete era, an essential part of my story but not the ending.

When I mention to Melinda our efforts to reframe, she told me about growing up in San Francisco. "My father," she said, "was also a San Francisco native. To him, whenever the fog horn sounded from the Bay, he thought of the times he'd been home sick from elementary school because that was the only time he could hear it. But to me, the fog horn symbolized warmth and freshness because I loved bundling up and walking outside in the city's thick fog. The point is — the fog horn itself was one hundred percent, completely neutral — neither good nor bad. But my father's and my *interpretations* of the fog horn were wholly different and affected our experience."

Maybe, I considered there in Michigan, "just relax" was my mother's version of "you're okay." Her delivery was harsh, dismissive. But the sentiment was similar to what that woman at the reservoir was teaching her little boy. Maybe my mother had been trying. That realization opened my heart a sliver, enough for me to feel a smidge different about my mother. Maybe it wasn't *just* Uncle Oscar who could unlock my understanding.

This shift in perspective, however slight, was most certainly a byproduct not just of meditation and reframing but of living on the road. A new way of looking at the world was emerging. I was starting to regard people in new ways, not just my sources but myself and my mother too.

That evening while I was vacuuming Irv, a text pinged in my pocket. "Did u call me. Get my voicemail?" Brad.

I paused the vacuum and sat at the dinette. Relieved at the silence, Dotty hopped from under the table into my lap.

"Sorry. Butt dial," I replied with a lie.

"Wish it hadn't been an accident." *I'll bet*, I thought, wondering again who the woman was who'd answered.

"Hows ur trip."

"Good!" I had no energy to fill him in on Derrick, my house, Uncle Oscar's precarious condition. "U?"

"I'm on a trip too. Visiting my daughter in Boston. Will u b in MA?"

I still had no idea what I was doing after Syracuse. "Not sure. Not anytime soon."

He sent a frown emoji and a picture of his daughter's huge chocolate lab on his lap. His smile was wide. And, man, that guy had a great head of hair for someone in his late fifties.

I hearted the photo and then did something I almost never do: I called my brother.

"Have you heard from Nathan?" I asked, my ostensible purpose for the call.

"He texted yesterday saying they spent the last week in Kyoto and were on their way back to Tokyo," he said, then turned down Metallica playing in the background. "Seen Uncle Oscar yet?"

"On my way. Not too much longer. Do you remember the trips we used to take to Syracuse?"

"'Course. I was high a lot as a kid but not that high."

I rolled my eyes. "What do you remember?"

He silenced the heavy metal altogether. "I remember it was always a nice break from mom even though she was there too. I remember how cold the lake was. I remember Derrick seeming like the coolest dude around, feeling lucky I was related to him."

"Yeah."

"What do you remember?" he asked.

"Pretty much the same."

We were quiet. I thought about Brian the professor, who noted how I preferred asking questions rather than answering them. So I dug deeper.

"Puzzles," I added. "I remember mom and Uncle Oscar and the other grown ups did tons of jigsaw puzzles on those vacations. She would sit for hours, trying different pieces, not giving up even when the other adults lost patience."

"I forgot about that. She seemed…relaxed when doing those puzzles. Wonder why she never did them back at home."

"Do you miss her?" I asked.

"No. So, anyway…." Leith's words suggested he was ready to hang up. Though we weren't close, I felt my spirit replenishing as we spoke and I wanted to keep it going.

"Wait," I said, "can I ask one more thing?"

"Sure," he said, though a hint of impatience seeped into his tone. There it was, my tendency to push. I recalled my breakfast with Derrick.

"This is kind of random. But do you have, like, a motto for life or anything?"

"Trying to sneak in some older sibling advice or something?"

"No, no," I said, trying to make my voice lighthearted even as I was regretting the question. "It's kind of, you know, a podcast-y question."

"You recording this?"

"What? No, of course not. I'm just…curious." *You're my brother. I want to know you.*

"Okay, fair enough. Let me think, let me think. A motto for life…." He hummed a little as he thought. "No, that's not it. Mmm…not that either. Well, that's probably not kosher to say…."

"Leith!" I forgot that my brother could be kind of funny.

"Okay, I got it."

"Great."

"You writing this down?"

"Leith!"

"Okay, here it is. Leith's motto for life: if you have pizza for dinner, put a glass of water next to your bed."

"*What?*"

"Seriously. Pizza makes you thirsty."

"That's your *motto for life*?"

"Hey, what's wrong with it?"

I thought for a moment. Simple. Practical. Not overthought or overwrought. Perhaps even metaphorical. I'd long judged my brother, but maybe he'd gotten life right after all.

"You know what?" I said, "It's not bad."

The next day around lunchtime, I parked Irv in a shady spot in Sylvania, Ohio just outside a cafe whose WiFi I could co-opt from inside the RV. I waited for the nearby church bells to finish their twelve rings before logging into Skype for my session with Melinda.

"I've listened to a few of your episodes," she began.

My cheeks flushed. I often forgot that it wasn't just relatives or Scottie listening to my show. "Oh?"

"Yes, I loved the one about the teenager who knits rainbow yarmulkes for LGBT rabbis."

"Oh, he was a kick," I said.

"Now that I'm familiar with your show, I can't help but wonder more about why you started Peeps."

"We haven't talked about this?" It seemed I was often explaining the concept of the show, especially to potential interviewees who weren't sure they wanted to answer my questions.

"No, we haven't."

"Well," I said and then took a deep breath and stretched my arms up to the ceiling. "If you've listened to some episodes, you know that Peeps is about people, about peeping into their lives. Even ordinary people have extraordinary stories. I've personally observed a direct, inverse correlation between obscurity and entertainment value. And I'd long noticed that there are, like, so many ways of living. I'm sure you see that in *your* job."

"Indeed." She didn't elaborate, a signal for me to continue.

"And there are jobs — like, say, ultrasound operators — that I don't know a thing about. Every time I walk through an airport, I think, *There are so many people I don't know.* I just want to explore what brings people to the jobs they have, the lives they live."

"Why the same questions every time?"

"Because those are questions I wonder about a lot. Plus, with the same seven questions, I can treat every source — from the fiercest congressional lobbyist to the meekest barista — with neutral curiosity instead of... judgment."

"From what I've heard so far, you've accomplished that. What, can I ask, is your favorite of the seven?"

"The question about people my sources never saw again."

"Why's that?"

"Because I think of it all the time. People who get stuck in your memory. People who you could never find no matter how hard you tried." There's no way Harris, for example, could ever reconnect with the woman he observed a few moments that one day on the bus. No matter how much money he had, no matter how good the investigator, he'd simply never be able to find her. But she remained there, in his mind.

"So what about you?"

"What about me what?"

"Who did *you* never see again?"

So many people, I thought. Alex's first preschool teacher, a Romanian grandmother who dutifully held his hand all day long for the entire first week of school and who moved away to Florida the next year. The girl in my Italian class in college who had my exact same name and similarly went by "Meggie" as a child.

"Well," I said with a half laugh. "I went to a Madonna concert during college. It was early January, the tail end of winter break. Most of my friends were still at home. Friends who were in town either didn't want to go or couldn't afford a ticket. I really couldn't afford one either but I loved Madonna so I was going no matter what. I bought the cheapest ticket, around sixty bucks, which was huge for me. A single, nosebleed seat. A pack of girls were in front of me. They were drunk. The girl right in front of me kept her arms in the air, swaying them to the music. In those seats, Madonna was just a tiny speck on the stage. This was so long ago there wasn't even a Jumbotron or anything. Anyway, every time this girl in front of me waved her arms, which was all the time, I had to move my body from side to side just to catch a glimpse of Madonna before she danced over to the other side of the stage. After about three songs, I couldn't take it any-more. I tapped the girl's shoulder and asked if she'd put her arms down. She gave me a dirty look but complied. I remember feeling like I was a hundred years old. There I was, at a pop concert *by myself*, asking someone to stop moving around so I could see. I've thought of that many, many times since then. Where's that girl now? Does she even remember that concert? The uptight girl behind her?"

Melinda seemed only mildly interested in the story and I felt embarrassed.

"Anyone else?" she said.

"Probably dozens."

"Anyone in particular?"

I was quiet and so was Melinda.

"Once in elementary school I was walking to the bus stop in the morning and a woman slowed her noisy, beat-up beige Datsun next to me, rolled down her window and asked if I wanted a ride."

"Did you know her?"

"No."

"What'd you do?"

"I said, 'No, thank you' and kept walking."

"Do you know *why* she offered you a ride? Was it raining?"

"No. Cool and misty but not raining."

"What happened next?"

I pulled my hair out of a ponytail and then collected it back into one. "She kept driving alongside me, really slowly. She said, 'C'mon, get in!' She had this fake, happy demeanor, kind of like how a babysitter behaves before the parents leave for the evening."

Melinda remained quiet, then said, "Did you?"

"Did I what? Get in? Of course not. This was the seventies. There were no mass shootings back then. The danger of our time was kidnapping. Patty Hearst and all."

"So what did you do?"

"I yelled, 'No!'"

"Were you scared?"

I nodded.

"Then what happened?"

I paused. "She let out this big maniacal cackle. Like she was laughing *at me*. Like I was such a square when all she wanted to do was give me a ride. Then she drove away." I sometimes heard that cackle in my nightmares.

"Did you tell anyone?"

"I told my mother that afternoon. When I got home from school."

"And?"

"She shrugged and said something like, 'No need to be dramatic. You're fine, right? It was probably just one of my friends trying to be nice.' But I knew that wasn't right. I asked her, 'Do you know anyone who drives a beat-up beige Datsun?' I knew she didn't. But, whatever. She was right. Nothing happened anyway."

"But you were scared."

My breath quickened. I rubbed my mouth to loosen the muscles of my face.

"Yes. For the rest of that school year, I ran to and from the bus stop every morning and every afternoon."

"So you took care of yourself."

"I suppose you could look at it that way. Anyway, I know it's impossible. But I would love to find that woman in the car now, ask her what that was all about. *Was* she just trying to be nice? Or was she, like, a Manson devotee or something? I'll never know."

I hoped Melinda couldn't see that I was trembling. To deflect, I picked Dotty up and waved her paw at the camera.

I'm okay, I told myself for the first time in my entire life. *I'm okay.*

Hello, peeps. I can hardly believe it's episode *fifty-two*. But here we are. Thanks for joining me as we discover the world in a grain of sand.

What a delight to meet Willie in Toledo, Ohio. Willie is the kind of person everyone should have in their life. Sunny, grateful and full of light, despite many reasons to be exactly the opposite. He speaks slowly, as if he has all the time in the world, and sports a short, curly beard that's grayer than the hair on his head. Together we watched the sun rise as I accompanied him during the first hours of his work shift on a recent Tuesday morning.

There are seven billion people in the world, Willie. What's it like to be you right now?

I got a good job at the Toledo Department of Recreation. Here thirty-two years. I work in the municipal parks department. Personally open every public park in the morning. The gates, the restrooms. I alert maintenance to tree issues, excessive litter, dead wildlife. I also supervise the gardeners at four of the parks. Up early every day. My rounds start at five. Early, yes, but the flip side is my day ends at two. Another worker closes all the parks. So I come home, take a short nap. Then I've got myself about a whole half day to do as I please before hitting the sack.

So what kinds of things do you do?

Watch TV. Go to sports games at the University of Toledo. Sometimes I grab a pop and just walk through one of the parks I opened earlier in the day. Just to see people enjoying them. Kids on swings, people playing tennis or basketball. Lately, I'm into bird watching. I'm keeping note of new birds I see. Recently, I added the American Tree Sparrow and the Northern

Flicker. On Saturday and Sunday mornings, I sell newspapers outside the Starbucks in my neighborhood. I know who likes the Times, who prefers the Journal. Nice way to spend a morning, talking to neighbors. One of my customers calls me the Mayor of West Central Boulevard. How 'bout that? It's a good life overall. I like to tell people I'm too blessed to be stressed.

Can you tell me a little about your background?

I served in the army during the Vietnam war. In a combat unit. I worked hard. The conditions were…difficult. I'm sure I don't have to explain. It was a crummy war. Saw much more than I wanted to. After two years of brutal work, I was expelled because one night I was having…I was sharing an…intimate moment…with one of my fellow soldiers. Consensual. I want to make that very clear. It wasn't the first time we were together. My unit commander discovered us. Both of us were on a plane — two separate planes in actuality — thirty-six hours later. Humiliating. Those were, you know, different times back then. Very different times. For the military, for, um, men like us. Very different times. Before that happened, my performance reviews were exemplary. That was the word used: exemplary. Still, I lost military benefits. Took me a long time to find a job after that. Even longer to find a job with decent enough health insurance to cover the counseling I needed to help me deal with what I'd seen in Vietnam, with what had happened.

I'm sorry you weren't treated better. That's really awful.

Yeah, it's alright.

Willie, what is an object you'd like to bring with you to the afterlife?

My prized possession, a letter from President Obama. Yes, personally signed by Number Forty-Four himself! He thanked me for my service. "Belatedly," he wrote. Receiving that letter was the best moment of my life. A letter from him, our nation's first Black president, the president who repealed Don't Ask Don't Tell, means more to me than even a letter from Johnson or Nixon would have at the time of my discharge. Got it framed. It's on my nightstand. Re-read it every single night before I go to sleep. It reminds me that I did nothing wrong. That I did good work. That I'm worth more than I was given credit for.

Lovely. And other than reading that letter, is there anything else you do every day?

Pray. Every damn day.

What was a pivot moment in your life?

'Bout twelve years ago, I got a brochure in the mail from a place called the Military Servicepersons Legal Defense Network. A group of volunteer lawyers. It had a headline along the lines of "Have You Been Denied Benefits Unfairly"? I contacted them. Told them my story. I was assigned a lawyer named Harriet Arthur. Nicest lady. She helped me file papers to appeal the characterization of my army discharge. A few months later, my discharge was officially upgraded. From "Undesirable" to "Honorable." The Pentagon described it as a move made "in the interests of justice." The letter from Obama arrived a few months after that. Harriet and I still keep in touch. I send her a card every year. She writes back. I have a little money now, thanks to retroactive benefits she was able to get me. Could probably retire soon, but I like what I'm doing. So I'm going to keep going. Least for awhile.

Who is someone you never saw again? Someone important to you, someone you saw or met or knew fleetingly.

The man I was, um, caught with. A few years ago, a friend showed me how to use the computers at the library. How to look people up online. The first name I searched was his. The top entry to appear on my screen was his obituary. He died in a car accident in Indiana years ago. A shame. He was forty-eight years old, married with kids. One of his daughters works for NASA.

What's your motto for life, Willie?

Like I said, "Too blessed to be stressed."

I can honestly say, my life is richer for meeting people like Willie, someone I never would have crossed paths with but for this show. Next time: a food scientist who spends autumn Saturdays inside a mascot costume on the football field at his alma mater.

CHAPTER FIFTEEN

C leveland is an underrated city, no longer deserving of the reputation it had back in the seventies and eighties of being crime-rid-
den and uncultured. Today, it's culturally diverse, pretty, and has
a foodie scene that even this native Californian admired. Though I'd heard
about the city's new millennium renaissance, I was still surprised by how
much I enjoyed my short stop there as I hurried to get to Uncle Oscar in
Syracuse before…well, I just hurried.

I plopped myself down in a cafe, one of the coziest, most delicious
cafes I've ever been to. I was settling in for a multi-hour production session. I could have done the work in the RV but I'd just finished a long driving stretch and was ready to be ensconced in, if not actually out exploring,
the world. I loved the solitude of life on the road, the coziness of being in
my own home no matter what city I was in. But every once in awhile, I
wanted to spread out, to feel the space around me expand, to be more than
five feet from where I slept.

I always felt a little guilty leaving Dotty in the RV. But Jeff had recently
emailed me an article titled "The 10 Best Apps for Your Feline." He'd sent it
in jest but I decided to see whether my little companion actually liked an

iPad. I downloaded an app called Fishes and Furs, with alternating video of fish tanks and mice in mazes, and soon realized that even a catnip-coated strip of raw salmon wouldn't have distracted Dotty from that screen. So I ventured out.

When I entered Brown Bear's Lair, which smelled of coffee and cocoa, I was pleased to discover a plush, oversized chair next to a square table. I ordered a large coffee and what turned out to be the best blackberry cobbler I've ever tasted. The big chair appealed to me because it was perfectly situated near the window and near a table big enough for my notebook, laptop, coffee, snack, and even my feet. I'd been traveling eastward so the shift in seasons seemed to be happening in speedy double-time, meaning I had to wear my new boots a lot, including on the quarter-mile walk along Cleveland's slushy sidewalks to the cafe. Something about those hiking boots made me feel different. When I walked down Fourth Street, passing Lola's BBQ and The Awe Bar, I felt like an adventurer of sorts: curious, independent and alert. The shoes were getting more comfortable, but I was still ready to sit down and plow through the production tasks for no fewer than four upcoming episodes.

I usually silence my phone while doing production because I've lost my place in raw audio too many times because of incoming calls or texts. But that morning, I'd forgotten. When my phone rang and I saw it was Alex, I welcomed the distraction. It had already taken me thirty minutes to write four mediocre sentences of an intro. I was eager for a break.

"Hi, handsome," I answered, transferring my headphones from my computer to my phone. I shifted to the right and swung my legs over the arm of the big chair, providing me an enjoyable view of the case of muffins to my right and the Cleveland streetscape out the window to my left.

"Meggie-Mom."

"What's new?"

"Well, uh, Sophie's birthday is coming up...."

"The girl you took to the formal after I visited?"

"Right."

"And you want to celebrate? Get her a gift?"

"Exactly. I want to, you know, hit the right note. Not too stuffy or serious since we're just, uh, newly dating. But nothing lame either."

"So no jewelry, no word-of-the-day calendars."

He laughed. "You just confirmed why I called you instead of Dad." I laughed inwardly myself thinking back to Jeff getting me a taser gun as a going away gift.

"Tell me a little about her," I said. "What kinds of things does she like to do?"

Alex told me about Sophie's hobbies, everything from yoga and knitting to baking and kickboxing. We decided a nice dinner out at a sushi restaurant and a three-class gift certificate to a popular Austin yoga studio would be a can't-miss gift.

"Thanks, Mom. That's perfect. I'll go get the gift certificate later today."

"How are you doing for money? Can I help you?"

My funds continued to dwindle. I'd heard nothing back from the third round of editors I'd contacted looking for freelance assignments. It wasn't just Uncle Oscar's health issues that created an urgency to my getting to Syracuse quickly, my depleting finances did too. But I'd spend every last penny on my son.

"I'm good, Mom. But thanks for the offer."

We hung up after he promised to report back on what Sophie thought of the gift. And just then a young woman stood before me.

"Sorry for interrupting you," she began.

I smiled as I awkwardly pressed myself upright in the chair. "No worries," I said, assuming she wanted to share the large table where I'd scattered all my stuff or, perhaps, to complain that I'd been speaking too loudly. "Would you like me to make room on the table?"

"What? Oh, no, no. I just wanted to introduce myself."

My mind was still on my boy and his stitches. "I'm sorry, have we met?" *Was she someone from the RV park?*

"No, well, I *feel* like we have. You're Meg from Peeps, right?"

I gaped at her, confused. How could she possibly have known that? Starting way back in my blog days, I never included a photo of myself online. Partly because I was self-conscious. Partly because I didn't want my sources having a preconceived idea of me before we met. Partly because Alex was young when I started the blog and I didn't want our privacy compromised. My profile "photo" had always been a cartoon avatar that a graphic design friend whipped up in about fifteen minutes.

"I recognized your voice," the woman continued with a giggle. "When you were on the phone." With her chin, she gestured to the phone still in my hand.

She recognized *my voice*? This complete stranger in a cozy cafe *in Cleveland*? I couldn't help but think of Aaron, the quilt collector, whose sister was an uber famous celebrity. This kind of thing must have happened to him all the time when he was with her.

"Wow." It was all I could say. Then seeing the woman's disappointment emerge, I realized it was not enough. "I mean," I added, standing up and extending my hand, "this has never happened to me before. Being recognized, I mean."

"Really?" She placed her mug on the corner of the table and sat in the wood chair next to my plush one. "My two best friends and I are obsessed with Peeps. We discuss it *all the time*."

I could feel my neck turn splotchy pink. I felt exposed and embarrassed and had a bizarre urge to apologize.

"Totally," she continued. "We have a text chain. We comment on every episode. *My* favorite was the one about the Uber driver who turns off his meter and gives a free ride to anyone using a cane as a way to honor the memory of his grandmother. One of my friends loved the one with the guy who said the person — I mean, people — he never saw again were two step-brothers who moved away after his dad and their mom got divorced. They'd been *related* for years and then they just disappeared! Liza, that's my other friend, loved the one about the woman who works as Snow White at Disneyland during the day and as a biker bar bartender at night. Liza's even adopted her life motto: 'Spend your life doing strange things with weird people.' She even commissioned an artist on Etsy to make her a pillow with those words. We now see people in a new way. We're all very different — but also as the same."

"That's—," I lifted my palms, asking the universe for the word to describe how I was feeling, how wonderful it was that someone had noticed, had benefited from the hours and hours I spent lining up sources, interviewing strangers, editing audio, writing intros. "Thank you. Wow."

"I got my mom into the show too. You know the one about the man who stands in at gay weddings, you know, as the best man or father of the bride for people whose families don't support them because they're gay? After that show, my mom reached out to this guy she went to high school with. I guess she hadn't been so nice to him because he was gay. He was out way back in the late seventies! She apologized for how she'd behaved. Now they're friends. They text like every day!"

I was speechless. A look of alarm crossed her face.

"You *are* Meg, aren't you?"

"Yes, yes! I'm sorry. I'm sure I seem like a weirdo or something. I mean, people email me. But I've never been recognized. And here I am, so far from...home."

Her expression transformed from alarm to one of warm smugness as she grabbed her mug, stood, and said, "Well, you should probably analyze your metrics. You're pretty freakin' popular."

She retreated with a playful sway, and my heartbeat thudded inside my ear drums.

During my eastward travels, I'd been focused on producing the best shows I could, finding new sources, securing the Pod Path grant and lining up some advertising. The increasing number of emails I received should have tipped me off that listenership was growing, but I hadn't spent much time on numbers.

I grabbed my laptop, sat back down in the oversized chair and logged onto my hosting service dashboard. A few minutes later, I learned my little show, the one I'd started because I was just personally interested in people, had more than *a half million* downloads. A world map with bright dots revealed the location of subscribers. The show had been downloaded as far away as the UK, Austria, Argentina and Japan. A graph showed the growth of subscribers over time. Since starting the RV trip and expanding my pool of sources, downloads spiked — just like those upward lines on an echocardiogram.

From that chair in the cafe, I texted Melinda to schedule a Skype session STAT.

"Of course, I'm flattered and all that," I told her that night as I sat at the dinette, Dotty kneading her paws on the back of my neck from her spot behind my shoulders. I was wearing the shirt I'd had on all day but below the Skype screen, I was in pajama bottoms and slippers. I'd already filled Melinda in on the accident in Alex's dorm room and was telling her about my interaction with the "fan" in the cafe. "But now that I know the extent of the audience…." I drifted off, shaking my head.

"What?" Melinda probed. "Didn't you assume people were listening?"

I shrugged. "Yes, of course. But I guess I just didn't realize the scope."

"Fair enough. But let's think about it this way: do you have a listener in mind when you create an episode?"

"I do."

Melinda paused, steadying her eyes on mine, as if to say, "And who might that be?"

"Well, when I put together a show, like writing the intro, editing the audio, I imagine I'm talking to Scottie. She and I think the same things are funny, touching, et cetera.... It keeps me from, I don't know, becoming inauthentic for trying too hard." I paused. "Plus," I admitted, "if it sucks, she'll still love me."

She slapped her palm onto her desk, making her computer screen shake a little. "Okay. Stick with that."

"But now I *know* it's not just Scottie. It's some person in Tokyo or London or—"

"Meg," she held up her palm to the screen, and I quieted, like a kid scolded by a librarian for talking too loudly. Maybe I deserved it. Who was I to be wound up about this? I needed to remind myself that, like Willie, I was too blessed to be stressed. That this is what people do with good podcasts — they listen, they tell their friends. Who was I to freak out for finding out that the show I worked so hard on, that I found so personally rewarding resonated with others too?

"Absolutely nothing has changed from this morning," Melinda continued. "You simply learned empirical information that was true yesterday. Just like me and my dad and the San Francisco fog horn. Your *interpretation* of that information is what's freaking you out."

She was right, of course. This was the Melinda version of "reframing," the could-this-bad-thing-actually-be-good practice Scottie and I were trying to adopt.

"It sounds ridiculous, I know. But now that I have proof that people, *a lot* of people, are listening, I feel so...exposed."

"Reassess the facts," Melinda said in her gentle, slow voice. "Yes, you're exposed. But here's an alternative, or at least an additional, interpretation: your work resonated with that woman and her friends. Isn't that what Peeps is all about? Linking people together?"

It's Meg, your host of the Peeps podcast where we find the world in a grain of sand. Before we dive into episode sixty-one, here's a fun update. Back in episode seventeen, we heard from Marcus, who told us about the boy who'd been his friend in grade school before abruptly moving away, the boy whose mother had leukemia back then. Believe it or not, that very boy — now a man like Marcus, of course — heard the episode and he, too, fondly remembered playing in that tree house in San Mateo, California. He reached out to me and, with Marcus's permission, I connected them. They've spoken on the phone and are both thrilled to have reconnected. The power of the podcast! And now for the show....

Seth and I met for a late lunch in Erie, Pennsylvania at a restaurant where he once worked as a waiter. The restaurant was technically closed at that hour between the lunch and dinner crowds, but Seth is still friends with the chef, who arranged for us to enjoy a meal and quiet conversation. In his early thirties, Seth has a boyish face and air of compassion. A Pennsylvania native, he pronounces "water" like "wooder." After our interview, we walked together towards the city's convention center where he was working that day. Along the way, he spotted someone he knew in a homeless encampment not far from the convention center parking lot. He handed the man a doggie bag from our lunch. "That guy used to be the wine sommelier at the place we just ate," Seth explained later. It was then that I suspected Seth hadn't finished all of his lunch on purpose.

Out of seven billion people, what's it like to be you right now?

I have the best job. I'm a sign language interpreter. I freelance. I get to work at the coolest places. Sometimes I'm needed at an amusement park or a theater. I once interpreted at Coachella. Another time I got to sign at a literary event with Stephen King! A cruise ship once hired me and I got paid to sign as we cruised through Alaska!

Tell me something about your background, about yourself.

I used to be a gambling expert. Specifically, roulette.

That means what, exactly?

Okay, so in my early twenties, my buddies and I would go to Atlantic City on weekends. Wicked fun. I became fascinated by roulette wheels. I studied them. Before long, I realized that each wheel has biases. Like a very subtle tendency to land on certain numbers. Not anything untoward by the house. Just the result of a mechanical defect or even just simple wear and tear. Once I noticed this, I memorized each wheel's nicks and scratches, other telltale identifiers. You can imagine what happened, right? Soon I was on a hot streak. My friends even nicknamed me "hot streak." Some of my buddies still call me that. Or "HS" in emails and texts and comments on my social media posts. Roulette wasn't my full-time job. I was working as a waiter here at the time. But I did win about eighty grand one year. I hopped casinos frequently so I wouldn't get banned. I did stand out, though, because I was a man.

What do you mean?

Well, women are what they call "escape" gamblers. That means that, generally speaking, of course, women like games based on luck. Slot machines and roulette, that kind of thing. Men, on the other hand, are "action" gamblers. They prefer blackjack, poker, craps. One night, I arrived to discover that my favorite casino had replaced all their roulette wheels. I took that as a sign from the universe to move on from my hobby. That was about ten years ago.

What's a physical object you'd like to bring with you to the afterlife?

Okay, so, I listen to your show. I knew this question was coming. I've racked my brain and couldn't think of anything. I realized: I'm good! I'll go empty handed.

Tell me one thing you do every day.

I do stretches for my wrists and fingers. As a sign language interpreter, my hands are my livelihood. I need to keep them healthy.

What was your pivot moment, Seth?

So after I quit my gambling gig — well, it wasn't an official gig, but you get the idea — I was trying to figure out what I wanted to do with my life. I was a good waiter and I liked the job. I liked interacting with the public. And I was making a decent living wage. But I wanted to do something more, like, helpful. More meaningful. I thought seriously about becoming a nurse. I could handle blood and guts but, sadly, not vomit. I figured that would be a deal breaker. Anyhow, two things happened in a single day that switched on the proverbial light bulb for me. In the morning, I went to a boxing class. During the cool down, the teacher, kind of a hippy-dippy guy, said, "As you go about your day, look for moments of stillness and remember that silence isn't empty; it's full of answers." I had no idea what he meant. Literally no idea.

Did you figure it out?

I did, at least for me. That night, I was at a bar, drinking a beer while waiting for my buddies. I noticed these two men at another table communicating in sign language. I was, like, mesmerized. Of course, I'd seen people sign before. Like someone at the front of an auditorium interpreting. But I hadn't seen two people have a conversation in ASL before. I watched them for a few minutes. They were laughing and signing rapidly. It was so animated and yet completely silent. I punched a message into the notes section of my phone and walked over and showed it to the two men. "Your sign language is beautiful," I wrote. I don't want to make it seem like I'm, you know, so great or anything. But the look on their faces showed that I'd made their day. Just to be noticed like that. To be complimented for what made them different. They looked at me with such, I don't know, warmth that I just knew right then what I wanted to do next in my life. So the boxing teacher was right. Silence was full of answers.

Who is someone you never saw again? And what I mean is—

Like I said, I listen to your show so I know the question. Got my answer. I have a dog, a Jack Russell named Astro. I was a big fan of Jetsons reruns as a kid. Anyway, I take him on a long walk every morning. Same route I've done for a long time. Years. For a time, I crossed paths with a guy walking his dog. An old black lab. He and Astro liked each other so every time we saw them, we'd stop. I'd chat with the man while the dogs sniffed and did what dogs do. Just a couple of minutes each morning. He was an older, a friendly guy. He's actually the person who recommended the boxing studio where I was that morning of my "pivot moment." Anyway, I'd see them the same time, the same place, for a couple of years. Then one day, they were just gone. I don't know if the man moved or his dog died or what.

What's your motto for life?

Try anything once.

Thank you, Seth. And thanks to you all for listening and for your encouragement and positive feedback and source suggestions for the show. I've got some great episodes lined up thanks to your connections.

CHAPTER SIXTEEN

I had sex with Seth.

It was the one and only time I'd even kissed a source, let alone slept with one. Though Peeps is a man-on-the-street podcast of my own invention, I still hold myself to strict standards of quality journalism, which definitely do not include physical intimacy with sources.

I wasn't even horny. My experience with Jimmy in New Orleans notwithstanding, Scottie and I jokingly called each other "LoLi," short for "Low Libido," as in, "Her name was LoLi, she was a showgirl...." But when I was with Seth, I just had this sense that chances were slipping away, and I wanted to grab hold before they did. Maybe it had something to do with Brad and having missed my chance with him before leaving LA. So I was determined to be fully present for those last chances, unlike how I'd been back in high school with the great-kissing Night Moves boy, the boy I'd naively assumed was a mere precursor to many more just like him when it turned out no one else had even come close.

When we walked together from our interview at the restaurant to his signing job at that Pennsylvania convention center, we bumped into his friend Matthew, the former sommelier, now homeless. We chatted with him for a few minutes after Seth handed over his bag of leftover food from our late lunch.

"Forgive me, but can I ask you, Matthew: how did you get here?" I said, glancing up at the freeway overpass, the roof that protected him from the elements. It was, I hoped, a more subtle way of probing his pivot moment. Everyone, I believed, has one, a time when everything shifted. How would my mother have answered? Had she once been nurturing and loving until something happened? Or had she simply been born, genetically predisposed, to be the way she was? And what was the pivot moment of my dad, a man I never knew?

"Didn't take much," Matthew said, his eyes clear and intent on mine. "A perfect storm. My roommate moved out and I couldn't find anyone to take over his spot. Student loans from Penn State caught up with me. My father needed to be moved to assisted living. One paycheck away from financial ruin?" Matthew said, and then pointed to his chest, "Exhibit A, right here." Then he spun around and gestured to the people living alongside him. "Former soldiers. Addicts. Mentally ill. Ivy League grads. Communists. We're as diverse here as you are out there."

Once again, I thanked the universe that I had Irv.

Seth had to get to his signing gig so we continued on towards the convention center. While we walked, I asked more about gambling and learned that he'd gotten into horse racing in recent months. I told him I'd never been to a race track, that I'd always wanted to go, that I was sure I'd find people to interview at such a place.

"I'm done with this job in an hour," he said with irresistible boyish enthusiasm. "Can you wait?"

So I did. Inside the convention center doors, I roamed the aisles of state-of-the-art fitness equipment. It turned out the convention was for gym owners. Seth was inside translating the keynote speech into ASL. That hour waiting for him was a boon for me because I set up interviews with a nineteen-year-old from Massachusetts who'd patented an electric jump rope and a South Carolina man who taught restorative yoga exclusively to first responders like EMTs and firefighters.

When I reconnected with Seth, I was in a great mood. My little show was doing so well that I'd been recognized by my voice in Cleveland. I was in Pennsylvania with a cute guy who, he may not have even realized, was probably twenty years younger than me. And we were heading to a race track, a slice of Americana I'd always wanted to see.

The track was cold and loud. My boots got splattered with the wet dirt everywhere. It smelled of horse manure and alcohol. I got the sense Seth spent a fair amount of time there because several people, from the security guard to the concessions worker, knew his name.

"Is there a way to game horse racing the way you did with roulette?" I asked.

Seth put his arm around me and winked. "I'm working on it."

I liked the way his arm felt around me. We ordered hot toddies and he explained how horse betting worked. I had no disposable income. Correction: I had no income. So I had no business gambling, as my costly diversion to the western Louisiana blackjack table proved. What did it say about me that I was not an "escape" gambler like most women, according to Seth, but an "action" gambler, drawn more to blackjack than to games of luck? But for the first time in weeks, probably since New Orleans, I wanted to throw caution to the wind. The next time Seth put his arm around my shoulder, I put mine around his waist.

I lost three hundred dollars in ninety minutes.

"I'm sorry, Meg," Seth said. "I haven't figured this all out yet." His brown eyes were sincere.

I shrugged like the money was negligible to me, though it wasn't.

"Wanna get out of here?" he said.

"I do."

With a firm but gentle hand behind my back, Seth led me to the side of the track building, an area hidden from the parking lot as well as from the wind and the upstate New York chill. With a mischievous smile, he took hold of my shoulders and gently backed me up against a wall, then took my face in his hands.

"Is this okay?" he asked.

The affirmative consent-seeking was a measure of our generational differences.

Good boy, Seth, I thought. This was already way better than my Viagra-fueled encounter with Jimmy, the farting drummer. Clearly, I was learning to make better choices.

I nodded.

He kissed me, a great kiss, perhaps as close to that perfect kissing I'd experienced as a high schooler as I'd experienced since. Better, even, than Brad. Seth kissed me long and slow and my whole body pulsed. Then everything sped up. I didn't care that we were outdoors. I didn't care that he was twenty years younger. I didn't care that I hardly knew him or that people might see us. I tore off my gloves, yanked up his sweater and felt his bare chest with my hands. He chewed lightly on my neck as he undid my pants and slid them gently below my knees. Seth was good with his hands, which was not surprising given that they were his livelihood.

"Come back to my place," he said, as we rebuckled our pants. He wrapped his arms around me and I nuzzled my face into his shoulder, which was thick and warm. He smelled of wool and a lit fireplace. "We can make some dinner…maybe watch a movie…."

My God, how I was tempted.

"That sounds…amazing, really," I said. "But I have to keep moving."

"Do you really *have* to?" he said, squeezing me tighter, warming me against the Pennsylvania winter. It had been a long time since I felt so small, so…desirable.

It took more strength than I thought I had but I pulled away from Seth, the wind whipping through the inches between us. "I do," I said, kissing him. "I wish I didn't, but I do. I have a lonely cat back at my RV and I need to get to my uncle. He's been in the hospital and…I just have to get to him."

I felt bad about losing so much money so quickly. I felt bad about compromising my journalistic principles by sleeping with a source. But, in great contrast to my night with Jimmy in New Orleans, I did not feel bad about the sex. Not at all.

Buffalo is as different from Santa Monica as any place on my travels. I'd never been to western New York, where I instantly felt the influence of Canada, a country I'd visited once for a conference with my old PR firm. Buffalo had a distinct Canadian feel and also the flavor of a stalwart and wholesome U.S. thanks to the General Mills plant and the fact that many people — from little kids to buff dudes heading to play hockey — carry around ice skates. In Southern California, everything felt new, even to people like me, who'd lived there for decades. But in Buffalo everything felt old. Fellow RV'ers recommended Spot Coffee so I grabbed a latte there on my first morning before wandering the streets. I enjoyed, as always, the clarity I felt being near water, this time a canal.

On the waterfront, just as I pulled my phone from my pocket to snap a photo of winter kayakers, it rang with a FaceTime call from Jeff.

"Hey," I answered.

"Hey." He hadn't shaved and I was struck by how white his emerging beard was. In my mind, we were still the same age we were when we met in Anthro 101 at UCLA.

When did he — did we — get so old?

"Tell me the latest," I said, bracing myself for the next construction delay or, worse, unexpected expenditure from the flood damage.

"What?" he said, running a palm over his chin. "Oh, all's on track with Spruce Street."

"Phew."

"Have a few minutes? I want to get your take on a conversation I just had with a new hire."

Jeff detailed an uncomfortable work situation and I chimed in with my two cents.

"That's perfect," Jeff said. "I'll do that. Thank you, Meg."

"With all you're handling for me right now, it's the least I can do."

"That may be true but you are just so good with this stuff."

"Oh, I don't know...."

"Seriously, Meg. You always say you're interested in people. But it's not just that. You're *good* with people."

My first interview that day was with Chad, a newly divorced dad. His split was acrimonious, but the one thing he and his ex did agree on was "nesting." I'd heard about the concept, in which divorced parents take turns staying with their kids in the house they'd once shared together so that the parents, rather than the kids, moved houses each half week. I'd assumed it was primarily a hippy California parenting trend. Chad showed me otherwise.

"My ex and me have just enough money to cover the mortgage on our Park Meadow house and a studio in Angola. That's where we take turns staying when we're not with the kids. I'm still dealing with how messy my ex is, and my sons live in a nicer place than I do," Chad said with hints of both bitterness and pride.

After I wrapped up with Chad, I lugged my recording equipment to the city center, where I interviewed Lee, the general manager of Buffalo's largest hotel. Lee and his family lived in the GM residence on the hotel's top floor, sharing the floor only with the Presidential Suite. The general manager's residence was the same square footage as my home in Santa Monica and the family enjoyed all the luxuries of the hotel's most distinguished guests, from free dry cleaning to daily housekeeping to room service at all hours.

"This feels enormous to me," I told Lee as he greeted me. While the residence struck me as profoundly luxurious — I mean, I could definitely get behind unlimited room service — it also felt wasteful.

"Oh, it's just about twenty-three-hundred square feet," he said. "My wife would love another bedroom."

"I've been living in a motor home the last few months. It's about the size of this," I said, sweeping my arm around the entryway.

Lee's pivot moment had been junior year of high school when he was diagnosed with anorexia. Though now in his thirties, he still had to apply the principles he learned in rehab at every single meal. "We need to stop referring to 'rehab' with shame or disdain, like it's a dirty word. Rehab," he said, "saved my life."

I considered driving to Niagara Falls after the interviews. But that would have postponed other pre-Syracuse tasks I'd assigned myself, including taking Irv to the car wash and spending a few hours at the laundromat. I'd heard from my cousin Lisa, Uncle Oscar's daughter, that he'd been moved from the ICU, but was still hospitalized undergoing tests.

So instead of Niagara Falls, I Yelped places to eat in Elmwood Village not far from where I parked Irv. I'd been craving a burger and reviews sent me to a nearby pub with live music. I laced up my hiking boots and walked over. The Buffalo air held a different kind of cold, a primal, almost prehistoric cold. How could my mother have grown up in upstate New York? Perhaps, I thought sarcastically, it was why *she* had been so cold. To take my mind off the temps, I launched into 5-4-3-2-1 as I walked.

I see an antique boat on the canal...

I hear the squawk of a cardinal...

The streets were quiet, though, probably because of the cold. It wasn't snowing, but I still yanked the hood of my jacket over my head, dulling any sounds I might hear. Given how barren it was on the streets, I only made it to 4 in the cognitive exercise before giving up. Zipping my coat all the way to my chin and raising the edge of my scarf to just under my eyes, I missed Los Angeles. The Erie Canal was pretty, but it was no ocean. I even missed LA's distinctly thick, polluted air.

A few moments later, I rounded the corner to find the pub. According to a poster taped to the door, a local band — the Malevolent Monkeys — was headlining.

Given its name, the Malevolent Monkeys wasn't the kind of band you'd expect. It wasn't metal or rock but instead an old-school folk band with three guys on guitars and a drummer. They sang slow, mournful ballads. During the fourth song, my burger arrived, as tasty as advertised. I even ordered a beer, something I didn't do often, to wash it down. After a few more songs, I decided to head back to Irv and Dotty. In the morning, I'd be on the final leg to Syracuse.

Before exiting the tavern, I bundled back up, and I kept my chin lowered as I plodded along the sidewalks, now dusted with a bit of snow. Half way up the block, the concrete seemed to ripple. Instantly, I felt unsteady on my feet and downright woozy. Pausing on the corner before crossing the street, I felt as if I was no longer on solid earth but instead on a rickety platform, the kind a trapeze artist might stand on before diving toward a partner's ankles. The sidewalk yanked me forward and back, the cars whooshing by attacked my equilibrium. I clutched the light pole on the corner. When the signal turned green, I gingerly stepped off the curb. The world reeled with a violence I'd never experienced. I stumbled backward and thumped onto the cement curb. I couldn't right my vision. The world swayed. Clamping my eyes shut didn't help. I curled into the fetal position right there on the sidewalk in Buffalo, three thousand miles from home.

"Lady, you okay?"

I opened one eye. The world jiggled and fluttered like a strip of film pulled loose from the projector. I squinted and saw a man double parked in a beat-up Taurus, not unlike the one my mother drove during my childhood.

"I don't...I'm dizzy."

"Drink too much?"

"What?" I hadn't even finished the single beer I'd ordered with my burger. "No. I just...I don't feel well all the sudden." The words sounded as if I had too much bubble gum in my mouth.

"Bad trip?"

In my five decades, I'd never even taken a hit of pot, let alone anything harder. Shaking my head no created a dissonant buzzing inside my head. I put my palms over my ears to quiet it.

"You don't look right, lady. Come with me."

It's a measure of how sick I felt that I complied with this strange man's command, especially given my experience as a kid with that woman who practically insisted I get into her car while I was walking to school. Or maybe I'd finally just become less afraid. In any event, amidst cars honking behind him, he carried me into his back seat, where I put my head down on the dirty worn leather. Everything continued to whirl. I planted one foot on the floor to try to stabilize my system the way we were taught to do when we'd had too much to drink in college. It didn't work.

"Here we are," said the man after what seemed like mere seconds. I'd lost all perspective of time. I pressed my torso up and looked through blurry eyes out the window, which was smeared with snowflakes. A neon sign read: EMERGENCY.

The man opened the back door and helped me stand. I promptly doubled over and vomited, splashing his shoes with the remnants of my dinner.

"Oh my God," I slurred, feeling the sour liquid in my nostrils as well as my mouth. "So sorry."

"Better my shoes than my car," he said, grasping my shoulders and guiding me, shuffling, through the automatic doors.

The next few minutes were a blur. I remember handing him my purse. I remember him speaking with the intake receptionist while I sat in the waiting room with my head in my hands.

Some time later, I glanced up. My insurance card was on top of my purse on the chair next to me. The man was nowhere to be found. That I never saw him again, that I wasn't able to thank him is one of my biggest regrets of the entire trip. I prided myself on asking good questions. I'd come to structure my whole life around that skill. But I'd never even learned his first name.

Sick as I was slumped in a chair in the ER waiting room, I couldn't help noticing a seventy-something woman cradling her right elbow with her left palm.

"I tripped," she said, her gold bracelets jingling as she moved her head back and forth. "Such a klutz."

Even feeling as rotten as I did, I observed the woman's cashmere hoodie, her designer jeans, the diamond on her left hand the size of a nickel. I could just imagine her life — country clubs, shopping excursions, relaxed mornings, home visits from a masseuse, a chef to cook vegan meals to support her remarkably slender physique for a woman her age. She was the kind of woman whose life revolved around appearances. Who, after all, wore lipstick to the ER?

"How ya doing, Mom?" said a woman who exited the nearby bathroom and sat down next to the wealthy senior.

Mom? Half the girl's head was shaved to her scalp and the other half was dyed neon green. She was what my mother would have called "chunky" and her outfit — jeans, an oversized camo t-shirt and ankle-high Doc Martens — wasn't, as my mother also would have said, doing her any favors. But the girl tenderly put her head on her mother's good shoulder and the woman smiled with contentment before wincing with pain and shifting her elbow.

I wanted to ask what the mom thought of her punk daughter, what the daughter thought of her overdone mom. They seemed so opposite and yet so connected. If I'd been in my right mind, I'd have struck up a conversation, maybe even asked to interview one of them for Peeps. Another wave of seasickness smacked me and I clutched the arm of my chair to steady myself. I clamped my eyes shut as the mother and daughter began to spin along with everything else in the room.

Was I having a stroke? Maybe I was dying.

Oh, God. Alex. Dotty — no one knew she was in my RV. She'd die too, from starvation. I'd never get the answers to my questions from Uncle Oscar. I'd come so close....

No! I demanded to myself. *You're okay. You're in a hospital.*

In triage, a male nurse who stood about six-foot-five took my vitals. My blood pressure went high and then low. My heart rate was rapid. He took an EKG, his hands warm as he popped the probes on and off my torso. Though I didn't understand the results, the printout reminded me of my echocardiogram route. Would I make it to my final destination?

The nurse left me in a room surrounded by other patients separated by curtains. One woman moaned. Another, translating for a relative who spoke Vietnamese, said, "He's bleeding profusely from his rectum."

I was trembling when the nurse checked on me so he brought me a blanket that he'd heated in a microwave.

"It shouldn't be too much longer," he said.

I yanked the blanket right up to my chin. Every time I opened my eyes, the tiles on the ceiling danced and wiggled.

You're okay, I told myself.

Eventually, a doctor with acne scars, wildly curly hair and a friendly but no-nonsense demeanor slid the curtain back and sat next to my bed.

"Did you hit your head or anything?" she asked, shining a pen light in my eyes.

"No."

"Any numbness in your limbs? Your face?"

I shook my head.

"Can you follow my finger with your eyes? Keep your head steady."

I eyed her finger as it moved about three inches to the left and then vomited.

"I'm ordering pictures and a scan."

I began to shake again. The nurse brought me another blanket. I thought again of Alex, Dotty.

What was happening?

Normally, I would have peppered the doctor with questions. What was she scanning for? A stroke? A brain tumor? Why did I feel like I was moving even though I was flat on my back? Was I going to make it out of here alive?

But it was all I could do to not throw up again.

The nurse drew three vials of blood. I flung my elbow pit over my eyes as he wheeled my bed from the room to the MRI machine and then to the CT scan. Despite my love of cozy spaces, I hated them both, the terrifying, closed-in, noisy MRI tube, the metallic taste of the dye required for the CT scan.

He wheeled me back to my shared room, where new neighbors had arrived, including one belligerent man who screamed over and over, "Don't touch me!"

My body quivered. This time, the nurse piled two heated blankets over me.

I'm okay, I repeated, while waiting for the results, as terrified as I'd been the day I'd run three red lights rushing Jeff to the hospital with chest pains.

The curly-haired doctor returned. "Blood work and scans are clear."

I cried with relief.

"Then why do I feel like I'm stuck in a washing machine?" I asked her.

"You've got labyrinthitis. It's what I thought when I first examined you but I wanted to rule out the worst. It's a harmless virus that sets up shop in the inner ear."

You buried the lede, I wanted to say.

"You're going to feel about as awful as you've ever felt," the doctor continued as she drew up my discharge papers, "but just that know you're fine — and you're not contagious. Do what you'd do for any virus. Rest, fluids. You should feel better in a week to ten days."

A week? I was supposed to see my uncle the very next day in Syracuse. What if Uncle Oscar took a turn for the worse and I never got the chance to ask him what I wanted to know?

"Seven to ten days — got it," I said, privately determined to disregard her advice and continue on to Syracuse as planned. I stood up and felt like I was trapped in a kaleidoscope screen saver. I had to right myself by smacking my palm to the wall.

"Do you have someone who can pick you up?" the doctor asked, hopping up from her chair to steady me.

"I...no," I said. "I'm from out of town. Here on business."

"Carla!" the doctor yelled out the door. Then she turned back to me. "Hand me your phone. I'm going to have a nurse call you an Uber. Make sure you get home safely."

By the time I got back to Irv — thankfully I'd marked my parking spot in my phone, something I'd gotten in the habit of doing since I was so unfamiliar with every place I was driving and parking — it was four-thirty in the morning. The sky was turning colors, announcing the approach of dawn. I tossed my purse on the floor and fell — literally fell — into bed. Poor Dotty hadn't even had dinner and it was already almost breakfast time. But she seemed to sense I wasn't well and didn't meow or circle her food dish like she normally did when hungry. Instead, she jumped gracefully onto the bed and curled up next to me, placing one paw on my cheek, which steadied my dizzy skull as I fell asleep.

CHAPTER SEVENTEEN

It was no fewer than nine days before I felt even remotely like myself. For more than a week, I couldn't do anything except lay down. I got six parking tickets, which I couldn't afford. And after three days of being holed up in the RV, I woke slick with sweat, menopausal night sweats or labyrinthitis, I didn't know, and discovered I was down to my last roll of toilet paper.

I had enough strength to walk to the RV next door, planting my palms along Irv's outside to keep myself upright. I explained to the family that I was ill and asked if they'd go to the store for me. I gave them my credit card — my actual credit card, to complete strangers — and plodded back to Irv. A bit later, they arrived with my toilet paper and other provisions, my credit card and a bouquet of flowers. Grateful I'd finally learned to open myself up to fellow travelers, I then slept for the next fifteen hours.

I did have one distinct stroke of luck: I'd gone to the sewage pump *right* before I'd gotten ill. Dotty, for her part, was in heaven, spending those nine days gazing at the falling snow out the window, playing on her kitten tree and snoozing alongside me. My tiny living space was the perfect place for me to recover. Since I felt like I was under water, being tossed amongst the waves, it was helpful to have everything I needed so accessible, to have walls and cabinets on either side of me to help me balance as I made my way from bed to bathroom to kitchen.

Uncle Oscar, it turned out, was getting better right alongside me. I'd texted my cousin Lisa to say my visit to Syracuse would be delayed. By the time I was well enough to drive, my uncle had been discharged from the hospital, having been diagnosed with small, reversible strokes and dehydration. Lisa and I ended up having a brief but nice chat. I learned she'd recently retired from her longtime job as a social worker and was taking classes in Italian and Middle Eastern history. It was an uplifting update, especially compared to the one Derrick had given about some of our other cousins.

Scottie entertained me with voicemails — I'd told her I was too dizzy to read texts — about how she'd gotten in the habit of emailing herself reminders like taking out the trash or scheduling an appointment and then moments later get excited when a "new message" alert came in, already forgetting that it was merely the message she'd just sent herself. I left her a return voicemail, letting her know that my music-loving son had started referring to meno*pause* as "meno-*play*."

Unlike most parent-child relationships, Alex had gotten into the habit of using Find My iPhone to check up on *me* rather than the other way around.

On my fourth day in Buffalo, the longest amount of time I'd spent in any one city, he texted, "U OK?"

"Sick." I replied with a frowny emoji.

Moments later, he FaceTimed me.

"Jesus, Mom, you look awful."

"I guess I forgot to teach you what not to say to a woman."

"Seriously, Mom. What's wrong?"

I filled him in.

"How about I fly up there and look after you? We can get a hotel room. Matzo ball soup, the whole shebang."

Dotty nuzzled against my neck. It was tempting to take my boy up on his offer. But I couldn't ask him to do that. Plus, where would Dotty be if we were in a hotel room?

"That's sweet. Really, I'm actually much better."

"Damn, if this is better, I can't imagine what it was like when you were worse."

"Remind me to give you that crash course on how to talk to women."

"Very funny."

"Really, though, I'm on the mend. The only thing I need from you is some photos of you enjoying college. That'll perk me up."

Eventually, I was well enough to sit upright, eat a complete meal rather than just crackers, and have a Skype session with Melinda.

"You've come a long way, haven't you?" she said when I updated her about my trip to the ER.

"Almost three thousand miles." I still couldn't believe it.

She shook her head. "That's not what I mean. If you'd been sick and alone and needing emergency medical care in a strange city when I first met you?" she said, widening her eyes. "That would have sent you into a downright tailspin."

I recalled the terror I'd felt in hospital triage before giving birth. And I thought of the heated blankets the tall nurse had to pile on top of me because I was shaking so badly. So I waved my hand, flicking her compliment towards the ceiling. "It's just a virus."

"Don't do that, Meg."

"Do what?" I whispered, feeling scolded.

"Stay with this ER visit, the virus that turned your plan upside down, literally. The brain scans, the uncertainty, being thrown wildly off course. As we know, you're not friends with the unexpected. You must have been afraid."

I remembered the terrifying thought that I might have some kind of brain tumor, that Alex might be motherless, that I might have frozen to death on the sidewalk if the man in the Taurus hadn't taken me to the hospital. But I didn't get where Melinda was going. Wasn't I trying to *stop* being afraid?

"I was nervous," I agreed.

"And what did you do when you were nervous?"

I glanced over my laptop screen to Dotty, who was batting a felt ball hanging from her kitten tree. "I sort of…talked to myself."

"What did you say?"

"I told myself that I was okay, that it was more likely than not to be something less serious than I feared, that the guy in the Taurus *had* stepped in so there was no use rehashing alternative endings."

She leaned towards her computer camera so her smile filled my screen. "Think about that," she said before a short pause. "I'm not suggesting that you try to never be afraid. That's not even possible. But you're establishing a new relationship to fear. Your tolerance for stress…it's expanding. As is your comfort zone."

I nodded, filing her words away so I could think more about them later.

Her expression grew self-satisfied. "*I've* known all along that you were capable of this. Now you're figuring it out for yourself."

Upon hearing Melinda's words, something like vulnerability, rather than pride, cloaked me. Feeling more confident managing scary things seemed like an invitation for bad things to test me. But I did also feel my body uncoil a little, my ears separating from my shoulders.

"Tell me about your next stop," Melinda said.

I was grateful for the change in topic. "I'm finally heading to Syracuse tomorrow, to meet with my mother's brother. I'm going to ask about their childhood, about our ancestors. I want to figure out how to move through the next phase of life."

She shook her head, her wavy hair jiggling across my screen. Another scolding. "You might learn some things that will explain why your mom wasn't a secure parent, why you crave certainty. But you may not. And it's okay *not to know*. Meg, your childhood, your mother, your fear — it's not necessarily something you can *understand* your way out of."

Then what the hell was all this for? I thought.

"What you *can* do," Melinda continued, "is change your narrative."

"What does that mean?"

"Whether your mom treated you badly because of something that happened in her own childhood or because of something to do with you, is, frankly, irrelevant. You've been telling yourself a story your whole life, that the people meant to keep you safe were not reliable. Your father died, your mother was neglectful, even hostile. So you've devoted your energy to keeping ahead of danger, of ensuring safety in an unsafe world. You know what that does?"

I shook my head.

"That keeps your mother at the center of your universe."

She was being too simplistic. So I challenged her. "I have this, I don't know, hunch that a sinister thread traveled through our family. I mean, look at my cousin Derrick: visiting with me one minute and hours later pulling the trigger on a pistol aimed at his skull." I grew nauseous as I spoke the words and had to cover my eyes.

"Your determination to find *the* answer is understandable, but not constructive," she said, her voice growing so loud I had to turn the volume down on my computer. "No matter what your uncle reveals, you'll never really know why your mom treated you the way she did. You're a story-teller, Meg. Tell yourself a new story."

In the morning, twenty miles outside of Syracuse, I stopped at a gas station where, in addition to filling Irv's tank, I checked the lug nuts and tire pressure and, once connected to shore power, checked my circuit breaker, fuses and battery voltage. A silver-haired man parked next to me at the maintenance area observed as I completed each of these tasks, which had gone from formidable several months ago to second nature now. As I drove away, the man nodded his head in apparent admiration and gave me a thumbs up.

From there, I drove into The Shadow Palace, my first and only luxury RV park of the trip, one that I had budgeted for before leaving Santa Monica. It was on every top ten list of luxury parks and happened to be right near my uncle's house. The park boasted a spa, gourmet market and state-of-the-art athletic club. Syracuse was an unlikely spot for such a fancy park but it was a destination for RV'ing Canadians heading south towards Florida. I treated myself to some pampering for getting this far.

Through the reception office window, I viewed to the left a rainbow of super fancy RVs, including a blue Mercedes van like the one I'd first seen back in Santa Monica and a Class A painted bright yellow. I pulled into my assigned spot next to a black and emerald Class C the same size as Irv. Its curtains were drawn so I wasn't able to wave hello to my new neighbor, as was now my custom whenever I arrived at RV parks. For a few minutes, I watched Dotty chase the red dot I controlled with a laser pointer and then made my way to the main building for a Korean salt scrub at the spa, a spur-of-the-moment splurge I hoped would rid me once and for all from the dregs of labyrinthitis. Scottie swore by salt scrubs. "You'll feel like a baby dolphin when it's over!"

I spent a few minutes in a sauna and then lay naked on a marble table waiting for my treatment to begin, feeling more like a human baby, defenseless and exposed. A woman entered wearing what looked like a wetsuit and began tossing buckets of water over me. Then she used mitted hands to exfoliate my body. I visualized layers of my skin falling to the tiled floor alongside skin fragments of the strangers being treated next to me. I felt sick then, but in an existential rather than labyrinthitis kind of way. I was finally at the door of my destination and didn't know if it would be the most enlightening or disappointing meeting of my life. Would what I learned from Uncle Oscar validate this journey or prove that it had all been a crazy idea, a confirmation that I was not meant for the kind of Big Life I coveted?

Welcome to episode sixty-nine of Peeps, where we see the world in a grain of sand. If you listened to episode forty-seven, you learned about Harris, who revealed that he was refusing cancer treatment because he'd long ago lost the will to live. Many of you wrote to me about how saddened you were by his story. I was too. I'm pleased to report that Harris's own brother also heard the episode. Learning for the first time of Harris's diagnosis, he reached out to him. Harris let me know that that he was deeply touched by his brother's gesture. Harris is still refusing treatment, but is now surrounded by his brother's family. So at least there's that. Harris, if you're listening, your peeps are here behind you.

In this episode we meet Hannah, a twenty-nine-year-old who lives in Avoca, New York. She's tiny — probably not even five, one — with long brown hair pulled into a low ponytail and enormous round glasses that give her a hipster, but not nerdy, vibe. Hannah looks younger than her age, but behind those funky glasses are the eyes of someone with an older spirit.

What's it like to be you right now?

I like to tell people I'm in first grade. I'm an attendant for a six-year-old girl with cerebral palsy. She goes to a fancy, progressive private school. I work directly for the family. I meet them at school in the morning, then help her maneuver through anything physical. Like transitioning from circle time on the floor to her desk for lessons. Or transporting her from home room to the music room. Or assisting during recess. That kind of thing. I've worked with this particular girl for about eighteen months. But I've been doing this work for, let's see, about five years now. I see first-hand how much education has changed since I was a kid. And I'm not even that old! I went to an all-girls Catholic school. The school I'm "going to" now is so much more, um, evolved. And fun. Believe it or not, I'm learning things in first grade!

Tell me something about you, your background.

Right after graduating from SUNY, I went into a management trainee program at a big corporation in St. Louis. Mistake number one — I should have spent a year as a ski instructor or something before diving right into corporate America. But, anyway, there were just six of us in that year's MT class: four guys, two women. The other girl was the niece of the CEO and dropped out of the program after a month because she got off the waiting list at Wharton. So pretty quickly it was just me and four guys. Long, loooonnnnggg story short, the place was a shit show. The guys were not only given better assignments but they were wined and dined by the executives. Taken to baseball games and concerts. I was never once invited. I worked harder than they did but got worse performance reviews. I had a short fling with one of the other MTs. Big mistake, I know. Later I learned that all the executives asked him what I was like in bed. I mean, I could tell you more stuff, worse stuff. But it's, like, painful for me to talk about and I'm sure you get the idea. I was outta there as soon as the program ended. Corporate America disgusted me. What really irks me now is this all happened long before the #metoo movement. I missed the whole thing. I'm kinda pissed about that, you know?

Explain what you mean.

Well, those assholes who excluded me, harassed me — like I said, I haven't even told you the half of it — they probably believe they're so "woke" now with their bogus HR training about consent and yadda yadda. Those guys probably remember nothing, not one thing they did that year.

That year they made my life hell. The year I lost 18 pounds because I couldn't eat. The year I had to take medication just to be able to sleep. If they did today what they did to me back then? They'd be fired. Probably even worse. I've thought about looking up statutes of limitations on these kinds of #metoo claims. But I don't want to have to relive that terrible year. So the system still works against women like me.

That's awful. Hopefully by sharing here, other women will feel less alone.

Maybe.

What's a physical object you'd bring into the afterlife if you could?

I love to read. I write down my favorite lines from novels and poems in notebooks. Anything that strikes me. Something lyrical or funny or clever. Or, more often than not, something that conveys a feeling I've had but never, you know, quite put into words. That's what the best writers do, put obscure feelings into words, making the reader feel less alone. Anyway, I've been keeping these notebooks since I was nine. My first entry was from a Judy Blume book. I've now got several notebooks filled. I've got one right here in my bag.... First quote? From a Billy Collins poem: "What a brazen wonder to be alive on earth amid the clockwork of all this motion." I could re-read these all day. But back to your question: I'd bring these beautiful words with me when I leave this earth.

What is one thing you do every day, Hannah?

Attend an AA meeting.

Thank you, um, for sharing that. Many people wouldn't.

No shame in doing right by your own self. No shame at all. It's what my sponsor's teaching me.

What was your life's pivot moment?

During that awful year I told you about, at the company in St. Louis, I made one friend. An assistant for one of the executives at the company. We both ate lunch in the employee break room. Believe me, I was looked down on for that. Management trainees were considered "above" eating in the break room. Fucked up, right? Anyway, he and I bonded when we discovered we both loved reality TV. We weren't romantic or anything. He's gay, as a matter of fact. He lived with his twin sister and the three of us hung out at their apartment watching baking competitions, Survivor, you name it. His sister did what I do now — working as an attendant for disabled kids. She'd come home exhausted, absolutely spent, every night. But she loved the work. The more I learned about it, the more interested I became. I knew I couldn't work for another big corporation. Just couldn't. I wanted to do something that mattered, even if it mattered just to one person. Meeting her is what led me to this life I have now.

Who is someone you never saw again? I'm talking about someone who passed away, someone you once knew but don't know anymore, someone you crossed paths with briefly.

Okay, one night in college I was at a fraternity party. I was with my roommate. She was well-known around campus because she was drop dead gorgeous. Legs up to here. Flawless, tanned skin without a freckle or a mole anywhere. Huge, straight teeth. She was a stunner. You know the type? Anyway, we're at this party, standing around with our red Solo cups, chatting with this guy, just the three of us. I don't remember what we were talking about. Something, you know, benign, something light, chit-chatty. I chimed in with a comment pertinent to whatever the innocuous topic was. The guy looked down at me and said, swear to God, "I wasn't talking to you." I was so utterly stunned I didn't know how to respond — neither did my friend. I mean, this asshole dismissed me from the conversation. I think I probably said, "Sorry." Come to think of it, that was actually another pivot moment in my life. Maybe that's why I remember it so vividly. Because it was a long time before I went to another party. For months I stayed in my dorm watching bad TV on Saturday nights. Even though I was in college. It's like that guy, I don't know, dropped me into a hole I had to dig myself out of. To be honest, I'm still digging. If you paid me a gazillion dollars, I wouldn't be able to pick that guy out of a lineup. But I wish I could find him. Find him and finally, finally tell him to go fuck himself.

What's your life motto?

One day at a time.

My thanks to Hannah.

Come back next time for episode seventy. I can hardly believe it's been seventy shows already. Maybe I shouldn't be so surprised. After all, there are seven billion people in the world — and every one of us has a story.

CHAPTER EIGHTEEN

In the morning, I showered, sat for meditation. I owed a call to the mold guy cleaning the Spruce Street house. But it would have to wait. My mind twisted and jumped so much that I periodically opened my eyes to confirm I was still right where I'd sat down. There I was. In Syracuse. About to see my Uncle Oscar.

It was forty degrees outside but I decided to bundle up and ride my bike the mile to my uncle's, the first time I'd removed it from Irv's back. I wore the rugged boots I'd purchased all those months ago, which had finally molded to my feet and had become as comfortable as my trusty Asics. I rode slowly, working on 5-4-3-2-1 as I pedaled along the sidewalks, damp with melted snow.

I see a narrow and tall red house…

I hear the rumble of a garbage truck…

Then I mentally rehearsed what I wanted to ask my uncle. For Peeps, my questions were the same seven every time. This was different.

My uncle lived in Brighton, close to the center of Syracuse. As I biked, I cataloged all that I'd done since leaving Santa Monica. I'd visited Alex and slept with two strangers. I'd met Leon and Brian the professor and countless others. I'd lost my cousin. I'd lost money. I'd gained confidence. I'd handled scary situations.

Part of me couldn't wait to point Irv towards the Pacific Ocean, to have the sun chasing me as I drove west. But I wondered whether Santa Monica would still feel like home since I'd begun to feel different from the woman who'd driven away from Spruce Street. I missed the familiarity and routine of life there, but I'd come to crave the lure of faraway places, the thrill of the unfamiliar.

I'd started doing more Peeps interviews on the fly, rather than planning them so far in advance. One of my recent favorites was with a guy I met in line at a Kroger in Michigan, an astrobiologist who'd survived childhood leukemia and now ran a small mineral museum. He hoped to bring a piece of Majorite, a mineral that stores oxygen, into the afterlife.

I'd also begun to see how I could be both afraid and brave at the same time. I was still cautious, no doubt. I chose to interview a Kentucky pilot on the ground rather than in her small plane, as she'd offered. And even in my vagabond existence, I clung to routine. I mostly ate the same things at the same time. I watched Seinfeld reruns before bed and before getting up in the morning, I checked the news, the weather and social media, in the same order, on my phone while lying on my left side.

But maybe I'd started to outgrow my life, the life I'd led for a long, long time. Maybe I was finally ready for my own version of a Big Life. I still didn't know what that was. A new job? A new relationship? A new, lighter way of being in the world? Something told me that I would know one way or the other once I got to the bottom of my mother's history, my family's history here in Syracuse with my uncle.

Reaching his house, I walked my bike up the path from the street and leaned it against the side of the house. Standing at the front door, I felt naked without my computer and podcasting equipment. I was not there to uncover someone else's life, but learn more my mother's and, by extension, my own.

Just as my knuckles were about to meet his front door, it opened. He looked much how I remembered: tall and handsome. His hair had thinned and he was frail but overall he looked pretty good for a man in his eighties who'd just been in the hospital. He wore a black V-neck sweater over a white button-down. All of the joy I felt when I saw him as a kid flooded me, all of that relief I felt being around safe, loving adults. I remembered how I'd always sob on the plane rides back home to Southern California, distraught that the three of us were alone again. I remember my mother rolling her eyes at my tears and then turning back to her magazine, the pages of which she'd sling quickly and noisily, not even reading. "Wicked Witch of the West," I remember thinking as we traveled in the sky towards California.

Behind Uncle Oscar stood a woman in a nurse's uniform, presumably the attendant my cousin hired to help him after his hospital stay. She gave me a silent wave and I smiled back. In the doorway, Uncle Oscar didn't embrace me but instead swooped his arm up and around as if to say, "Come in." I stepped inside, into the house that he, my mother and their other brother — Derrick's father — grew up in and inherited from my grandparents. It was homey and warm. The bits of snow on my boots melted instantly, creating puddles in his entryway.

"I'm so sorry!" I gasped.

I moved to whip off my wet boots, placing my right ankle on my left knee and reaching with my right arm to steady myself against the wall. But instead of the wall, my hand hit something leaned up against it, which then crashed to the floor. A broom.

"Meggie," he said, as the attendant scooped up the broom. "No worries. You're not in California anymore. Here upstate, we've got tile entryways and brooms by the front door for all of the snow and dirt we track in."

"Of course," I said, tucking my boots neatly alongside other shoes underneath a bench. I peeled off more layers — my scarf, my jacket, my hat, my fleece, all of which I'd purchased solely for this trip with this exact spot, my mother's childhood home, as my destination. The heater rumbled as it kicked on. The house smelled of cinnamon and menthol.

"I told Ursula, here, that my niece from California was coming for a visit and she told me I better have oat milk or kale juice or something called kombucha to serve you," he said, leading me into the living room sunken down two stairs, mid-century style. Ursula held his forearm as he lowered onto the sofa. I sat next to him. On the coffee table was an acrylic tray holding a tea pot and a file folder. "But I don't know where to find shit like that. So we made good, old-fashioned tea. Hope that works."

"It definitely does," I laughed. "Thank you."

"It's been a long time, Meggie," he said, while Ursula poured golden liquid into two mismatched cups.

"I know. I'm very sorry about Auntie Am." Oscar's wife Amelia had died from Parkinson's the year before.

"Yes, yes, thank you," he said, with a wistful smile.

"I remember her so fondly," I added. Auntie Am was my favorite of my two aunts. Barely taller than five feet, she was loud and bawdy and affectionate. By the time I was eleven, I towered over her. When she hugged me, which she did often, the top of her head landed under my chin. She hugged me longer than anyone else and slapped my butt at the conclusion of each embrace. "I've always loved that tush, Meggie," she'd say.

"Every once in awhile," I continued, "I try to recreate her boysenberry cobbler. She gave me the recipe when I got married and even though I follow it exactly, it's never as good as hers was."

"Ah, well, probably the boysenberries. New England boysenberries. Nothin' like 'em. No offense to California produce!"

"None taken."

"And I'm sorry about your mom, Meggie. I wish I'd been able to be with you for the service."

"Thank you. I understand — it's not easy making the cross-country trek. And my condolences to you too — you knew my mother longer than I did," I said, placing my palm on his hand.

He nodded.

"Really, though, how *are* you, Uncle Oscar? I'm so glad you're home from the hospital."

"Me too. It was touch and go for a bit. But I'm feeling great. Ursula has been doing some physical therapy with me. Pretty soon she won't have a job here anymore!"

"Well, for your sake, I hope that's true." I paused. "Tell me more about your life these days."

"You always were full of questions, Meggie! I work to keep busy. I play bridge. And when my slipped disc permits, I play golf. I hang out with the grandkids. That kind of thing."

I'd traveled to Syracuse for a utilitarian reason: to untangle my mother's past. But I underestimated how good it would feel to simply be with my uncle, to feel the belonging and warmth I'd experienced with him and our extended family when I was a kid.

"Here," he said, handing me a manila envelope, my third package of mail forwarded from Jeff. I tucked it into my bag without opening it.

"So, Meggie," he said, "Tell me why you're here."

"Well, as I mentioned to you in my emails, I was hoping you could talk to me about your background and my mother's. Tell me about the childhood you shared."

Oscar reached forward to the file folder on the coffee table. It was a bit bent, as if it had been stuffed into a drawer. On the outside, it said FAMILY. From it, he pulled a disheveled stack of papers and photos. They crinkled from his touch and I felt my scalp tingle. "I can't even remember what I've got in here, but it'll help me answer your question."

In no particular order, he began passing me photos and mementos.

"Here we are at Seabreeze Amusement Park." He shared a black-and-white picture of my mother between her two brothers. All three were holding cotton candy above their heads like trophies. "What's this? Oh, I think this is your mother's report card from third grade." He handed over a piece of paper barely larger than an index card. My mother had earned all A's and one B- in penmanship. The comments included words like: "Conscientious. Good citizen."

"Oh," Uncle Oscar said, laughing. "Here's one of us at Whitelope Lodge. We went for a week every summer. Loved that place. Haven't thought of it in years."

My uncle seemed to be enjoying himself as he handed me photo after photo. My mother in bathing suits, on sleds, holding a "runner up" ribbon, and, in one, a puppy. In all of them, she was smiling. I did note that the older she was, the more likely she was to be turning the side of her face with her under-eye mole away from the camera lens.

With each picture he passed, my uncle seemed to be recalling a happy childhood, a far cry from how my mother had described it to me. And in each of the pictures, she didn't look troubled. She didn't even look pensive. She looked happy.

"Uncle Oscar," I said, placing a photo from her first day of sixth grade onto the coffee table. "My mother always made comments about her childhood, implying it hadn't been happy. You know, Pop-Pop's extramarital affairs. Your mother's instability. And she'd say things like, 'You're lucky I don't whack you like my dad whacked me. Or threaten you the way my mother did!'"

He inhaled. "Well, yes, that did happen."

I felt awkward about probing, but this is what I'd come here for. "A lot?"

Uncle Oscar raised his chin and looked skyward before responding. "What's a lot? I don't know. I only grew up in one family. What do I compare it to? It wasn't easy, sometimes, sure. But overall, we were a normal family. Auntie Am's father left her family — left them penniless, no less — when she was seven. The next-door neighbors," he continued, leaning his head to the left, "grew up with an older brother who molested them. So I guess Pop-Pop's philandering, our mother's rage, it felt kind of mild. It's hackneyed for someone my age to say, but things were different back then."

He struck me as sincere. If there's anything I learned from the hundreds of interviews I've done, it's an ability to detect insincerity. Uncle Oscar didn't seem to mind my questions so I decided to shift directions.

"I've been doing research," I said, "about something called epigenetics. It's the notion that trauma may have a genetic impact on future children, future generations even. I'm no scientist but the idea is that, say, the grandson of someone who experienced profound stress in a concentration camp may have depression and anxiety even if he himself has not experienced any trauma."

Uncle Oscar shook his head, confused, which I expected. I was still confused myself. I held up a finger and pulled my own file out of my bag. I read out loud from some of the notes I'd taken while making my way through *Transgenerational Transmission of Environmental Information*.

"Um, so, like the lives of ancestors, even deceased ancestors, can influence our own day-to-day behaviors," I read from my notes. "Our thoughts, our experiences, may persevere genetically. It's like a ripple effect down to our progeny."

My uncle nodded blankly, as if this didn't apply to his life at all. "Is this for a blog post you're working on?"

"Um," I hesitated, "so I'm doing a podcast now rather than a blog but...no, this isn't for that. I'm trying to understand my mother."

"Understand what, exactly?"

So many memories flooded to my prefrontal cortex. The night when I was eight and my brother and I were fighting and my mother screamed her oft-repeated line, "I didn't sign up for this!" But then, for the first time, she added, "I resign!" and stormed out the front door and didn't return until after school the next day. I spent thirty-six hours petrified about being put into foster care or, worse, being left alone to fend for ourselves.

How to encapsulate my childhood in a few words?

"It may not have been apparent during our once-a-year visits, but she wasn't a…loving mother. She didn't take care of us."

I racked my brain for a singular illustration. There were no hugs in my childhood. I remember not one. No stories read. Her ferocious anger. The put-downs and dismissals. The nasty way she'd pretend not to hear me and then call me "needy" when I fought harder to get her attention. The way she'd minimize my feelings, telling me to get over it. Then I landed on a prime example.

"Want to know how Leith first got into pot?" I said. "From her, our mother. She gave — no, she *sold* it to him. He was eleven."

Uncle Oscar lowered his eyes to his lap.

"So her…neglect…it's impacted how I feel about the world," I continued. "I'm fearful, I try to make everything safe. It's exhausting, actually. So I'm trying to understand the origins of it all, to see if I can somehow undo it."

"Meggie," he said, looking me square in the eye and speaking with authority, with a strength that belied his being in the ICU just days before. "For growing up in the forties and fifties, ours was a pretty regular childhood."

"How can you say that?"

"It had ups and downs, some unhappy moments."

"But your parents—"

"Our parents were flawed, like your mother was. But no more so than other families we grew up with. I say this not to deny your epig— whatever it's called — theory. Perhaps it's true. But your mother's childhood was not a traumatic one. People can be raised in the same house and

turn out differently. Look at you and your brother. The same is true for me
and your mom."

I thought of my recent exchanges with my cousin Lisa, Uncle Oscar's
daughter. She was helping to take care of him. He had been a good parent,
she a good daughter. Uncle Oscar was more than his childhood. There was
no pattern of abuse traveling through generations. My grandparents were
no more responsible for my wounds than a stranger was.

"What about Derrick?" I asked, a last-ditch effort to prove my theory. Maybe Uncle Oscar's brother had somehow genetically transmitted
trauma onto my cousin.

For the first time, suffering flashed on Uncle Oscar's face.

I remembered the motto of Maya, the fertility specialist: don't be
a dick. What was I doing? My selfish questions had probably hastened
Derrick's death by suicide and here I was going on again.

"Terrible," he said about the sudden death his nephew. "But you
know he'd been diagnosed with early onset Alzheimer's, right?"

Answers began to fall into place, just in a wholly unexpected way.
Like doing a jigsaw puzzle upside down, with the grey cardboard side facing up and the picture hidden.

Oh, Derrick, I thought, clamping my eyes shut. *I'm so sorry for what
you were going through.* That my cousin chose to keep his breakfast plans
with me amidst everything he was dealing with, perhaps even knowing
that day would be his last, filled me with a deep gratitude and a tender
sadness that brought tears to my eyes.

"I didn't know," I said, reaching over to place my hand once again on
top of my uncle's.

We were quiet together for a few moments.

"Want to see the rest of these?" he finally said after a deep inhale,
pointing his chin to the photos we hadn't looked at yet.

I nodded.

I saw more snippets from my mother's past — taking a bow on stage after performing in a high school play, the first head shot she'd gotten for her acting resume, a photo of our whole extended family during one of our summer visits in the seventies.

"Here's one from your parents' wedding. A small affair," he said.

My mother had never shared photos from her wedding. I didn't even know they existed. My father looked sturdy and happy as he clutched his right arm around her. She wore an ivory suit and an unsettled expression. I flipped the photo over. "2-10-68," was written on the back.

"What's this?" I asked.

"Well, that's the date. I remember because your father wanted to get married on Valentine's Day but that year it fell on a weekday. So they settled on the weekend before."

I felt something rush over me, overtaking me the way Scottie had described her first hot flash.

"They got married in February? February, 1968?"

"Yes, I remember because it was the Olympics. I listened to the radio at the airport waiting for my flights to and from California for the wedding."

I was born in July 1968. That meant my mother was pregnant with me when they got married. They probably got married *because* she was pregnant with me. It sounds ridiculous now. But those were the days when women couldn't even get a credit card without a husband co-signing. That was five whole years before Roe v. Wade.

I'd never before considered the sequence of events, never even thought to ask. Had my mother even loved my father? Maybe he'd been a fling and she blamed me for tying her down, her first born an unrelenting reminder of the life she would never have.

Raw sadness, decades in the making, floated from the deepest core of my being to the surface of my skin. I felt sorry for the child I'd been, for having to deal with a mother who was mean, disinterested, dismissive.

But for the first time in fifty-one years, I also felt sorry for my mother.

"Mister Oscar," my uncle's nurse said, stepping down into the sunken living room. She held out a glass of water and a teeny paper cup, which she jiggled, indicating it was time to take the pills it contained.

He swallowed the meds and handed the water glass back to her.

"It's best for you to rest now," she said.

What? I'd planned to spend most of the day with my uncle. We'd barely gotten started. I was ready to protest, to tell the nurse how long I'd been waiting to speak to my uncle, how far I'd driven to arrive here today. But then Uncle Oscar took a deep breath and nodded and I saw for the first time how old he really was.

"Yes," he said, wearily. "You're probably right."

I wanted to object, but I could see our conversation had already taken a lot out of him. Though I desperately wanted to keep talking, I took my uncle's left arm as he stood while the nurse took his right. With our assistance, he took two slow steps, then halted.

"One more thing," he said, turning to face me. "I lived a different life than your mother did and maybe this is why: somehow I knew that if I didn't forgive my parents for their mistakes, I'd be stuck. Auntie Am used to say, 'Anger digs two graves.' I heard what you said today. Your mother was not a good mother. But what you can do is stop returning to the scene of the crime. Death ends a life but not a relationship. That's given me great comfort since Auntie Am died. But the same is true for you. Your mom is gone now. It's probably time you ended your relationship with her."

I hugged Uncle Oscar.

"Thank you," I said. To the nurse, I added, "I'll let myself out."

Just outside his front door, I got back on my bike. As I rode back to Irv and Dotty, I considered my uncle's words.

Even if epigenetics had played a role in how my mother parented, in the end, it made no difference. The origin of my feelings about the world as unsafe...what did it matter? And then my mind flashed to, of all things, Hillary Clinton during the Benghazi hearings. "We had four dead Americans," she'd said. "Whether because of a protest or random violence, *what difference, at this point, does it make?*"

Maybe things would have been different if my mom had been able to fulfill her dreams of being on TV or if my father had lived to help raise us. But, as Melinda often said, "If my aunt had balls, she'd be my uncle. Wouldn't you rather live in the real world?" Recovering from my childhood, I understood from my uncle, was my responsibility.

As I pedaled, I observed clouds in the distance crisscrossing and dancing across the sky. "You're right, Uncle Oscar," I whispered to the wind. "You're absolutely right."

I slept so soundly that when my phone rang the next morning, I was in the exact same position I'd fallen asleep in. The call was from Uncle Oscar, inviting me back to his house that morning before his doctor's appointment.

Forty-five minutes later, Ursula the nurse brought me into the kitchen where he was in a bathrobe eating eggs. He didn't get up, but did look ruddier, more rested than the previous day.

"Meggie," he said, and I noticed for the first time how similar his deep voice was to my son's. "Thanks for coming back today."

"I'm glad you're feeling well enough for another visit."

He gestured for me to sit down and then to the eggs. I shook my head in a wordless, "No, thank you." I put my hand on his. "Thanks for showing me all those old photos yesterday and for inviting me back today, especially given that you just got out of the hospital. Sorry if my questions were unpleasant."

"Don't be silly, Meggie," he said, removing his hand from under mine and then placing it on top of mine. "You've given me a lot to think about. About my parents. About your mom and Leith. Even Derrick."

I cringed. "I really shouldn't have brought some of that up. I didn't mean to upset you. I—"

"No, no," he interrupted. "When you hit my age, it can be interesting to look at old things a new way. But I wanted to tell you something else."

Had he realized, as I had, that given my birth date, my parents were forced to have a shotgun wedding?

"Okay," I said.

"You," he said, pointing a forkful of eggs at me, "are not fearful. As a matter of fact, you're quite fearless. How many women your age could do this kind of cross-country trip? By themselves? And *a podcast*? I had no idea. Putting work out there to strangers. Forgive my French, but that takes balls."

I laughed. "That's sweet."

"I mean it," he said, sternly. "I don't think you got the answers you wanted from me yesterday. But you *asked the questions*. That's brave. That's not being guided by fear, that's diving head first into life."

The nurse entered the kitchen. "Mister Oscar," she said, "time to start getting dressed for your appointment."

I stood and kissed Uncle Oscar on the cheek before nodding to the nurse that I'd let myself out.

Three thousand miles and many months on the road? Worth it.

CHAPTER NINETEEN

"**H**ow was it?" Alex asked.

I was back in Kansas City, once again half-way between Syracuse and Los Angeles, lounging at the dinette in the motor home with my feet up and Dotty snoring on my lap. I hadn't changed my clothes since Derrick's funeral that morning. I was wearing black slacks with red loafers, my ankles exposed to the elements, which I didn't mind because it was unseasonably warm in KC. I'd even spotted a few yellow wildflowers sprouting from sidewalk cracks as I walked back to Irv from the service.

"It was nice," I said, rubbing Dotty's soft ears between my finger and thumb. "There were lots of people there so Claire and the girls should have plenty of support going forward. And I was able to reconnect with some other cousins I haven't seen in about twenty years."

"Cool," Alex said. His husky voice, far deeper than Jeff's, still startled me sometimes. In my head, he was still little enough for me to rest my elbow on the top of his head — our little gag in those years — when waiting in line at Ralph's. Now our physical gag was him planting his palm on my forehead, extending his arm and commanding me to run towards him.

With almost no effort, he could prevent me from doing anything but run in place, making me look like a frustrated cartoon character.

"Did you learn more about what happened, exactly?" he asked.

What *had* happened, exactly? To Derrick, to my mother, to me. Was it all connected or just...life?

There are things we will never know for certain. Why someone — like the man who took me to the hospital in Buffalo — crossed our path but didn't stay. I'll never, ever know whether that woman who tried to give me a ride to school had dark intentions. I was trying to make friends with uncertainty. Scottie had a friend who regularly saw a medium and she asked if I wanted the person's name so I could attempt to connect with my mother or Derrick. I declined. I was done with future tellers and the like.

I'd also stopped trying to find answers to unanswerable questions through science. When I left Syracuse, I ditched *Transgenerational Transmission of Environmental Information*, plopping it into a recycling bin in a Washington, D.C. suburb. I let go of epigenetics and began formulating my own theory: that we're all a patchwork of traumas and joys, of parenting failures and our own autonomy, an unpredictable, unscientific blend of nature and nurture. I was who I was both because of and in spite of my mother. I'd probably spend the next fifty years a cautious person, more fearful than average. But I'd begun paying attention recently. I started confronting my habit of hashing out every "what if" scenario, of forcing myself to live through things that aren't even happening. "Hello, fear, I see you," I'd started responding in my head. "I choose to ignore you right now."

When I Skyped with Melinda after learning that I'd been born just five months after my parents married, that perhaps my mother blamed me for how her life had turned out, she said, "You have to accept that you were the villain in your mother's story even though you did nothing wrong. She got to have her narrative and you get to have yours."

Alex, my boy, so capable, wise and solid, was a huge lynchpin in my narrative, I realized. If there was any genetic component to the disturbing way my mother was parented or the way I was, it seems to have stopped with me. Alex got my Uncle Oscar's baritone, but not my mother's cruelty or my anxiety. The evidence had been right before my eyes, in both Alex and Nathan, my brother's son. They were both sweet, motivated, good with people.

"I learned a little bit," I said to Alex. "Derrick had health issues I wasn't aware of. And not enough help to deal with them."

"Sad."

"Yes, and it's an important reminder that if you ever—"

"Mom," he stopped me, his voice taking on that occasional whine he had as a teen when I'd remind him to put on sunscreen or get enough sleep. "Life lesson not necessary."

"I know. But remember, you can always come to me if—"

"*Of course*, Meggie-Mom."

We hung up, and I slipped off my red loafers and slacks and changed into yoga pants for the next leg of my trip. My westward travels had a slower pace and, with the exception of the stop in Kansas City, merely a loose itinerary. I'd become more spontaneous about Peeps interviews, asking people I met along the way if I could interview them right then and there. One example: in a Starbucks in Harrisburg, Pennsylvania, I began chatting with a woman in line behind me. She was about my age and wore a diamond tennis bracelet and a huge diamond cross around her neck. Her flawless French manicure shined under the cafe lights as she reached for her latte. She was the kind of woman that Jeff would dismiss as high-maintenance and vapid. But after she agreed to spend a few minutes at a table being recorded for an interview, I learned that she worked as a notary for a bank, meeting borrowers at their homes to sign loan agreements. She listened to nearly a hundred audiobooks a year because every Saturday she drove fifty miles to have lunch with her ninety-year-old father. Her life motto? "I have lots of time but none to waste."

As I was changing out of my clothes after talking with Alex, my phone beeped with a text from Scottie, who shared a link for a YouTube video demonstrating exercises to firm up neck skin.

"I'm telling U, Meggie," she wrote, "it's all about the neck. If your face is firm but your neck is saggy, forget it."

Then she added, "Remember to kegel. Maintaining a strong internal core is critical at our age, even if our bellies r looking like yesterday's oatmeal."

My best friend's admonition took on a double meaning for me. My pelvic floor needed to stay tight, of course. But my true internal core — my essence — needed strength too. That's what 5-4-3-2-1 and meditation were helping me do. The practices helped me understand that the way I was parented was part of my story, but it wasn't my core.

"1 more thing," Scottie wrote, "I just heard a chin hair say 'See u next week!' when I plucked it.'"

A text from Jeff popped in right after Scottie's. "I'm heading to the post office tomorrow," he wrote. "Need me to send u anything from home?"

"Nope. All good," I replied. "But thx for asking."

Reconstruction on my Santa Monica house was adhering to the stereotype: taking twice as long and costing twice as much as promised. I was headed West, but I wouldn't be able to go home for awhile. Yet it was no longer scary because I was not the same Meg who left those months ago. I'd get home eventually and when I did, I'd discover how *this* Meg Newlin would operate in that world. In the meantime, I was excited to explore new places on the drive, such as Montana. I still had to be frugal with water and I still wiped down counters and vacuumed Irv's floors daily, but I loosened up in other ways. I only set an alarm clock if I needed to be somewhere early. I resisted the instinct to say no when offered to try something new, even eating Snoots in Missouri.

I realized how much I'd isolated myself over the years. Driving away from my life in Los Angeles was an act of bravery, yes, but also a distinct act of isolation. Driving west, I began spending more and more time with motor home neighbors, no longer the first to leave gatherings in parking lots and RV parks. I discovered a new confidence and stood up for myself more. When one of my sources kept interrupting me, I didn't politely shrug it off like I'd done in the past. I reminded him that I was in charge of the interview, not him. And when he described a woman at his workplace as someone who needed to "grow a pair" and remarked that his son needed to stop being such a "pussy," I replied, "Did you know the average vagina has a circumference the size of a quarter and yet can expand to expel a human roughly the size of a watermelon?" And not only did I manage to say such a thing, I didn't edit it out of the episode later. Listener feedback was 7:1 in favor of my response.

Brad messaged me after listening to that episode, the first time we'd touched base in several weeks. "Fierce!" he texted. "I like it." I told him I was on my way home, likely detouring through the Pacific Northwest, and he asked if I wanted any company. We made a plan to meet up at the Bridge of the Gods, the section of the Pacific Crest Trail that connects Washington and Oregon.

That night of Derrick's funeral, I sat in my jammies at the dinette, twinkly lights I'd strung in the kitchen illuminating my map, which I was scanning in preparation for the next drive, a long stretch from Missouri to a small town in southeastern Nebraska. I now used my yellow highlighter to trace the route *after* I'd completed each stretch, letting myself create wiggly, nonsensical lines as I meandered westward. I hoped to find a source or two to interview, but I'd become okay with not knowing where or when my next episodes would emerge. The last months on the road confirmed that as long as someone was willing to talk with me, I could produce engaging interviews.

ERIN GORDON

It had become easier and easier to get people to talk with me too. After the woman recognized me in the Cleveland cafe, I checked my stats every few days. I wasn't obsessive, just curious. The Peeps audience grew each week and I was receiving more and more messages from listeners who'd been touched by the stories they heard. One man emailed to say that Peeps made him feel connected to the world, made him realize that his own life mattered. The day before my stop in Kansas City, a literary and media agent emailed me, and it was on my list of things to do to give her a call when I drove north the next morning.

Welcome back, everyone. I'm Sheryl Shoun and you're watching Oregon's KCAE television. For those of you just joining us at Chromatic Studios here in Portland, I've had the pleasure of talking with Megan Newlin, host of the wildly popular Peeps podcast. What fun it's been to interview the interviewer! She's at the tail end of a multi-month trek across the U.S. in an RV she nicknamed Irv. She's been wonderfully candid with us, revealing her mistakes, her disappointments as well as her triumphs.

Thanks for spending so much time here, Meg. Your honesty, your vulnerability — we can all learn from it. I've got to tell you...my five-year-old daughter has a favorite way of describing people she likes. She says, "They have hearts in their eyes." I confess that I never quite understood what she meant until talking with you today. You've an...energy about you. Do you think it's because of Peeps?

That's sweet. Thank you. If anyone does get that feeling about me, I'd credit the Peeps subjects and listeners for the effect they've had on me. And I'd credit this trip. When I drove away from Santa Monica all those months ago, I probably had question marks in my eyes!

Spending so much time alone but also meeting people from all over and reconnecting with extended family, it's just.... Well, I guess I've kind of found my place in the world. There are upsides to middle age, I've discovered. Don't let anyone convince you that you can't reinvent yourself after fifty. And if you don't believe me, listen to the episode I did with Fera, a sixty-something video game champ! I'm still not a fearless person, but if I can take risks amid my fear, anyone can.

Any regrets?

Always! I had a little lapse in judgment with a drummer in New Orleans.

Well now, I wonder if he'll watch this.

Me too. Actually, someone who I truly hope sees this is a man from Buffalo who drove me to the hospital when I was ill. If you're watching, don't be someone I "never saw again." I want to thank you!

So you're now within a few hundred miles of home. What's next?

Dotty and I are sticking with Irv awhile longer. My house in Santa Monica is undergoing some renovations, but Los Angeles will be our home base. I'm eager to spend time with old friends. As my therapist Melinda says, "Sometimes we must walk away to come back."

What else is on your agenda?

A few weeks ago a media agent reached out to me. She's a longtime fan of Peeps, back to the blog days. She convinced me that I have an opportunity to use the Peeps platform to reach more people, to grow what she called "the Peeps community."

I wasn't sure, at first. I didn't want to dilute the concept. I mean, the whole notion of Peeps is that it's *intimate*. But the Peeps podcast won't change. The only thing that's changing — and you're hearing it here first! — is we're adding some live Peeps shows. I just realized how tawdry that sounds! Not peep shows but *Peeps shows*.

The first live show is scheduled for April in San Francisco. Best of all: fifty percent of all proceeds from every single show will be donated to local suicide prevention organizations and organizations that support individuals experiencing homelessness.

Wow, that's *big*! I'm sure I speak for all Peeps fans when I say we look forward to its continued evolution. When you bring your live show to Portland, I'll be in the front row! So, Meg, it's time to wrap up. We'll conclude, of course, with your own final question: What, Meg Newlin, is your life motto?

Ah, well, this actually became my final Peeps question for selfish reasons: I'd long been seeking my own motto and hadn't found it yet. I always assumed that one day I'd hear a source's motto and know immediately that I should adopt it as my own. But surprisingly that hasn't happened. I've loved learning all my sources' mottos. And I've applied many of them to my own life at one point or another. In fact, that's just it — I take with me a little piece from each person I've interviewed. Every one of them stays with me somehow.

The RV journey was part of *my* life. It belonged to me. But you were there too: all the Peeps sources, all the listeners. Whenever I feel afraid or confused, I tap into the richness of humanity, that undeniable linking of all our lives. And then I move forward again, not just passively living out this second half of my life but propelling towards it.

So I've finally landed on my motto. Just one word. It is, simply: *Connect.*

QUESTIONS
FOR DISCUSSION

1. Themes of self-discovery are usually reserved for YA novels. How does PEEPS reimagine those themes for a middle-aged woman?

2. PEEPS is a journey story in the tradition of *The Wizard of Oz* and Cheryl Strayed's *Wild*. What symbols from and references to those iconic stories did you spot in PEEPS?

3. How did Meg's relationships with her loved ones change during her journey?

4. Do you believe epigenetics has played a role in your life? How so?

5. Which PEEPS podcast interview resonated with you the most? Why?

6. How would *you* answer Meg's seven questions?

7. At the end of the story, Meg seems destined for a Big Life. What do you believe is next for her?

ACKNOWLEGEMENTS

Thank you to the generous friends and family, many of whom read multiple drafts, who helped bring PEEPS to life: Emmy Etlin, Tali Levy, Bruce Berrol, Jill Chanen, Sheila Gordon, Kelli Herzog Anderson, Kerryn Schwarz, Willow Older, Megan Pickett, Robin Meyerowitz, Allison Gruettner Stuart, Jill Schecter, Amy Mason Doan, Mary Hossfeld, Michael Krasny, Keith Scribner, Mark Armstrong, Lori Corenthal, and Lucy Sanna. Literary agents Uwe Stender and Maria Whelan also gave me wonderful, actionable feedback.

Dr. Jeb, Elaine Mowday and Elizabeth Springer remind me to put publishing in perspective. Thank you to the Rainbow Kittens, the Peloton Gals, Aimee Gordon and so many other friends for your support and encouragement.

Thank you, most of all, to C, A and E for making all my dreams come true.

ABOUT THE AUTHOR

A "recovering" lawyer and longtime legal affairs journalist, Erin Gordon lives in San Francisco. Learn more at ErinGordonAuthor.com.

If you enjoyed this story, the author would be thrilled if you shared your enthusiasm with fellow readers.